DRY INK PUBLICATIONS

His Name is Peck

A Novel by Justin Bradley

First published by Dry Ink Publications 2025

First edition

This book was professionally typeset on Reedsy.
Find out more at reedsy.com

For everyone.

Contents

Acknowledgments

I would like to thank everyone who helped make the completion of this book a reality. Thank you so much to my beta readers, who offered thoughtful notes and feedback and helped me to grow. And of course, thank you to those who pushed me to soldier through and finish. I couldn't have done it without all of you.

It was fun. It was difficult. In the end, though, I found that the real treasure was the journey itself.

Thank you all.

Prologue

1985.

Chicago.

Mayor Harold "Harry" Washington's office.

Mayor Washington's office door slammed shut with a thunderous bang. Closed behind it was a brewing argument that seeped through the thick, solid core mahogany barrier into the otherwise peaceful room beyond. A palpable silence washed over the staff of secretaries and advisors as they continued to shuffle papers and answer ringing phones, all while quietly straining to catch a word or phrase coming from the clash of men's voices inside. It had all built up to this—the arguments, the court orders, property destruction, and the toxic cloud. It had all finally come to an explosive head, and one could hear a pin drop as the office staff waited to see who would be victorious.

Office managers and staff writers were among those who exchanged curious glances, each doing their best not to seem like they were straining to catch the fragments of the argument filtering through the closed door. Everyone knew what this was about. They had all seen the reports. They had read the papers. Many of them had fielded more than one phone call from the Environmental Protection Agency, specifically from Stanley Peck, regarding the accusations of lies, fraud, and deceit.

Mayor Washington's authoritative voice cut through the door of his office as if it were cardboard, clashing with the defiant comebacks of the CleanCycle BioSystems staff, particularly that of its chief operating officer, Leonardo Vincent. All the while, Stanley Peck's rigid and resolute declarations could be heard at the center of the verbal storm. Much like the rest of the city, the people of the mayor's office found the news reports of a new biowaste disposal technology to be intriguing at the very least and a flight of fancy at the very worst. There had been something of a city divide about this new company. Some were waiting to see if it could deliver, while others denounced it entirely. But now there had been an explosion, property damage, and a toxic cloud looming over the sky, to say nothing about the news coverage looking for a villain to crucify. Mayor Washington had called for the owners and operators of this new startup company, CleanCycle BioSystems, but the man who followed them in, Stanley Peck of the Environmental Protection Agency, was clearly not a fan or supporter of these new and self-proclaimed '*eco heroes*.' He was far from impressed, and he was certainly not a believer.

Muffled words continued to strain their way through Mayor Washington's door, picked out as the office staff listened intently. Snippets of a debate over unprecedented levels of city power usage and unfiled reports clearly made it through.

Issues of public safety and accusations of illegal dumping were being hurled like daggers. Then, everything fell silent.

Finally, Mayor Washington's mahogany door whipped open, and EPA officer Stanley Peck emerged, his brown-bearded face etched with frustration and indignation. He had lost. No one in the office knew exactly *what* he had lost, but the mayor had made his choice, and CleanCycle BioSystems had evidently won the battle. The office door closed behind him, leaving Stanley Peck ejected and defeated. He looked about the room, doing his best to mask his embarrassment with a show of dignified pride. The secretaries and advisors, the staff writers, and the office managers couldn't force themselves to focus directly on him. Rather, they just looked blankly in his general direction or tried to avoid eye contact with Stanley Peck altogether.

Echoes of the office fight whirled around in Stanley's head as he stood motionless, contemplating his next few moments. All the mayor's staff and other city officials had been against him, or at least hadn't helped defend him. Each of the CleanCycle BioSystems staff had been against him. Some even held him up as a criminal. But it was Leonardo Vincent, '*Leo*' to friends and bloodthirsty reporters, the chief operating officer of CleanCycle BioSystems and figurehead of Stanley Peck's crusade, who had taken extra delight in taking personal shots at Stanley. It was Leo Vincent who, out of spiteful pettiness, had hurled a particularly nasty insult at Stanley, calling him '*a human ball sack*' in front of the mayor and his entire advisory staff. It was Leo Vincent whom Stanley Peck blamed—for everything.

Stanley closed his eyes as he worked to center himself. He did his best to wash away Mayor Washington's echoing words of rejection that were dancing around his mind like a vicious tango. It wasn't quite over yet, after all, and he knew it. He still had to stop at the EPA home office and meet with his boss, the director of operations. And there was little wonder in his head about how *that* conversation would end. And then there was home. But there was no running from it. There was no avoiding the storm that was coming. The forecast called for a personal hurricane.

Stanley steeled himself against the imposing thoughts, as best as he could, anyway. He took a deep breath, forcing the thoughts away, though they kept rolling back like debris pushed around by a leaf blower. Ash and soot from the earlier explosion still covered his suit, but Stanley stood proudly as if he were ready to meet a king or a president. He ran his fingers through his dusty brown hair, and with a firm tug, Stanley straightened his tie and squared his shoulders. He mapped the office with his eyes, aimed for the exit, and walked purposefully away from the battlefield behind the mayor's door, his head held high.

No one said a word as Stanley passed by their desks. Everyone's eyes followed with a mix of curiosity, compassion, and even pity as he slowly marched to the door. But Stanley Peck gave them none of his attention. Instead, he kept his gaze fixed on the path before him. Despite his defeat and public shame, there was still a glimmer of defiance in Stanley's eyes, a determination that refused to be extinguished in the face of such a beating.

He thought he was right.

* * *

Stanley Peck's rearview mirror reflected the sprawling Chicago landscape as he merged onto the freeway and pointed his aging blue Volvo towards the nearby suburbs, towards home. He watched with relief as the skyscrapers faded in the distance. The highways gave way to suburban streets, and the congestion of commuting cars around him finally eased. At last, the familiar sight of two-story and single-story homes filled Stanley's vision. Finally, all that remained was a sense of calm as the evening sky replaced the day. The tension that had been gripping Stanley's shoulders like a vise at last loosened its hold.

The day's battles felt like a memory, replaced by the tranquility of *this* world, removed from busy city life and the problems it held. The comments and attacks of Mayor Washington and Leo Vincent that were replaying on a loop in Stanley's head had finally grown quiet. House after house passed by until finally Stanley pulled into his driveway. He was home at last, safe from all the belittlement and persecution. The hint of a smile slowly crept onto Stanley's dirty face. But just as it did, the demons in his mind charged back in. Though he tried to stop it, the start of Stanley's smile transformed back into his familiar grimace.

Stanley stepped out of his car, a knot firmly taking root in his stomach. Just like walking out of the mayor's office and facing his EPA supervisor, Stanley knew there was no escaping walking through that front door. He had to face it. Every step felt as if there were weights attached to his feet. His heart pounded like a jackhammer as he brought the key to the lock, and metal touched metal.

Stanley swung open the door and whipped it shut as if someone was chasing him. He leaned back against its cool surface, silently pleading for the lifeless piece of wood to help keep him steady—it helped. It was quiet inside. The ride home was mostly quiet, too, but the house was quieter still. Stanley closed his eyes. It wouldn't be long now, he knew.

Then, just as Stanley finally drifted into the solitude of his thoughts, a voice broke the silence. "Daddy!"

Stanley blinked his eyes open, startled with surprise as his daughter's voice broke through the silence. Her bare footsteps quickly closed in on him from down the hallway. With an endearing, half-crooked grin spread across her face, she leapt onto his shoulder and wrapped her arms around him. The heat from her welcomed embrace warmed Stanley's bones. He smiled and knelt down on one knee.

"Hi, Lizzy," Stanley said as he smiled affectionately, no sign of the grimace that overtook him in the driveway. "How was your day?"

Elizabeth's soft, five-year-old voice was like a cool drink to Stanley on a warm summer day. They exchanged pleasantries about her school day and what she had played with some of her friends. For those few minutes, Stanley was free. He allowed himself to get lost in the simplicity of her world and simple stories and problems, the innocence of childhood proving a welcome reprieve from the complexities of his own terrible day. But that proved short-lived as the focus inevitably turned back to him.

"How was *your* day, Daddy?" Lizzy inquired eagerly.

"Oh, just a day like any other at work," he said.

As if on cue, Stanley's wife, Kate, appeared from the living room. He felt himself sink into the floor as their eyes met and shared a momentary glance. Kate searched Stanley's face for answers. She could read him like a book, always could. Even though her review of his face told her everything she needed to know, Kate still went through the motions.

"Everything OK?" she asked.

"I, ah... I lost my...," Stanley's words trailed off as the weight of his failures hung heavy in the living room air.

Kate's expression was distant as she absorbed his words. She stopped Stanley before he could finish his sentence, reaching out her hand and touching Elizabeth on the shoulder. "Elizabeth, honey," Kate said, "why don't you go play in your room while Daddy and I figure out dinner?"

Elizabeth offered no argument and headed off down the hallway to her room, completely and blissfully unaware of the doom quietly unfolding in the Peck family living room. Stanley and Kate regarded each other as they both waited to hear Lizzy's door click shut.

"I can't keep doing this, Stanley," Kate said as she turned and headed deeper into the living room. She stopped in front of the bay window, looking out into the darkness.

Stanley's face sank as he took in Kate's words. It wasn't a question. It wasn't something she was thinking about. She had made a statement. "What do you mean?" Stanley asked as he followed behind her.

"You never quit, Stanley," Kate said, still facing away. "You just never quit. And we pay the price with you." She threw her hands into the air. "It's already all over the news, you know. Those people are the heroes of Chicago. And you're the one who said they were the bad guys. You stood on top of your ivory tower and proclaimed to the world that those CleanCycle people were liars, that they were frauds. And now they're out there fighting for the people—and you've lost your job."

Stanley stood silently as he stared at Kate's back. He waited for the right words, the right phrases, to come to mind. In the end, all he could get out were five lonely words. "I thought I was right."

The tension in the air massed around Stanley as Kate whipped around to face him, the few feet between them seeming as vast as the Sahara Desert. The soft glow of the solitary lamp in the room cast heavy shadows across their faces.

"It's just never enough for you, Stanley," Kate said. Her words cut through the air like a knife and burrowed into Stanley's chest. "Today, it was these CleanCycle people. Yesterday, it was Leo Vincent. Before that, it was something else and some other guy. It just never ends. You've always got to win. You've always got to be right."

"It's who I am, Kate," Stanley said. "It's *what* I am."

Kate pointed her finger at Stanley. "No! It's what you *choose* to do, not who you are."

Stanley's jaw clenched involuntarily. He knew she was right. She usually was. "I don't know how to be any other way, honey," he said, his voice breaking ever so slightly.

Kate lowered her head as her eyes filled with tears. "Well, that's just not enough, Stanley," she insisted. "Not anymore."

Stanley fought against the defiant look that started lighting up his face. He would have taken it back if he could have, but he couldn't. "So what are you saying?" he asked. "Are you giving up? Is that what you're saying?"

Kate scoffed as she fired back at Stanley's dismissive questions, "Oh, don't you dare try to turn this around on me!" She noticed her volume and quickly lowered her voice so it wouldn't echo down the hall. "I've always stood by you,

Stanley, even when plenty of people told me to run for cover, but I always stayed. I always defended you. So don't you dare try and turn this around on me like this is because of me"

"Well, bravo to you, honey," Stanley said as his eyes finally betrayed him, and his entire face committed to the spiteful words he was saying. He could hear himself talking as if it were an out-of-body experience. It was like it was someone else speaking, like some monster was using his mouth like a weapon. He wanted to stop, but he knew it was too late, though. He wanted to wrap his arms around Kate and plead for whatever was left. But he didn't. He couldn't. "So you stood by your husband," Stanley said, venom in his voice, "until it was just too damn inconvenient for you. Wife of the friggin' Year."

Kate's eyes blazed with a volatile blend of hurt and fury. Her hands balled into fists at her sides as she closed some of the distance between them. "Inconvenient?" she repeated. Her voice trembled as the weight of years past came crashing down on her. With one throwaway remark, Stanley robbed Kate of any goodwill she may have had. With one thoughtless comment, he had reduced her dedication and her pain to nothing. "Stanley, do you have any idea what I've endured for you? Do you even care? I stood by you when you went back to school to get your environmental degrees. And I didn't say anything when we moved to Chicago when you got your EPA job. I left my family. I left my friends. Because you promised it would be worth it. And every time you went to pick a fight with someone—your boss, the neighbors, now this Leo Vincent guy—I had to clean up the mess back here. I was the one making excuses for you, telling Lizzy her daddy was just '*passionate*' when she asked why people didn't like him.

I'm the one who had to explain or justify everything people ever said about you."

Stanley opened his mouth to interrupt, but Kate quickly raised her hand, silencing him before he could fire another shot. "No, no! You don't get to make this about *you*—again." Kate let out an exhaustive breath as she looked up to the ceiling, then back to Stanley. "I've spent years watching you chase your crusades. And I believed in you, Stanley, I really did. I thought you were fighting for something bigger, something that mattered. But now? Now I finally see it's not about justice or truth at all. It's about you needing to be the one who's right, no matter who gets hurt." Kate took a moment and looked around the room. She stopped as she focused on their family portrait hanging above the fireplace. "Lizzy deserves better than a father who's always at war with the world, Stanley. And I deserve better than a husband who doesn't see what he's destroying."

Stanley's face quivered, his defiant expression crumbling under the weight of his wife's words. "Kate," he stammered. "I didn't mean to hurt you. You have to know I never meant for that. I was just trying to do my job. It's all I've ever tried to do. Those CleanCycle people—they were dangerous, reckless. I couldn't just stand by and let them..."

"Let them what, Stanley?!" Kate cut in. "Save the city? Because that's what they're doing. And you? You're the one who looks like a..." She paused, holding herself back before some truly hurtful words made their way out. Kate centered herself before continuing. "You've lost everything. And for what? Pride? Ego? Tell me, Stanley, what was it all for?"

He looked away, his jaw tightening under the pressure. Though he tried, Stanley couldn't muster the strength to meet

Kate's unyielding gaze. "I thought I was doing the right thing, honey," he mumbled. The words sounded hollow even to him.

Kate let out a bitter laugh as she wiped a falling tear from her cheek. "The right thing? You don't even know what that means anymore. You're so caught up in your own battles that you've forgotten what you're fighting for. And I can't keep waiting for you to figure that out for yourself, Stanley. I can't keep hoping you'll change when you've made it so clear to me you don't know how."

Stanley's chest tightened. He had never had a heart attack, but he was sure this must be what it felt like as it started. A sense of panic started rising as he sensed what was coming. "Kate, please," Stanley fumbled. "We can fix this. For Lizzy. For us, I'll try, I swear."

Kate shook her head, her expression softening but completely resolute. "I'm tired, Stanley. I'm so tired."

Stanley let go of the tension in his body as he looked back at his wife. "I don't know what I'm supposed to do, Kate. I don't know what I'm supposed to say."

Kate stepped closer. She kept her voice low, still making sure her words didn't travel down the hall. "I don't think there's anything you can say, Stanley." She rubbed her eyes, clearing them of the tears that had built up. "You know Lizzy's friends at school are already asking her why her daddy's on the news and why people are calling him a laughingstock and a liar. I had to sit her down today and explain why her daddy might not have a job anymore." Kate pressed her gaze into Stanley's eyes. "Do you know how that felt? To see her try to reconcile who her father is versus the man people tell her he is?"

Stanley lost a breath as the image of Elizabeth's confused face hit him like a sucker punch. "I didn't know she was hearing things like that," he said as he wiped his hands down his face. "I'll talk to her. I'll make it right."

"Make it right?" Kate's voice broke as the tears started spilling over. "How, Stanley? By fighting all the people who've said these things about you? I didn't tell you that to hurt you. But you can't talk your way out of this. You can't fix what's broken by doubling down. I've watched you do this our entire marriage—pick a fight, lose, and then swear you'll do better next time. But you don't. You just find another hill to die on. And I can't follow you up there anymore. I won't let Lizzy grow up thinking this is what love looks like, that this is what family looks like."

Stanley's shoulders dropped. It was so quiet, yet he couldn't hear anything. It seemed so loud. But he knew that was only in his head. His ears were ringing as he quietly pleaded, "Kate, I love you. I love Lizzy. You're everything to me. Isn't that enough?"

Kate shook her head. "It should be, Stanley. It used to be. But love doesn't mean standing by while you destroy yourself and take us with you. I need a partner, not a martyr. And right now, I don't know if you can be that."

Stanley held his gaze on Kate, waiting for her next comeback, her next round of assaults and emotional unloading. He was ready, he thought, ready as he could be for whatever she was going to hit him with next. He felt so numb he was sure he wouldn't even feel it hit. But she said nothing more. No quick comeback or another example of where he had gone wrong. She didn't even offer a dirty look. She just closed her eyes and lowered her head.

"I'm leaving, Stanley," she finally said.

Stanley quickly opened his mouth, but nothing came out.

Not a word. Nothing. Stanley Peck had been rendered silent. He felt as if the world had stopped turning, his heart sinking to his feet as if strapped to a thousand-pound weight. There were so many things he wanted to say, so many apologies he wanted to offer. But Stanley knew there was no point. He knew Kate, and if she had come to a place where she said those words, then there was no argument he could make, no apology, no grand promise that would turn it around. All of her pain and hurt had brought her to say the words he was always afraid she would say. Stanley had always feared this day would come, and now it finally had. He or Kate might not leave the house that night, but it was over, and he knew it.

As Kate turned and walked away, leaving him alone in the empty living room, Stanley resigned himself to her departure, the echoes of his failures reverberating in her retreating steps.

Chapter One

That night, Stanley got himself settled in the guest room downstairs. How strange it felt to be a guest in his own house as Kate slept upstairs in their bed. But it was only temporary. Soon enough, he wouldn't even be a guest there. He would be gone. Stanley stepped into the connected bathroom and turned the shower knob full tilt. Steam quickly billowed from the shower stall and filled the room. He stripped down and stood motionless in front of the mirror. He perched himself on the edge of the sink. Life as he knew it was over, gone. What would replace it, he couldn't begin to imagine. He regarded his reflection in the mirror. Rich brown hair and a tightly trimmed brown beard. He looked worn. Young, but worn.

The fog from the steam of the shower slowly but steadily covered the mirror and the reflection of Stanley Peck. He watched himself as he disappeared.

Then, with a deliberate sweep of his hand, Stanley cleared away a swath of condensation from the mirror, revealing his reflection staring back at him once again. The guest bathroom, with its cutesy knick-knacks and well-balanced color scheme, was gone. In its place was a smaller washroom, devoid of any fancy personal decorations. And it wasn't quite the youthful face Stanley remembered either. Also gone was the brown beard that had covered his gaunt cheeks and chin. Wrinkles and age lines, unwanted gifts of passing years, were all that remained. His neatly trimmed and luscious brown hair was now gray and long and unruly.

Forty years had passed. Chicago. The mayor's office. CleanCycle BioSystems. Leo Vincent. It was all forty long years ago.

Stanley squinted and frowned in dissatisfaction as he studied his reflection in the mirror. His eyes lingered on the lines etched into his weathered face, scars of a life lived and the choices that made them. Yet, amidst the wrinkles and gray hairs, a sense of pride snuck through, a quiet resilience that had carried him through the darkest days of those past forty years. So practiced, so manicured was this demeanor that, for a moment, he almost believed it himself.

Almost.

"Who are you?" he asked himself.

"You're Stanley Peck," he answered himself.

Stanley let out a frustrated sigh, turned away from the mirror, and stepped into the living room. The apartment was small, with just two bedrooms, a living room, and a kitchen. It was all he really needed. It had been all he needed for a long time now. Much like the bathroom, Stanley's second-floor apartment was light on decorations and personal flourishes. A few pictures hung on the walls, the generic kind featuring mountains and rivers, accented by a couple of fake potted plants of various sizes. It was quiet, a benefit of being a senior citizens' retirement community. And Stanley liked it quiet.

He looked around the room, internally wrestling with

himself about what to do with his action-packed morning. Before long, Stanley let his attention fall upon the collection of family pictures on the mantel of his red brick fireplace. There were pictures of his family, his ex-wife Kate, their daughter Elizabeth, and himself—forty years ago. There was a picture of him and his daughter at a park. He also had pictures of his daughter years later at her college graduation, with Stanley at her side, as well as her mother—and her new husband. His gaze moved from the pictures to his living room window. He stepped over and stood in front of it, pulling the shades to the side, revealing a new day.

Stanley pulled in a deep breath of air as he surveyed the town of Redmain from just inside his balcony. Scattered homes, random businesses, some grocery stores, and a mall. He couldn't quite see the end of town, the full distance of it, but he knew it was there. No skyscrapers. No suburbs. Just a small town in Southern California, surrounded mostly by dirt and tumbleweeds. Stanley continued to hold that breath—then choked on it as he coughed a rather unpleasant cough.

* * *

A while later, Stanley emerged from his modest apartment, locked the door behind him, and started down the long walkway towards the stairs. He passed Mrs. Collins from apartment twenty-five, who was watering her collection of plants in front of her window. She smiled at Stanley. He smiled back. Mr. Bolton from apartment sixteen zipped by Stanley as he enjoyed a brisk morning power walk around the walkway of the complex. They exchanged a mock two-finger salute as they crossed each other's paths. These were both familiar sights to Stanley, those little sorts of idiosyncrasies that come from people living near each other.

When Stanley reached the main road, the quaint storefronts and cozy homes and apartment buildings of the small town of Redmain stretched out before him, a striking contrast to the crowded and bustling city he once called home. This was his normal now, though, and had been for many years. Stanley had stayed in Chicago until Elizabeth had reached eighteen and gone away to college. After that, he moved west, as far as he could reasonably go, where people might not know his name or remember his story. But no matter how far he went, no matter how incognito he tried to be, Stanley Peck's notoriety always followed him. And Redmain was, sadly, no exception.

Stanley started down the sidewalk towards his destination, *Beans & Brew*, the only decent coffee house in town, he often thought. With each step he took, Stanley mumbled to himself a bitter litany of grievances that seemed to echo off the walls of the quiet buildings.

"Leo Vincent, I'm gonna get you!" he muttered under his breath.

"Vincent, you'll regret the day you ever met me!"

"Remember me, Leo Vincent? Oh, I bet you do!"

"I'm comin' for you, Vincent! Just you wait!"

As he walked and vented his forty years of frustrations, Stanley passed by the familiar sights of the town—a row of charming independent cafes and diners, a quaint bookstore with a faded sign, a walking path with rustling trees, and quiet benches where elderly couples gathered to reminisce. It was a town mostly gone in the days of 2025, a throwback to simpler times. Stanley had found Redmain some years ago when the odd jobs he had found over the years had dried up, and as such, was forced into early retirement. Now it was home.

"You listen here, Vincent," Stanley continued talking to himself, his words growing louder with each repetition. "I'm going to ruin you! You better believe it!"

The sleepy town of Redmain remained mostly oblivious to Stanley's routine tirade. The streets were all but deserted at that early hour, save for the occasional passerby who glanced at him curiously before shaking their head and hurrying on their way, more than a little reluctant to disturb the local crackpot. This was standard fare for Stanley these days, venting out loud his anger at the man who he felt ruined him as he walked to wherever he might be going.

"Thought you saw the last of Stanley Peck, huh?" Stanley said to himself and the empty streets, his voice bouncing off the brick facades of the buildings. "I'm like a bad penny, Vincent. I always come back!"

* * *

Stanley placed his order with the young barista behind the counter, then stepped over and waited at the pickup station for his coffee. He surveyed the various patrons of the coffee shop as he took in the perfection that was the smell of brewing coffee. He observed what looked like a couple, two buddies, and a trio of people who looked like they were on their way to work. None of them looked at him, of course, at least not for long. No one ever really looked at Stanley unless they were watching him talk to himself or were about to hurl an insult his way. But no one ever *really* looked at him. Redmain was a small town, the kind where most people knew most everyone. And most everyone knew Stanley Peck, or at least they thought they did. The old nutcase, who looked more than a little off and talked to himself—a lot.

Realizing enough time had passed, Stanley looked back at the pickup station and saw his coffee placed next to him. Traditionally, the server would call out the customer's name, alerting them that their order was ready. But not this time. Not for Stanley.

"Thanks for letting me know," Stanley harrumphed as he reached for his drink, shooting a passing dirty look at the barista behind the counter.

He stepped away and lifted the cup to take a sip. As he brought it closer to his mouth, Stanley spotted the name written on the side of the cup, the name the barista had asked for when he ordered, the name they were supposed to call out when the order was ready. But it didn't say '*Stanley*,' as he had told the young girl. Instead, it said the name he knew the people of this friendly town, full of nice people, called him behind his back, and sometimes even to his face. '*Pecker*.' Not '*Stanley*,' not even '*Peck*,' which he might have understood and more easily ignored. No, they called him '*Pecker*.' A fairly uninspired bastardization of his name that, much like his famous story, had followed him most everywhere he went.

Stanley fired another angry look back at the employees behind the counter. They didn't really look back at him, just giggled within their group while half-looking in his direction. He sneered, then put on his sunglasses and walked out. Stanley didn't get more than a few feet outside when he noticed a newspaper sitting on a table. Someone must have left it behind as they finished their coffee earlier. With little else to do, Stanley sat down and picked up the paper.

Stanley sat nursing his coffee for a while as he idly flipped through the pages of the current edition of the *Redmain Gazette*. The stories were typical of a small town, with nothing that extended past the town's geographical limits, but they provided Stanley a quiet distraction as he sipped on his daily caffeine delivery system. The chatter of patrons walking in and out of the shop buzzed around him, but Stanley found himself lost in the printed pages as he searched for some semblance of meaning in the mundane news of this sleepy little town.

The front page touted an article about the mayor of Redmain, Jim Mass. Stanley skimmed the byline, which read, "*Mayor Mass Cuts In*!" The picture that accompanied the article was of the mayor at a public event, holding a comically enormous set of scissors that he was using to cut a ceremonial ribbon. A smaller picture next to it showed Mayor Mass shaking hands with someone very official and important-looking. Stanley ignored the text and focused on the picture itself. Mass, a tall man with an imposing frame, sported a perfect politician's smile, or so Stanley thought. He found it immediately off-putting and switched his focus to the other man, who Stanley believed was a state congressman, if he remembered his local politicians correctly, which he was sure he probably didn't.

Stanley flipped past the front page, uninterested in the goings-on of Redmain's important people and events. He scanned the sports section. *The Padres* won another one, Stanley read. If only he had even a passing interest in sports. He thumbed his way through the stocks page. The Dow Jones was down, Stanley noted. Perhaps that would have been interesting if he had been involved in stocks and trading, which he wasn't. After a few minutes of reading and page-turning, finding nothing that could hold his attention for more than a minute, Stanley's eyes landed on a headline tucked away in the business section: *"New Industrial Company, ParaWorks, Passes Full Inspection."* Intrigued, Stanley leaned in closer and scanned the article for details.

ParaWorks, a multinational corporation specializing in industrial manufacturing, had announced plans to open a new facility on the outskirts of town, coincidentally not too far from Stanley's modest apartment complex. The article quoted Mayor Jim Mass's comments that the new project would bring a variety of economic benefits with the new venture—jobs for residents, increased tax revenue for the city, that sort of thing. Recognizing the name ParaWorks, Stanley flipped back to the front page and realized the ribbon-cutting ceremony Mayor Mass had attended was for the construction site of that very same company. Stanley scratched his forehead as he wondered how he hadn't heard of this. Redmain wasn't big, and this was big news. Of course, Stanley realized he hadn't picked up the *Redmain Gazette* since the last time he used a public bathroom, and his attention was elsewhere at the time.

Stanley made his way back to the business section, lightly dusted over a few lines, and was about to turn the page when something caught his attention. Amid the small print of the article was a reference to the environmental impact assessment for the town of Redmain by the EPA, which was basically a standard check on the effects of the ParaWorks facility on the ecosystem of the town. To Stanley, it was like a bright red flag waving in the breeze, although to most people it probably would have been passed over as a forgettable footnote. Of course, being a former employee of the Environmental Protection Agency, Stanley was well aware of how crucial environmental impact assessments are and what could result from neglecting or failing to act upon them. He bent a little way forward and gave the words his full attention.

The terminology of the article was not exactly clear-cut, and the information was minimal, yet Stanley still couldn't shake the impression that there was more behind the article than met the eye. It wasn't any particular fact or detail that cried foul, not exactly. But something didn't seem right. Stanley made a mental note to look into it further, to dig deeper into the glossy facade of ParaWork's corporate promises and catchy slogans. Then, as quickly as the thought had come, Stanley remembered he didn't work for the EPA any longer. He didn't work at all, as a matter of fact. The fire that had so quickly lit up his eyes faded like a struck match quickly blown out by a gust of wind.

Stanley tossed the paper down on the table, got up, and started his walk home.

* * *

Redmain's streets were busier as Stanley made his way home, a fact that didn't stop him from continuing his daily disparagement of his arch-nemesis, Leo Vincent. He kept working diligently to perfect his insults and comebacks for a showdown that would likely never happen.

"You'll show me?" Stanley asked. "Ha! I'll show you, Vincent!"

"You thought I gave up? Ha ha! No, no! I was always here, Vincent. Always here!"

"Vincent!"

"Vincent!"

As Stanley trudged along the familiar streets of Redmain, lost in his thoughts of personal victories, he hadn't noticed that he had veered off from his normal route home and was taking an alternate path back to his apartment. When the familiar setting became all too *unfamiliar*, Stanley's eyes caught sight of something he hadn't seen before in this town that never changed—a large sign erected on a vacant lot, which itself was on the edge of town. It read, '*Coming Soon to the Town of Redmain: ParaWorks! A New Industrial Facility*.'

Stanley scowled as he took in the massive sign. It was big, ten feet by ten feet, and planted in full view of anyone passing by. With a furrowed brow, he approached the sign, his mind racing with thoughts of the *potential* environmental impact of such a facility on a small town like Redmain. As he stood before the sign, Stanley's eyes fell upon the pristine, natural beauty of the landscape, the site of this new industrial facility. It was a desert landscape and plain, very plain, but it was beautiful in its own simple way. Untouched by man, stretching unobstructed to the mountains. Sites like these were rare in 2025. Population and construction were taking them all away. But the town of Redmain still had them. They surrounded it, in fact.

Stanley had worked at the EPA for many, many years. He hadn't seen it all, but he had seen most of it. With his knowledge of environmental issues, contaminants, and chemical impacts, Stanley knew all too well the potential dangers posed by industrial development—pollution, habitat destruction, deforestation—parking garages.

Stanley took in the surrounding area as he stood pondering. His mind raced with images of bulldozers cracking a water main, oil spilling out, and displaced townspeople. He had flash after flash of what could be, what might be, and what horrors could befall this area and this town. And as he surveyed the scene before him, Stanley felt that familiar sense of determination creeping into his blood like adrenaline. He ignited a fire within him. He felt strong, like he used to. Not on his watch, Stanley thought.

Then, with a vocal harrumph, Stanley shook his head free of the returning thoughts and feelings and continued on his way, pushing aside his silly concerns and wild imagination. He flicked the lid off his coffee cup and tossed the remaining brown liquid at the ParaWorks sign. He dropped the empty cup on the ground and continued grumpily away—only to return moments later, pick up the coffee cup, and throw it in a nearby trash can.

Once an EPA man, always an EPA man.

Stanley started home again, diving right back into the insults and comebacks he was working on before he saw the sign.

"Let me tell you something, Vincent," he mumbled to himself. "*You*, sir, are a human ball sack!"

Chapter Two

It was late morning by the time Stanley shuffled back into his apartment. Somewhere in the back of his mind, he was still working on the article he had read at *Beans and Brew*, but he kept pushing it away from his conscious thoughts. Not his job anymore, Stanley kept reminding himself. He kicked off his flip-flops and tossed his keys onto the kitchen counter. It's not worth thinking about, Stanley thought as the sound of his old-school landline phone pierced the silence with its shrill ring. Stanley crossed the room and looked at the caller ID display. His heart skipped a beat when he read his daughter's name.

"Hey there, sweetheart," Stanley said. "How's my baby girl doing?"

A warm chuckle echoed through the phone. "I'm 45, Dad. Hardly a baby anymore."

Stanley beamed with delight at the sound of his daughter's voice. In the years since Chicago, Elizabeth had become Stanley's only source of happiness. His ex-wife, Kate, had thankfully not fought his request for 50/50 custody, so Stanley could continue to be a genuine part of his daughter's life, a reality that not all fathers have.

"You'll always be my little girl, honey," Stanley said with a smile. "So, tell me everything. How's the new job treating you? Are you running things yet?"

Elizabeth laughed from the other end of the line. "It's pretty good so far. Getting used to California instead of Chicago. I'm definitely at the bottom of the totem pole though," she said. "I never expected to be moving, not to a different part of the field this late, but I'm loving it though, and I've made some amazing new friends."

Stanley climbed onto one of the bar stools in his kitchenette. "Well, entertainment law isn't something you can just jump into," he said. "Family law was your bread and butter for a long time. It's going to take a while to get a handle on things. Be patient. Be diligent. I know you'll do great things. But I'm glad you're making new friends out there. That's good."

As they continued to chat, Elizabeth shared all the details about her new job. She talked about the challenges it presented, the opportunities it offered, and the genuine sense of worth she felt doing something that helped people. It was like stepping back in time for Stanley as he listened to the excitement in her voice. He found it all too familiar. He had felt the same way all those years ago when he was young and starting his new career with the EPA. It seemed like another lifetime, Stanley thought. Another life.

"I'm so proud of you, sweetheart," Stanley said before shifting to a more cautious tone. "And how's Mom?"

Over the years, Stanley and Kate had found a cordial place in which to function, where they could focus their attention on their daughter. Stanley was always grateful that she hadn't fought him for custody of Elizabeth. She could have. She may have even wanted to. But she never did. From there, Stanley began his long process of healing, which derailed slightly when Elizabeth told him that Kate had moved on. But as the years passed by, he found his peace with it, or at least he tried to convince himself of it. The subject was never completely pain-free, though.

There was a momentary pause on the other end of the line as if Elizabeth was thinking and choosing her words carefully. "She's—she's doing okay," Elizabeth finally said. "She and Robert just got back from a trip to Spain."

A quick, albeit hurtful, laugh erupted out of Stanley's mouth before he could stop it. But he reined it in quickly. "Oh, Spain! Wow, that's really something!"

"Dad, I'm sorry," Elizabeth said quickly. "I wouldn't have said anything, but..."

Stanley cut Elizabeth off mid-sentence. "No, no. It's fine, Lizzy. I'm glad she's doing well. And Robert too." Stanley swallowed, trying to keep the gulp quiet. "He's a good guy."

There was an awkward silence for a few seconds before Elizabeth continued. "So, Dad. What about you? Anything new?"

"Oh, you know, same old story, same old Dad," he said vaguely with not too successful evasion. "Nothing much to report here. Yesterday happened yesterday, but that was the same as the day before that one, kiddo."

For a moment, Elizabeth said nothing. She didn't need to. Her concern was obvious, even from miles away. "Dad, I know you. I know when something's cooking, even if you won't admit it," she said. "I can hear it in your voice. Tell me. What's up?"

Stanley let out a long exhale. Elizabeth knew him too well. "Well..." Stanley trailed off, wondering if he should even mention it, but ultimately gave in. "I just read an article in the *Gazette*. Seems there's a new company coming into town, something called ParaWorks." He started rolling the phone cord around his finger. "They're planning to set up shop on the outskirts of town. New jobs. An influx of money. You know, that sort of thing. Funny thing is, I can't shake the feeling that something isn't right. Something seems… off."

"What do you mean, Dad?" she asked, her curiosity piqued.

Stanley hesitated, unsure of how much of his thoughts to give in to. This kind of thinking led to divorce, early retirement, and an apartment in the middle of nowhere. But as usual, he couldn't keep things from Elizabeth.

"I don't know, sweetheart," he admitted. "I wish I could explain it. But I have a funny feeling about it. I was thinking of maybe looking into it. Maybe."

The silence on Elizabeth's end of the line spoke volumes. "Just promise me you'll be careful, Dad," she said, "whatever you do."

"I will, sweetheart," Stanley promised. "Don't worry about me. It's nothing. I'm sure I'll wake up tomorrow and have forgotten all about it."

Stanley and Elizabeth talked for another hour, catching up on the latest happenings in each other's lives. Stanley felt such pride in Elizabeth's accomplishments. He always had. She had become so much like him in so many ways. Dogid. Tough. Relentless. That worried Stanley sometimes, even though she was 45 and far from helpless. But Elizabeth seemed to navigate the tricky waters of office politics far better than Stanley ever did.

CHAPTER TWO

* * *

The rest of Stanley's day evaporated like a puddle on the sidewalk during a hot summer day. He paid some bills, watched some television, and did nothing of any relevance. Such were his days, and such were his nights. Normally, anyway. But this night was different. As Stanley lay in bed, he couldn't shake himself free of the thoughts that had been plaguing him all day and all evening. Try as he might, sleep eluded him as his brain practiced mental acrobatics. His mind was never far from that article and the thoughts about the ParaWorks company coming to town.

Stanley tossed and turned restlessly, the events of the past creeping into his thoughts like unwelcome guests crashing a party. Memories of his time in Chicago, of Leo Vincent, the explosion at the CleanCycle BioSystems plant, the toxic cloud, the mayor's office, the news reports, and that damn statue. It was all so long ago, but he could recall every detail as if it had just happened yesterday. The memories flooded his mind and darkened his expression as the bitter reminders of his choices and their consequences seemed to taunt him with the life he had left behind, the life that he had lost.

Stanley's thoughts drifted back to the start of it all—forty years ago. The CleanCycle BioSystems office and operations plant in 1985 was a fortress of glass and steel, a three-floor, remodeled packaging plant from the turn of the century. CleanCycle BioSystems was, according to its own promotional literature, a new start-up company that processed and disposed of hazardous materials using a new, closely guarded secret process that was cheaper and more efficient than existing means. The building itself was just large enough to be imposing in the older industrial area on the outskirts of Chicago proper.

Stanley Peck, EPA officer, walked up to the main office door, clipboard clutched like a shield, his regulation suit crisp but slightly too tight around the shoulders. His instincts said this '*secret process*' was a sham, a lie, a dangerous environmental risk, and he was there to prove it. He was there to prove he could see through CleanCycle BioSystems' smoke and mirrors and expose what he believed to be their fraudulent business claims. Stanley delivered four sharp knocks on the door, each a pointed declaration of his righteousness.

A man swung the door open before Stanley could knock a fifth time. There stood Leonardo Vincent, sporting a perfectly tailored suit and with charisma oozing out of his pores. He looked Stanley up and down, not bothering to hide his judgment. "Can I help you?" he asked.

"Yes, you can," he said as he stepped forward. "My name is Stanley Peck, and I'm here on behalf of the Environmental Protection Agency."

"Well, that certainly sounds very important," Vincent quipped as he extended his hand and stepped aside to admit Stanley into the office. "I'm Leonardo Vincent. But my friends call me Leo."

Stanley ignored Leo's hand, his steely eyes fixed on his prey, and stepped into the slightly disheveled office. "This isn't a social visit, Leo. I'm here on official business."

Leo retracted his hand and sneered. "That'll be Mr. Vincent, I think," he said as he closed the door behind Stanley and made his way over to his desk, plopping into his chair.

"Mr. Vincent," Stanley said. "As the figurehead of Clean-

Cycle BioSystems, you're the one ultimately responsible for its operations. Is that correct?"

"I prefer managing CEO," Vincent said with not a small amount of snark. "But yes, that's true. I'm responsible for the operations here."

"And just what operations exactly do you manage?" Stanley asked.

Vincent held Stanley's gaze. "We use a specially designed high-pressure and heat process to treat hazardous material and dispose of it safely." He smiled. "Simply put, that is."

Stanley slapped his clipboard onto the desk like a judge's gavel. "Come on, Vincent. Skip the sales pitch and the brochure. Your processing technology—how does it work? How do you handle residuals? What are the protocols? Walk me through it." Stanley's voice was a blade, each word soaked in the certainty that he already knew better, no matter what Vincent said.

Leo propped himself up on one of his armrests, his grin unshaken and arrogant as a king. "Walk you through it? Stan..." Vincent used the abbreviation of Stanley's name like a weapon. "You wouldn't understand the poetry of our process if I painted it on the walls."

"Oh, I don't know about that," Stanley countered. "I've been around the block. I've seen things. Give me a shot."

Vincent all but snarled at Stanley. "Alright, Mr. EPA man. We take waste, nasty, toxic stuff, and lock it in a loop so tight even Mother Nature would blush. Some heat, some pressure, and bam! Safe as your grandma's apple pie."

"Is that the best you can do?" Stanley asked. "What are the technical details?"

"You wouldn't understand them."

"Mr. Vincent," Stanley said, "it would be in your best interest to cooperate with me."

"And why is the EPA interested in my business, Mr. Peck?" Vincent asked.

Stanley didn't skip a beat. "Because we want to know what you're doing here," Stanley said. "And I am very concerned about the environmental impact of your operations here."

"*You're* concerned?" Vincent asked.

Stanley paused. "*We* are concerned."

Leo Vincent shifted in his chair, ever so slightly uncomfortable. "Well, they're trade secrets, *our* technical details. We're still in the process of securing a patent, so I'm not at liberty to reveal our technical specs to the EPA, you, or anyone else."

Stanley nodded disapprovingly. "I see. And you created this new process, did you?"

"We did."

"And you have the numbers to back all of this up?" Stanley asked.

"It's science, Peck, not accounting."

"And the city of Chicago provided you with a license to operate this '*process*' within city limits?" Stanley asked.

Vincent spun around and grabbed a decanter from the table behind his desk and poured himself a drink. The clink of the glass echoed in the space between the two men. No offer for Stanley. "We are operating under a provisional permit while we wait for full state licensure. But you can check that yourself. Chicago loves what we're offering, Mr. EPA." Vincent smiled. "We're golden."

"I see," Stanley said. "And this process you perform, is it on site? Here in this building?"

"Yes, it is."

"May I see it?" Stanley asked.

Vincent shook his head. "What's your problem, Mr. EPA? Why are you pushing this?"

"Because I think your operation is a sham, Mr. Vincent," Stanley said. "Your claims of a '*new process*' that makes hazardous materials safer for disposal, and at a cheaper cost than your competitors, sound *way* too good to be true. The city may love you, but the EPA wants to examine the environmental impact of your *supposed* process. *I* want to examine it." Stanley straightened his posture. "Particularly, I want to explore your handling of dangerous, hazardous byproducts resulting from your *secretive* process, as well as the disposal chain of your operation and whether it involves illegal dumping of materials or the release of airborne toxins."

Vincent's eyes fired daggers at Stanley. "We have a valid permit from…"

Stanley's eyes narrowed, and his determination hardened into a vicious sneer that could curdle milk as he cut Vincent off. "Your permit's a loophole, Vincent. You haven't filed your '*process*' with the patent office. You haven't completed the checks and safety lists from the city. Your secrecy stinks worse than your claims."

Vincent puffed up his chest. "Secrecy?! It's called innovation and corporate protection, Peck!"

Stanley leaned in and matched Leo Vincent's aggression with calculated restraint. "We can do this the hard way, or we can do it easily. But I *will* see your operation, Mr. Vincent."

Leo leaned back in his chair. "Go chase a litterbug, Mr. EPA."

Stanley stood and snapped up his clipboard from Vincent's desk, his sneer gone, replaced by a calm and controlled expression. "This isn't over, Mr. Vincent. I'll be back with a court order and a magnifying glass. You can't hide from me." Stanley turned on his heel and headed for the door.

Behind him, Leo Vincent's voice cut through each step. "Bring it on, Peck! And don't forget to bring a flashlight. You'll need it to find your head after I shove it up your ass!"

Stanley slammed the office door behind him, leaving Leo Vincent's taunting laughter and threatening words like an annoying tick burrowing into his ears.

Lying in his bed, Stanley blinked his eyes free of the forty-year-old memories. He turned to his side and scoffed. Who would have thought that a simple visit to some bullshit company would lead to such an unadulterated mess? And yet, here he was, a world away from the hectic streets of Chicago, still grappling with what had happened and the consequences of his actions all those years ago.

Then Stanley's thoughts returned to the newspaper article he had read earlier. A sense of apprehension washed over him. He just couldn't shake the feeling that something wasn't right. But as much as Stanley tried to push the thoughts aside, they continued to gnaw at him like a persistent itch, refusing to be ignored unless scratched. With an exhaustive sigh, Stanley prayed for sleep as he buried his head beneath his pillow.

Chapter Three

It wasn't too far away, Stanley thought. It would only take the better part of the morning, maybe the afternoon if things went well. The county EPA office was just a few towns over in Atherton. He didn't need to do much, just provide a friendly push for someone to look up a report and read some files. Nothing major, Stanley thought. Shouldn't be a big deal.

Stanley stood patiently at the bus stop. The crisp morning air nipped at his cheeks as he waited for the next bus to arrive. The street was quiet except for the occasional car that drove by. No one could hear as Stanley mumbled under his nose his daily rant towards that one particular man who made his head twitch from time to time.

"Remember me, Leo? Betcha do," Stanley said, almost like he was sleepwalking.

"I've got something for ya, Vincent." Stanley rammed his fist into his palm. "How do you like that, Leo?"

"You'll rue the day, Vincent!"

Stanley's verbal bashing of Leo Vincent got cut off as the bus rumbled to a stop in front of him. He climbed up the three steps, paid his coin fee, and took a seat near the back. His mind still buzzed with nerves. The only thing that helped soothe his racing thoughts were the comeback fits that poured out of his mouth like free-flowing lava from an active, spurting volcano. Stanley paid the awkward glances from the other bus riders no mind. He was used to people looking. It didn't bother him—most of the time, anyway.

* * *

The journey to the local county EPA office took about 45 minutes. When he stepped off the bus, Stanley regarded the office with a sense of apprehension. No turning back now. The bus was already gone, after all. No, he made his choice. He would say what he needed to say. Besides, the bus back to Redmain wouldn't be back until 12:35.

Stanley whipped off his sunglasses like a detective on one of those silly shows and stepped inside. He approached the reception desk, where he found a tired-looking clerk who greeted him with a forced smile.

"Do you have an appointment, sir?" she asked.

Stanley wondered if she could look more bored and uninterested if she tried, but he resisted asking and shook his head. "No, no appointment. Just here to save the world," he quipped, earning a half-hearted chuckle from the clerk, who nodded absently and motioned for Stanley to take a seat in the waiting area.

As he settled into one of the many hard plastic chairs he had to choose from, Stanley noticed a familiar sense of dread creeping in. Maybe this wasn't such a good idea after all, he wondered. Stanley looked at his watch. 10:14. 129 minutes until the return bus, he thought. This was going to be a long wait.

After what seemed like an eternity, although it was only nine minutes, a door at the end of the hallway swung open. A tall woman with dark hair emerged. Her crisp business suit, black-rimmed glasses, and no-nonsense demeanor marked her as the EPA branch officer.

"Mr. Peck?" she called.

Stanley stood, cleared his throat, and approached her with his hand extended in greeting. "Yes, ah, that's me. I'm Stanley Peck."

The woman nodded, her expression unreadable, at least to Stanley.

"I'm Louise Talbot, the local EPA representative."

She smiled, but it was hardly sincere. Stanley was well acquainted with that kind of gesture. Stanley had given it more times than he could count or even remember. He felt defeated before she spoke her next words.

"Follow me, please," she said.

As they entered her office, Stanley took a seat facing Talbot's desk and immediately leaned forward and started talking before the EPA representative could ease into her seat. "Ms. Talbot, first let me say I really appreciate you taking the time to see me. I'm sure you must be busy, so I'll get straight to the point." Stanley adjusted a bit in his seat. "I have to tell you I'm a little concerned about the environmental impact of the new industrial facility, ParaWorks, that's supposed to be set up in the town of Redmain. You see, I have a background with the EPA, and I can tell you there are red flags all over this. In fact, I..."

Ms. Talbot raised her hand and waved over the start of Stanley's next sentence. "Hold on, hold on, Mr. Peck. Slow down a moment, please."

Stanley looked up and took a deep, calming breath. He did his best to calm his rate of speech before finally starting again. "I apologize, Ms. Talbot. I know I can come on strong sometimes. Let me start again, please."

Ms. Talbot gave Stanley a gracious nod and allowed him to continue.

"Redmain is a small town, not too far from here," Stanley began. "I've lived there for a while now. It's the kind of town where most people who live there work jobs, not careers. Nothing like New York or Chicago. It's just Redmain. The sort of town where people would welcome with open arms the money that a big industrial complex like ParaWorks would offer. A town where no one would ask too many questions. But I read the report that the local paper published. It had dry statistics and numbers that wouldn't mean anything to most people. But I've seen reports like that. Hundreds of them! And something was—off. I'd have to see more to tell you exactly what. But there were a lot of T's not crossed and a lot of I's not dotted. I got the distinct impression that corners were being cut."

Ms. Talbot raised an eyebrow, unable to hide her skepticism. "Mr. Peck, I understand and respect your concerns. I know all about Redmain and ParaWorks going up there. But local and state authorities reviewed and approved all the reports. Many of them passed through this very office."

"Yes, yes, I understand that," Stanley said, speeding up his speech again. "I don't mean to imply that anyone here isn't doing his or her job."

Ms. Talbot shook her head. "I didn't take it that way, Mr. Peck."

"Good, good," Stanley said. "It's just—I've seen this happen before. This new barrel of cash comes rolling into town, and people are so welcoming of it they don't read the fine print."

"Fine print?" Talbot asked.

"Yes," Stanley said, "the fine print. The report in the article mentioned the gas emissions being within safety margins, the depth of the penetration into the soil, and the plan for the disposal of toxic chemicals. All the standard things you'd expect to see, but what about the distance to the water table? What about the long-term effect of their emissions on the ozone? Where is that data? There's a lot missing, or only half-answered."

Stanley sat up straight, a rush of confidence fueling his posture. For a moment, he felt like he used to when confronting someone. He felt strong. He felt right. It had been a long time since he had felt that way. It felt good. He locked eyes with Ms. Talbot as if daring her to question him about data and statistics. Talbot met his gaze but didn't take the bait that Stanley's eyes offered her.

"Again, Mr. Peck, I have to tell you," Talbot said, "that '*fine print*' went through this office and the main office. The city officials of Redmain itself read those reports. Mayor Jim Mass and the city planner, Alan Hargrove, read those reports. They didn't have any objections. They passed everything through. No concerns of any kind."

"Of course they didn't," Stanley said. "Politicians and bean counters aren't worried about environmental issues. They're worried about..."

Talbot cut him off again. "What are *you* worried about, Mr.

Peck? Exactly? What exact harm do you think ParaWorks is going to have on Redmain?"

Stanley froze. He didn't know what to say. Ms. Talbot was asking reasonable questions, he knew. But he didn't have the answers Ms. Talbot was looking for. All he had were suspicions, questions rooted in what wasn't there, rather than what was. He was so used to pushing forward with a feeling, and that feeling being backed by his position. He wasn't at all used to being on the other side of the desk.

"I…" Stanley stammered. "You're asking for specifics that I don't have. I just read that report in the newspaper, and I noticed a lot of information was missing. It's not that anything there was specifically wrong, just that things were missing."

"Missing?" Talbot questioned. "What was missing?"

"I just told you. You aren't listening," Stanley said. "What about the mineral report? The longevity report?"

Talbot sat forward in her chair and leaned over her desk, closing the distance between herself and Stanley. "Mr. Peck, you were looking at a truncated report in a small-town newspaper. Data like you're talking about wouldn't mean anything to the average reader. You saw something missing, and you immediately cried foul. But you're jumping the gun here. And maybe you're just a little too close to things like this to be objective."

Stanley looked up and locked eyes with Ms. Talbot. "What does that mean, exactly?"

In what felt like an eternal pause, Talbot leaned back in her seat. Every creak of her chair cut through the silence before she finally spoke. "Look, Mr. Peck. I know who you are. Every EPA agent this side of the moon knows who you are."

Stanley closed his eyes as he nodded. There it is, he thought.

There it is. "Oh, I see," he said. "And because I had a bad last day, all my years of service go out the window? Is that it?"

Ms. Talbot shook her head and took a breath. "It's so much more than that, Mr. Peck." She grudgingly gestured to the wall behind Stanley. He had been so quick to sit and start talking that he had missed seeing the 8x10 picture mixed among the various corporate rules and HR guidelines arranged on the wall. It was the famous picture of Uncle Sam pointing. Only this time, instead of saying *'I want you for the U.S. Army,'* it read, in big bold letters, *'Don't be a Pecker!'* And in place of Uncle Sam's face was a photoshopped face—of Stanley Peck.

A wave of nausea washed over Stanley. His heart began to race, and a layer of sweat sizzled all over his body. He struggled to push back down the vomit that was rising in the back of his throat. The memories flooded Stanley's mind. That day in Chicago. The mayor's office. Leo Vincent. His wife. His daughter. Everything. Stanley lowered his head, as if resigning himself to the firing squad of his past. No matter *what* he had been, no matter *who* he had been, this is who he was *now*. He was a cautionary tale. It made him sick.

"I'm sorry, Mr. Peck," Talbot said as her face sank. She could see the damage that picture had just done. And she very much regretted gesturing for Stanley to see it.

Stanley clenched his fists. "You don't understand," he said. "No one understood. I was trying to protect the public, trying to do my job. CleanCycle BioSystems…" He half laughed at the mention of their name. "They claimed to dispose of toxic waste in some secretive way, using technology no one knew about. Why would I believe that? Why would anyone believe that? They looked like con men. I thought they were illegally dumping materials somewhere and claiming the residuals were clean. So, I got my court order and demanded to see proof of this new technology. And what did I see? They called it a '*high-pressure system*' or something like that. It all sounded made up. They were drawing excessive power from the city grid, and whatever else they had there wasn't properly coded or approved of. They were a danger, a menace! At least they looked like they were. It was my job to question them. Real or not, what they had in that warehouse was dangerous. I had a responsibility, a duty." Stanley's eyes glossed over as he replayed the memories in his mind. "Then that explosion, the cloud, the statue. Everything got out of control so fast."

Stanley closed his eyes and shook his head. Talbot, who had been listening intently to Stanley's telling of the famous story, almost stood to walk over to him—almost.

"I called them liars, and they saved the city," Stanley said. "It cost me almost everything. But it doesn't mean I was wrong, Ms. Talbot. What I did was right." He took a long breath, then refocused and looked directly into Talbot's eyes. "I'm asking you to put aside the past and look at this with impartial eyes, please. I've seen this sort of thing before, and I know the signs. Companies like these cut corners to save money. And it's the environment and the people who pay the price."

Talbot sighed and leaned back in her chair. "Mr. Peck, I'm sorry about what happened to you. I truly am. It's not fair. But you've got to understand that our team has thoroughly vetted the ParaWorks plans, and the city officials verified the data themselves. We've taken every precaution to ensure that everything is up to standard."

"Standards can be manipulated," Stanley insisted, his voice rising slightly. "Please, just look at the reports with me, or let me look at them. There has to be something we can find, some discrepancy. I'm not asking for much, just a little bit of your time."

"Mr. Peck..."

He cut her off. "Stanley. It's just Stanley."

Talbot's expression softened slightly, but she remained firm. "Stanley, I get it. I really do. But my hands are tied. The reports are clear, and we've followed every protocol. I can't just open an investigation because of a hunch—especially *your* hunch."

Stanley leaned forward. His voice took on a desperate tone. "It's not just a hunch, Ms. Talbot. It's experience. I've seen how these things can play out. Just give me a chance to prove it. I'll do all the legwork. I just need access. If there's something there, I'll find it."

Talbot shook her head. "I'm sorry, Stanley. I can't authorize that. We have procedures for a reason, and I have to follow them. You, of all people, know that. I can't yell '*smoke*' when there's no sign of a fire."

Stanley stood up, defeated. "I knew this was a mistake."

Talbot furrowed her brow. "I beg your pardon?"

"I should have expected this," Stanley said. "I should have known."

"I'm not the bad guy, Stanley," Ms. Talbot replied.

Stanley nodded his head and extended his hand to Ms. Talbot. She stood and took his hand.

"Neither was I," Stanley said.

* * *

As Stanley walked out of the office, he couldn't shake off a miserable sense of déjà vu. Once again, his warnings were dismissed. And yet again, he walked out of an office empty-handed. The bus arrived promptly, and he stepped aboard. He took a seat and readied himself for the ride home. As the bus pulled away, Stanley closed his eyes. The image of the Uncle Sam picture, or the Uncle Stanley picture to be more accurate, flashed through his mind. That's all he was now. Maybe that's all he ever was.

"All for what?" he thought to himself.

All for nothing.

* * *

Though he himself was unaware of it, Louise had watched Stanley leave the office. She stood at the back of her hallway and watched as Stanley sat down at the bus stop outside of the EPA office. Like everyone in her organization, Louise knew the general history of Stanley Peck, the events of Chicago, even that he had lost his family because of it. So public was his downfall that many people knew the personal details of his life and how he essentially lived in exile at this point in his life.

Still, there was something about Stanley that most people found hard to ignore. It wasn't his persistence or even his hard-headedness, although he was most definitely both of those things. It was his passion, his conviction, his determination, and that certain twinkle in his eye that people often found convincing. Louise Talbot stepped back into her office with just those sorts of thoughts running through her mind.

Atherton wasn't all that far from Redmain. It was close enough, in fact, that Louise had heard of Stanley's living there. She also knew most thought of him as the local nutcase, the odd man that talked to himself on the way to wherever he was going. She was equally aware there were no reports of Stanley Peck causing a scene, stirring up trouble where there was none to be found, and no incidents of making accusations against anyone or anything that might be considered slanderous, as his Chicago reputation would have people believe.

When Stanley stood up and left Louise's office, she was sure that was it. That was the end of it. A strange encounter with the famous Stanley Peck. She felt bad about the 'Uncle Stanley' picture, but assumed that when the office door closed behind him, that would be the last she considered his claims and questions. Yet, as Louise slid back into her chair, she found herself—considering. Was it his passion, his conviction, his utter determination that made Louise open her internal EPA search engine? She didn't really know, but Louise found herself typing in '*ParaWorks*' and '*Redmain*' into the search field just the same.

A list of files and documents scrolled across her screen. Louise spotted an entry for the ground penetration report filed with the EPA three months ago. She looked around the room as though she were doing something she shouldn't. Louise double-tapped the mouse, and the report filled her screen. She started reading, her practiced eyes taking in the dry statistical information, disregarding what was standard, and ignoring what was irrelevant. Then, an entry caught Louise's attention.

She squinted her eyes and cocked her head. "Wait a second. What?"

Chapter Four

Stanley could still smell the exhaust from the bus pulling away as he unlocked his apartment door and stepped inside. The quiet instantly surrounded him. It was as if he had just jumped into a pool of water, and it was suffocating. The meeting with Louise Talbot played over and over in his mind in a vicious loop, and it had been on full blast the entire bus ride home. It's not that she was rude or even impolite, Stanley thought, but she dismissed him just the same. He couldn't shake the image of that damn Uncle Sam poster with his face taped onto it, quietly mocking him and reminding him of his failures.

Stanley tossed his apartment keys onto the kitchen counter and hung his jacket on the back of one of the dining room chairs. He meandered around the small living room, eventually looking through a collection of books in a small bookcase and running his finger along the shelf, checking for dust. He picked up a magazine that he had left on the couch and thumbed randomly through the pages, only to drop it back onto the coffee table a moment later. Stanley tried to settle into his old, worn armchair, but the soft comfort it usually offered now seemed like sitting on rocks. He grabbed the TV remote and flipped through the local channels, but nothing could hold his interest.

Stanley turned off the TV and tossed the remote across the room and onto the couch. He pushed himself back in the chair and ran his hands down his face. When he opened his eyes, his gaze landed on a framed photo of his daughter on the mantelpiece. Her endearing smile was still a little crooked, but bright and inviting nonetheless. Stanley got up and walked over to the fireplace. He picked up the framed photo and traced her image with his finger.

The silence of the apartment grew louder in Stanley's ears. It pressed down on him so hard he felt like he couldn't breathe. He set the picture of Elizabeth back down and groaned in frustration. He started pacing the room, his thoughts a chaotic jumble. The meeting with Talbot, her polite but unmistakable dismissal, the *'Uncle Stanley'* poster, and the memories of his past failures all swirled together in his thoughts like an abstract painter throwing color randomly on a canvas.

Finally, Stanley threw his hands up in exasperation. "I need a drink," he said to himself as he grabbed keys, ripped his jacket from the back of the chair, and powered out the door.

* * *

The brisk evening air cooled Stanley's skin as he walked down the street, his footsteps heavy and slow as he returned to his daily rant towards a certain man.

"Oh yeah, Vincent?" Stanley said under his breath as he walked. "Feeling hungry, are ya?" Stanley clenched a fist and waved it into the air. "Well, let me give you a piece of this knuckle sandwich!" He took a hard swing at the evening breeze. "How'd that taste, Vincent?"

Stanley was only a few insults deep by the time he made his way to *Everett's Place,* a local bar a few blocks away that offered a surprisingly decent selection of drinks and a quiet corner to lose oneself in. Stanley had been there more than a few times as he whiled away an evening, listening to the jukebox in the corner.

Stanley pushed open the stereotypically creaky door and stepped inside. The familiar scent of stale beer and cigarette smoke hit him like a smack to the face. Normally, Stanley wouldn't consider himself a bar guy, but Everett, the owner and operator, was always nice to him. So, *Everett's Place* was a semi-regular home away from home. He made his way to the bar and slumped onto a stool.

"Hey, Everett," Stanley mumbled, waving a finger for attention.

"What'll it be, Stan?" Everett asked as he walked towards Stanley's end of the bar, a subtle limp in his stride.

"Whiskey," Stanley said. "Make it a double."

Everett nodded, poured the double whiskey, and slid it over. Stanley took a breath and upended the glass, savoring the familiar alcohol burn as it went down. The warmth of the whiskey spread through his chest, momentarily dulling the ache inside as it worked its way into his bloodstream.

Stanley waved Everett over again. "I'll take another one of those."

Everett looked Stanley up and down before squinting his eyes and asked, "This a shot or a bottle night?"

Stanley pulled his frown up to meet the bartender's gaze. He paused just long enough for the image of the re-faced '*Uncle Stanley*' to flash across his mind. "I think we're looking at a bottle night, Everett."

"Pace yourself, Stan," Everett said. "I'm not tellin' you your business, but I don't have money for a cab ride today, okay?"

Stanley winked. "Hey, I paid you back for that cab ride. And thank you, but pour away, please."

Everett shook his head and topped off Stanley's shot glass, smartly leaving the bottle nearby but just out of Stanley's reach. "Alright, alright. I'm not your pappy."

Stanley upended the shot and delighted in the sound of the empty glass kissing the wooden surface of the bar as he looked up to the television mounted in the corner. He watched a complete tire commercial and was about to look away when the next advertisement took over with a splash of red and white across the screen. Patriotic music played in the background, and the camera pulled back from an American flag to reveal a man standing by a window. Stanley quickly recognized the man as Mayor Jim Mass. "*Hello there, my friends,*" Mayor Mass said. "*Times have been hard on Redmain, but those times are over. Soon, we'll break ground on a new industrial plant that will change our little town. I've worked tirelessly to make sure that this new venture brings jobs, opportunities, and most of all—progress.*" The corner of Stanley's upper lip curled at the sight of such a polished politician. "*Just remember, I've got your back,*" Mass continued. "*I'm looking out for you, and I'm looking out for this town. I'll see you around*!" The commercial ended with a close-up on Mayor Jim Mass's smile, an image that made Stanley scowl and turn back to his empty shot glass.

"Everett," Stanley said. "I'm gonna need another over here."

As the evening wore on, Stanley continued to down one whiskey shot after another, and the once full whiskey bottle was now nearing the end of its life. The bar had filled with the usual crowd, mostly locals looking to unwind after a long day, and the random loner at a table or at the bar. Even though most people who sat at the bar were looking for some idle conversation, Stanley had kept to himself, but as the alcohol slowly but surely clouded his mind, his tongue loosened up.

Eventually, Stanley turned to the man sitting next to him, a young man nursing a beer with a few of his friends. "Hey, buddy. You know, I used to work for the EPA," Stanley slurred, his words barely rolling off his tongue.

The young man looked away from his friends and at Stanley with little to no interest. He raised his beer in a mock toast. "Oh yeah? Very impressive, pal."

"Damn right, it was!" Stanley stated emphatically, drawing the attention of the young man's friends, who chuckled at Stanley's grand statement.

"Everyone knows about the police department and the fire department," Stanley said, "or about the doctors, the teachers, and even the damn meter maids. But no one knows about the EPA guy—or woman. Everyone knows about the garbage man who takes your trash. But just *who* do you think makes sure that trash gets properly disposed of according to local and state guidelines?"

Stanley paused for an answer, and the group of four young men stared back at him blankly.

"Me!" Stanley said, pointing his finger in the air. "Guys like me. That's who!"

One man in the group spoke up. "So... you're a garbage man? Do you drive the truck or something?"

Stanley looked around as if shocked these men didn't know what he was talking about. "No, young man. I'm not a garbage man. I'm an EPA man! The Environmental Protection Agency!" He drifted off. "Well, I was, anyway."

The nearest of the young men nodded politely to Stanley, but he didn't see him looking back at his friends, quietly chuckling at the drunken tirade. He also didn't notice the men waving their hands at their buddy, encouraging Stanley to continue.

The man rolled his eyes at his friends and turned back to Stanley. "What happened, pal? You didn't get fired for drinkin' on the job, did ya?"

Stanley chuckled bitterly. "What happened? I'll tell you what happened! Ever hear of *'The Great Plume of '85'*?"

The man furrowed his brow, clearly unsure whether Stanley was joking. "The what?"

"The Great Plume of 1985!" Stanley repeated, louder this time, drawing the attention of a few more patrons. "A giant cloud of toxic death that nearly killed a suburb of Chicago back in '85. You're telling me you've never heard of that?"

Unbeknownst to Stanley as he continued his story at the bar, at that moment, none other than Louise Talbot had walked into *Everett's Place.* She looked around and sat at a nearby table. Coincidentally, Louise was there to meet a friend for a weekly info dump of their week. However, when she noticed Stanley Peck at the bar, it piqued Louise's interest.

She watched as the young man next to Stanley shook his head, still looking confused. "Are you serious? That crazy thing, like, 40 years ago?"

"Oh, I'm dead serious," Stanley said, a manic gleam in his eyes. "You see, back then, I was in charge of investigating this group of so-called *'eco-heroes.'* Bunch of frauds, if you asked me, but they had the press fooled. They had everyone fooled. But not me. Not Stanley Peck!"

Stanley took another swig of whiskey. The alcohol did its work, further fueling the fire of his rant. "So there I was," Stanley said, "trying to shut them down, doing my job, when all hell broke loose. Smoke and gas, chaos in the streets. And then a really unfortunate incident with a statue, and I'm public enemy number one!"

The crowd around the bar started to whisper and murmur. Some chuckled, while others looked on skeptically. At her table, Louise leaned in slightly, intrigued, despite herself.

"Everyone thinks those CleanCycle guys were heroes," Stanley said, his voice rising even more. "But they were reckless! And me? I was just trying to protect people, you know. Do my job. But no, I'm the villain in the story. The one everyone hates." Stanley slammed his shot glass down on the bar, spilling out some of the remaining whiskey. "Lost my job, my family, everything, all because of that mess. And for what? For trying to do the right thing."

Across the length of the establishment, Louise's friend arrived and sat down next to her. She was about to speak, but Louise waved her hand and made the "*shh*" sign as she continued to strain to listen to Stanley's story.

"So here I am," Stanley said. "I ran away. Now I'm stuck a million miles from everything I had, sitting on a bar stool in '*Nowhere City*' pouring it out to strangers and..." Stanley shifted himself closer to the young man closest to him. "Say, what is your name anyway, friend?"

The young man looked back at his friends and chuckled before turning back to the very inebriated Stanley. Before he could reply, Everett stepped over and leaned in. He covered the top of the shot glass with his hand and gave Stanley a sympathetic look.

"Maybe it's time to call it a night, Stan," Everett said, keeping his voice low.

Before Stanley could respond, the young man next to him whipped his head back to his friends, then back to Stanley with recognition in his eyes. "Hey, I know who you are!" the young man said. "You're that *'Peck'* guy that everyone talks about." He laughed. "Pecker! That's right. You're the Pecker Man, aren't you?!"

For a moment, just a moment, Stanley had thought someone was really listening to him. For a moment, he had allowed himself to think this young man might just be young enough not to know too much about Chicago and certainly nothing about Stanley Peck. And maybe he didn't. Maybe he knew nothing about Stanley, not really, anyway. But in the end, Stanley Peck was who he was. There was no escape.

"There it is," Stanley said, his head hanging now. He shook his head, his bone-weary sadness giving way to anger. "Yeah, maybe you're right, Everett. Time to go."

Stanley stumbled off the bar stool and started making his way to the door. A few tables away, Louise continued to watch Stanley closely. Perhaps he was a cautionary tale, an example of what *not* to do. But he was also a person, a person who had lost everything trying to do what he believed was right, even if he ended up being wrong. Louise turned back to her friend, who was looking at her curiously.

"What was that all about?" her friend asked.

"Oh, just an old story," Louise said as the wheels started turning in her mind.

Across the bar, Stanley pushed the door open and stepped

out into the chilly night air. He wobbled, but took a deep breath to steady himself. The memories of those events in Chicago were never far from his mind, and they were in full force that night. Stanley did his best to wash the memories away with a shake of his head as he walked toward his apartment. His footsteps echoed in the quiet Redmain streets.

As he half-walked and half-stumbled, Stanley noticed a piece of newspaper fluttering along the sidewalk, caught in the cool evening breeze. He bent down unsteadily and picked it up. Stanley squinted as he focused his vision to look at the picture and read the bolded headline. His blood boiled as he saw a familiar face staring back at him. The article was about Leo Vincent, who was being given the keys to the city in Chicago.

Stanley's vision blurred with rage and alcohol. "Vincent…" he growled, crumpling the newspaper in his fist.

In a fit of drunken defiance, Stanley tossed the balled-up newspaper page to the ground and unzipped his pants. He took careful aim at Leo Vincent's face as the paper unraveled.

"Here's some of my vengeance, Vincent," Stanley mumbled. "How does it taste, sir?!"

Stanley then let loose a stream of pee onto the newspaper, muttering curses under his breath. He was so lost in his delightful relief that he didn't notice the approaching police car until it was too late.

"Hey! What do you think you're doing?" a police officer asked as he stepped out of the police cruiser.

Stanley quickly zipped up and turned, startled. He stumbled, nearly falling over. "Just giving Vincent the respect he deserves," he slurred, giggling to himself.

The officer scowled, thoroughly unimpressed with Stanley's

answer. "Public urination is a crime, you know, sir. Step over here, please."

Stanley didn't resist as the officer turned him around, cuffed him, and led him to the patrol car. As he was being placed in the backseat, he glanced back at the crumpled, urine-soaked newspaper on the ground. The face of Leo Vincent seemed to mock him even now.

Back at *Everett's Place,* Louise Talbot watched from the doorway as the scene unfolded. She shook her head, feeling a curious mix of pity and curiosity. Stanley Peck, once a man of principle and duty, had been reduced to a drunken crackpot in a small-town bar. She couldn't help but wonder—what if?

As the patrol car pulled away, Stanley leaned his head against the window, the cold glass soothing his heated skin.

"Who are you?" he asked himself. "You're Stanley Peck."

Chapter Five

Stanley groaned a spectacular groan as he slowly opened his eyes, the painful shine of overhead lights glaring in his face. The cold, hard surface beneath him was a smarting reminder he had not spent the night in the comfort of his own bed, and the air around him was heavy with the smell of days-old sweat and generic disinfectant. Together, these clues stacked up as irrefutable evidence that Stanley was, in fact, not in his apartment. He pulled himself up and sat against the wall, his head pounding from the previous night's drinking, and squinted his eyes against the harsh fluorescent lights that flickered above him. The muffled sounds of police radios and distant conversations made their way down the hall and through the metal bars of his holding cell.

"Oh, sweet Jesus," Stanley mumbled before letting out a guttural belch.

He rubbed his temples as he tried to piece together the events that had brought him there. His memory was a blur of whiskey, anger, and of the urine-soaked yet triumphant face of Leo Vincent staring up at him from a crumpled-up newspaper. Stanley sighed, wondering when the guy with the jackhammer would stop working on his head.

As if on cue, the sound of footsteps echoed from down the hall, growing louder as they approached Stanley's holding cell. He looked up, and his eyes widened in surprise as he focused his vision on the sight of none other than EPA representative Louise Talbot. She stopped in front of the cell and shook her head, both disappointed and amused.

"Good morning, Mr. Peck," she said.

Stanley blinked, and confusion washed across his face. "Ms. Talbot?" he questioned. "What on earth are you doing here?"

"I've come to bail you out," Talbot answered.

Stanley's confusion deepened. "What? Why? How did you even know I was here?"

Talbot raised an eyebrow. "I was at *Everett's Place* last night. Saw the whole thing. I figured you might need a little help this morning."

Stanley's mind raced. He hadn't seen her at the bar. And he certainly hadn't listed her as an emergency contact. This was all very unusual, at least for Stanley. No one ever offered to help him.

"Why would you bail me out?" he asked. "We barely know each other. In fact, I'm pretty sure you don't even like me."

Talbot's expression softened slightly. "Let's just say I've been thinking about what you said. After you left my office yesterday, I pulled up some of the records, and I noticed some things didn't quite make sense. I brought the records for ParaWorks with me. I thought we could look at them together." She paused, letting Stanley take it in. "If you're still interested, that is."

Stanley's eyes opened wide with excitement. "Yes!"

"Good," Talbot said. "You must be hungry. How does breakfast sound?"

Stanley's stomach growled in response. He remembered he hadn't eaten since around lunchtime the previous day. "Yeah, I could eat. And maybe some coffee. Lots of coffee."

Ms. Talbot gestured to a guard just out of sight. The officer on duty stepped over, unlocked the cell, and escorted Stanley to the front desk, where he signed a release form and collected his meager belongings.

The fresh morning air was a welcome relief as they stepped out of the police station. Stanley turned to his new benefactor, still trying to wrap his mind around this sudden turn of events.

"I don't really understand why," Stanley said, "but thank you, Ms. Talbot."

She smiled. "Call me Louise."

* * *

Stanley and Louise walked to a nearby diner, the kind with vinyl booths and the comforting smell of sizzling bacon wafting from the kitchen. The bell above the door jingled as they entered, and a friendly waitress with a name tag stamped '*Dale*' greeted them with a smile in between gum smacks.

"Just the two of you?" she said. "Grab any booth you like." She gestured to the nearly empty dining area and grabbed a few menus.

Stanley and Louise chose a booth by the window. The waitress dropped the menus on the table and poured them both steaming cups of hot coffee. Stanley took a grateful sip, the warm caffeine starting its journey into his bloodstream. He glanced at Louise, who was already studying the menu. After a moment, Stanley looked up, noticing that the waitress, Dale, was still standing beside their table. Dale, an older woman in her 50s, smiled and glanced down at the yet-unpacked folders Stanley and Louise had brought in with them.

"Oh, don't mind me, kids," Dale, the waitress, said. "I'm nosy by nature. Always like knowin' about my customers."

Louise smiled back, then looked to Stanley for the next move.

"Thank you, Dale," Stanley said, looking at her name tag. "I think we'll need a few minutes, though."

Dale took another quick look at the stack of paperwork Stanley and Louise had brought in, then headed back to the register.

"So," Stanley began, setting his cup down. "You were at the bar last night. Must have been quite a show. It's hard to believe that display changed your mind."

Louise looked up, her eyes thoughtful. "It was definitely a show, but that's not why I'm here. Not entirely, anyway. When I looked up the ParaWorks file, I noticed that some of the numbers were definitely in the unsafe zone. It was the kind of thing I would have expected to see further documentation on, but there wasn't anything. So, I started thinking, or wondering. Then, after you were driven away, I couldn't shake the feeling that maybe I was too quick to dismiss you. I thought maybe there could be more to your story than I'd initially thought." Talbot lifted a thick folder out of her bag and plopped it down. It hit the table like a pile of bricks. "So, I figured it couldn't hurt to take a closer look."

Stanley nodded. "Well, I appreciate it. Really, I do."

They ordered breakfast. Pancakes and bacon for Stanley and a veggie omelet for Louise. As they waited for their food,

Louise opened a file and started spreading out its contents on the table. To the uninitiated, it probably looked like pages and pages in another language. But this was a language they both spoke fluently.

"This is everything my office has for ParaWorks," Louise said. "I've looked them over, but I want to hear your thoughts."

With that, Stanley started at the papers. His fingers danced across the files as his eyes scanned the documents. His brow furrowed, and he tapped a finger on the pages. He read and read. The food came, and the food went. Minutes stretched into hours. Stanley and Louise went through every page, every line, every bit of data.

It was all beginning to seem hopeless. Then, Stanley's eyes opened wide. "Here!" he shouted. "This section about the water table—do you see it?"

Louise scanned the page twice before looking back up at Stanley. She shook her head. "I don't see anything."

Stanley pointed to a chunk of data in the center of the page. "I knew I saw numbers that seemed off to me. It's very sneaky, but it's there. You just have to know what you're looking for."

Louise shrugged her shoulders, clearly mystified about what Stanley was getting at.

"Look here." Stanley turned to another document, a hydrogeological survey. "The infrastructure for the facility stops short of the depth of the water table. That's good, of course." Stanley directed Louise's attention to another page on another report. "But look at this report here. Redmain's water table is unusually close to ground level."

In the middle of Stanley's observation of the reports, Dale, the waitress, had made her way back to the table and was silently pouring more coffee into Louise's cup as Stanley continued. “Most people assume that the water table for a desert is quite low, but that isn’t always the case, especially when that desert is located close to mountain ranges, which Redmain just so happens to be.”

Dale, having finished Louise’s coffee top off, stood at the edge of the table, nodding her head to Stanley’s comments. “Mmm hmm. Mmm hmm. You shouldn’t never assume, I always say.”

Stanley glanced at Dale curiously as she moved over to Stanley’s coffee cup and started pouring—slowly. The wheels started turning in Louise’s mind. “And because Redmain has a high water table, if any structural elements from the facility breach or leak, they could contaminate the water supply?”

“Oh, honey,” Dale interjected as she dripped the last few drops of coffee into Stanley’s cup and chomped at her gum. “That don’t sound good at all.”

“No, no, it’s not,” Stanley said. “But there’s more.” He gestured again to the original document but stopped as he looked up to Dale with as polite a look as he could muster. “I think we’re good here,” he said with a crooked smile.

Dale, still smacking away at her gum and looking terribly disappointed, side-eyed Stanley as she headed off.

Stanley continued. “This report here gives statistical data on Redmain’s natural risk factors, like floods, wind conditions, fire, that sort of thing. But this is where it gets interesting. Redmain is basically flat land. It’s not like an urban city or mid-country town with a lot of tall buildings or natural bumps and valleys. It’s essentially flat. And Redmain itself even has building codes that prevent any construction from being over a certain number of feet.” Stanley gestured out the window of the cafe, revealing the rather uninspired and relatively flat landscape. "You know, to preserve the view," he said with no small amount of irony.

Louise leaned in, her eyes widening as she looked at the highlighted section. "And look at this last comment here," she said, excitedly gesturing at the document. "With its historically high winds and lack of natural or unnatural barriers, the city of Redmain is at higher than average risk from natural disaster, and its high water table presents a risk of contamination in the event of floods, fire, or other unnatural intrusions."

Stanley threw his hands up. "Redmain is just too high-risk! At first, it might seem like an ideal site, but it has so many factors that tip the scale."

Louise put the paperwork down, a confused look on her face. "I just don't understand. It seems so obvious. How could we not see it?"

Stanley lowered his head. "Because you weren't supposed to see it."

Louise grimaced. "What?"

"You're not payin' attention, honey," a voice cut in.

Both Stanley and Louise looked up to find Dale yet again at their table, this time not holding any coffee to refill with. Dale stood, head cocked to one side as she attempted to read the document Stanley was holding, still chewing away at her gum. "The devil's in the details. That's what he's sayin'." She pointed arbitrarily at the landscape out the window. "Sounds like we're a dangerous place to build certain things, and people should've said that, but it's bein' covered in all sorts of fancy talk."

Stanley nodded his head in bemusement at the waitress's assessment. "That's very observant of you, Dale, and quite correct."

"Oh, yeah, my ex-husband was like that," Dale said, slightly louder than she needed to be. "He'd always say somethin' nasty with somethin' good, thinkin' I wouldn't notice, but..."

Stanley cut Dale off mid-word. "Uh, Dale," he said, trying to find a friendly tone, "could we maybe have a few minutes to go over some things?"

After what seemed to be a minor eternity, Dale leaned in, recognition hitting her like a freight train. "You mean alone?"

Stanley nodded and smiled. "If you don't mind."

Dale chewed her gum a few times before replying. "Sure, honey. You go ahead on."

Stanley shook his head and smirked as Dale walked away. Then he returned to Louise and continued. "You see, it's easy to miss if you're not looking for it. The data itself isn't meant to be connected. And they bury it under layers of assurances about secure infrastructure and state-of-the-art technology. Someone probably hoped the two things wouldn't ever get put together. And maybe nothing will ever happen, but it could. Any number of natural or man-made disasters could spread the nastiness of an industrial facility like ParaWorks all over Redmain. Floods could erode the soil and reach the water table. Fire or winds could carry contaminants anywhere. The codes are all met. The 'I's' are dotted. The 'T's' are crossed. But the right hand doesn't seem to know what the left hand is doing. And that's a huge red flag. On paper, each thing by itself is manageable. But it's all about risk, Louise. What *could* happen? What *might* happen?"

Louise dropped her head into her hands. She suddenly felt the pressure of responsibility squeezing the backs of her eye sockets. "I see it. I do," she said. "But it's far from a smoking gun. I mean, this is just theory or conjecture at this point."

"You're right. That's true," Stanley agreed. "But we put this together over coffee, Louise. There's no way no one else did too. Someone out there knows this, and someone out there is part of an effort to keep it quiet."

Louise squinted in naïve confusion. "Is it possible this could have been honestly missed? Just a clerical mistake or something like that?"

"With data like this?" Stanley scoffed as he leaned in closer. "Like you said, it's not a smoking gun, but information like this would have been presented to Redmain officials. They would have had to sign a knowledge waiver and consent form in order for the plans to move forward. No one may have broken the law, but they knew the risk, and the published data is careful to keep the information in the right hand far away from the information in the left." Stanley straightened his posture. "Like I said, you weren't supposed to notice. It's hidden in plain sight. But it's meant to be missed. And that smells like…"

Louise cut him off. "Like a conspiracy."

Stanley shook his head. "Careful. Don't be a Pecker," he said with a wink.

Louise sighed, thinking of the altered Uncle Sam picture in her office. "I'm sorry about that, Stanley. That poster in my office. It wasn't fair what they did to you."

A long pause hung over the table before Stanley replied. "It's in the past."

"No, it's not," Louise said. "It's right here in our present. It's hanging on my office wall. But it's coming down, I promise. And I'll bring this to the main office tomorrow. I'm sure they'll start an investigation. Someone will answer for this."

Stanley smiled. "I love the attitude, kid. But we need proof.

They'll need proof—proof that Redmain knew about the risk and agreed to let ParaWorks start construction despite it. Anything else is just—words."

"Okay," Louise said. "How do we get that?"

Stanley winked. "We go old school."

Louise laughed openly. "Old school?"

Stanley frowned, sure he had used the expression properly. "My daughter Elizabeth says that. At least she says that's what I am."

Louise smiled. "You're most definitely that, Stanley."

He smiled at her, then refocused on the business at hand. "Whoever signed off on this didn't do it in an email. It's on paper somewhere. *Old school.* We just have to find it."

"All right. How do we do that?" Louise asked.

Stanley's eyes gleamed. "We might find something at the construction site itself. It has a building office set up there. We'll have to go there and throw our weight around."

Louise cocked her head. "*Our* weight?"

Stanley sighed. "Sorry. Old habits." He took a long breath. "Your weight. This is *your* case, Louise."

Louise smiled, excitement and apprehension on her face. "Oh no. We're in this together, Stanley." She thought for a second. "Let's do it."

Stanley grinned, feeling a renewed sense of purpose wash across his soul as he stood from the booth. "That's the spirit!"

"One thing though," Louise said, reaching out and grabbing Stanley's arm. "Before we go—you need a shower."

Stanley squinted his eyes at Louise, then leaned into his armpit and took a long sniff. He immediately pulled away and looked back at the local EPA rep with a sad look of agreement. "You might be right."

From across the diner, Dale chimed in one last time. "Oh, she's right, honey!"

Stanley nodded and waved to the waitress. "Thank you, Dale."

Dale smiled and waved back. "Sure thing, honey. Y'all don't be strangers if you need a meetin' place again. I'm here to help anytime."

Stanley held the door open as Louise stepped out, but paused as he turned and said to Dale, "Thank you, honey. We'll be sure to call you."

Chapter Six

Stanley and Louise sat in Louise's brown Buick, parked just outside the ParaWorks construction site. The industrial landscape loomed before them, made of massive piles of steel, concrete packs, and other building materials. Off to the side was a double-wide portable building that housed the site's construction office. This was their target. They could sketch the building with their eyes closed, as they had both been staring at it for about fifteen minutes, silently working up the courage to get out and do what they had gone there to do.

Stanley lowered the passenger window and adjusted his tie in the rearview mirror. His suit was from many years ago, looked more than a little dated, and served as a cool reminder of Stanley's older self. Besides his shower, Louise even talked Stanley into getting a fresh haircut. The clean lines of his new dew lent him an air of authority he hadn't felt in years. Stanley smiled at himself in the mirror, then wiped it away, replacing it with a stern business sneer. The old Stanley Peck was back in business.

"You know, it's been a long time since I did something like this," Stanley said.

Louise turned to him and offered a reassuring smile. "Well, you look the part at least. Just like the old days, right?"

Stanley nodded and took a deep breath, then looked down at his suit. "Yeah, in the old days this suit fit a whole lot better." Stanley adjusted himself in his seat and looked at Louise. "Look, I know you could have done this without me. Thanks for bringing me along."

Louise looked Stanley over and straightened the out-of-date name badge attached to his lapel. Immortalized behind a yellowing laminated cover was a picture of Stanley from 40-plus years ago. Louise smiled as he pulled her hands away. "I told you, we're in this together."

Stanley only smiled in response. He wanted to say something, but he couldn't. He wanted to tell her how much it meant to him that someone was taking him seriously again. But he was afraid, afraid that speaking it aloud would somehow make it real and then make it go away. Instead, he just awkwardly smiled. Louise may have noticed, probably did, but she didn't say a word.

They stepped out of the car and walked towards the main office. The gravel crunched under their feet. Stanley's heart raced as the double-wide trailer got bigger and bigger. But he steadied himself, trying to tap back into the confidence he once wielded with ease. Louise, however, was getting more and more nervous with each passing step. Stanley may have lived for moments like this, but not Louise. This was something new for her.

The construction office was a modest double-wide trailer, perched on concrete blocks and surrounded by the organized chaos of a new work site. Stanley knocked on the door with authority. As the duo waited for someone to answer, Stanley looked over at Louise. He noticed her nervousness as she nibbled on her lower lip.

"Hey, don't be nervous," Stanley said. "Just remember, pop-ins like this are pretty normal. As long as we act like it is too, everything will be fine."

Louise nodded in agreement as the door handle turned and a burly man in a hard hat and a high-visibility vest emerged. "Can I help you?" the man asked, eyeing them with confusion.

Stanley smiled his best fake smile and extended his hand. "Good morning, sir. I'm Stanley Peck, and this is Louise Talbot. We're with the Environmental Protection Agency. We're here for a routine inspection of your files and records."

The man's expression shifted slightly as he shook Stanley's outstretched hand. "Bob Jackson, site manager," the man said as he scratched his head and cleared his throat. "I haven't heard about any inspections today. Of course, why would anyone in the fancy main offices tell the head contractor anything?"

Louise stepped forward despite her nerves, her tone professional but friendly. "It's a bit last-minute, I'm afraid. Probably why the main office didn't reach out to you. We're doing a series of unscheduled inspections to ensure compliance with local building codes and site safety. Just a precautionary measure, you understand."

Bob nodded slowly. "Well, at least you're tellin' me what's goin' on. It's more than those corporate asses bother to do." He moved out of the way. "Well, come on in, and I'll see what I can do for you."

Stanley and Louise followed Bob into the trailer, which was crammed with desks, filing cabinets, and blueprints spread across every available surface. The area inside the double-wide was mostly an open floor plan, except for the two small offices in the far left corner. The walls were bare, save for a single re-election poster of Mayor Jim Mass, no doubt hung there as a '*thank you*' for the business support. Bob gestured for them to take a seat at a small table in the open area while he rummaged through a filing cabinet on the far right side of the trailer.

Stanley looked over at Louise, who gave him a subtle nod as if to say she was doing better with her nerves. When they were for sure out of Bob's earshot, Stanley leaned in close to his new partner. "Careful there, kid," Stanley whispered. "The EPA doesn't do safety."

Louise started biting at her lower lip again. "Shit. Damn," she whispered back. "I knew that. I know that. I'm just nervous."

Stanley leaned in closer, nudging Louise's shoulder with his own. "I know you are. But you're with Stanley Peck. Now unclench your muscles and act like you're in charge here."

Louise took a deep breath as Bob went through the top three drawers of a file cabinet. Stanley nudged Louise, drawing her attention to the fourth drawer at the bottom, which had a lock on it. Bob completed his search of the drawers, ignoring the locked one completely. He returned with a stack of papers and laid them out on the table in front of Stanley and Louise.

"Here are the latest site compliance reports," Bob said, a bit exasperated. "Look, I'm just an earthmover around here, so I really don't know what else you might need."

Stanley side-eyed Louise, who looked a bit frozen. He jumped in quickly. "We'll need to see any environmental impact assessments you might have and any material safety data sheets—to start with, that is."

Bob's eyes darted between them. "Impact assessments?" He looked a little confused, either at the request or about what the specific documents were, but responded quickly. "Oh, yeah, sure. Let me go look."

"And we'll need a space to review the records," Stanley called out as Bob headed back to the file cabinets. He pointed over to one of the small offices at the opposite end of the trailer. "We'll take that room over there."

Stanley picked up the reports and walked Louise and him over to the small office. He set the paperwork down and pulled a chair out for the clearly nervous Ms. Talbot. "Have a seat, my dear," Stanley said playfully.

Louise took the seat and leafed through the first folder in front of her. Stanley took a seat next to her and started with another folder, quietly watching as Bob started rummaging through another file cabinet. The locked drawer, Stanley noted, was still being ignored.

"Remember," Stanley said, "we're looking for signatures. Someone from Redmain had to sign off on this build. Someone, somewhere, put pen to paper. *That's* what we need."

Before Stanley and Louise got more than a page into the documents, Bob popped into the small room, a short stack of files in his hands. "I hope this is more of what you need. I would have had this stuff pulled for you if someone had told me you were coming."

Louise reached out and took the files. She mustered her best tough voice and said, "Everything looks good here, Bob. But there are a few other specific documents we need to verify."

Stanley did his best to hide a smirk as Bob began to sweat a bit.

"Like what, Ma'am?" Bob asked.

Louise continued, her voice steady. "We need to see the detailed hydrogeological surveys and the foundational integrity assessments for the primary facility. Given the building site's proximity to the water table, it's crucial we review those."

Bob hesitated as he took off his hard hat and ran his fingers through his thinning hair. "Oh, well, those documents are a bit more sensitive. I'd need authorization from the main office to release them. Guess I could give them a call. I think I've got their number over here somewhere."

Stanley could see that he and Louise were pushing their boundaries. He leaned forward, his expression serious but not confrontational. "We really do thank you for your help, Bob, and we appreciate your cooperation. Our job is just to ensure that everything is aboveboard. If there are any issues, it's better we catch them now rather than later."

Louise said, her tone softer, "We're not here to cause trouble, Bob. Just to make sure everything's safe and compliant. And we can't do that without seeing those documents. But if it's going to take that long to get approval, we'll just have to go directly to the ParaWorks main office and get what we need." Louise looked at Stanley. "Isn't that right, Mr. Peck?"

Stanley froze for a moment, truly taken by Louise's sudden aggression. He shook himself of the surprise and answered authoritatively. "Yes, Ms. Talbot. That's unfortunately very true."

Bob scratched his head, clearly torn. "Well… I don't want to set anyone back. I mean, it serves those bigwigs at the corporate office right to be delayed by not telling their head contractor what's goin' on, but I guess if you're going to get to them anyway, there's no point in slowing *your* work down."

Louise shook her head. "That's good thinking, Bob." She smiled. "We're all on the same team here."

"All of us here at ground level, at least," Stanley added.

Bob flashed Stanley and Louise a quick, two-fingered salute, then stepped out to look for the rest of the documents as Stanley and Louise exchanged relieved glances. Stanley leaned in close to whisper again.

"Slow your roll, Rambo," he said. "I love your energy, but pace yourself."

Louise cocked her head at Stanley. "*Slow my roll?* Let me guess, your daughter taught you that, didn't she?"

Stanley grinned. "Did I say it wrong?"

Louise chuckled and smiled. "No, you got it right."

"Alright," Bob said as he walked back into the small office. This time, with even more paperwork, this time in binders, in his hands. "This is everything we have here on site. I sure hope it helps you all. We gotta stick together, us ground-level people."

Stanley smiled at the self-proclaimed '*earth mover*.' "Thank you, Bob," Stanley said. "We'll let you know if you need anything else."

Bob plopped the paperwork on the desk and awkwardly backed out of the room. He fiddled around in the office for a minute but ultimately stepped out of the office trailer. Stanley watched as Bob started scanning the various piles of building materials outside, noting them on a clipboard.

"Did you see the locked file drawer over there?" Stanley asked Louise.

"Yeah," she agreed. "He went through every drawer in the place except that one."

"I wonder what might be in there," Stanley said as he stood up. "Keep an eye on Bob out there and let me know if he comes back."

Louise perched herself up to better watch the window as Stanley made his way over to the mysterious locked file drawer in the next room. He bent down and gave it a good pull, which of course did nothing. He looked around the room, hoping to spot a key or a set of keys somewhere. Nothing.

"Do you see any keys over there?" Stanley quietly called out to his partner.

Louise quickly looked around. "No, there's nothing here."

Stanley harrumphed. "What we need could very well be in this drawer. We've got to find a way into this thing."

Louise bit at her lower lip. Still watching Bob through the window, she crossed the length of the trailer to the file cabinet. "Now *you* keep an eye on Bob," she said. "I might be able to get in there."

Stanley stood and faced Louise inquisitively. "You can't muscle that thing open. I tried."

Louise reached into her purse and pulled out a small pouch. She opened it, dug through it, and revealed a thin metal tool about three inches long. "Who said anything about muscles?" Louise quipped as she knelt down and started working the lock with her newly brandished tool.

Stanley watched in amazement as Louise looked to be finding the secrets of the lock with the practiced hand of someone who had most definitely done this before. "What the hell is this, Houdini? How can you do that?"

Louise looked up at Stanley. "Don't watch me," she said nervously, "watch Bob!"

Stanley did as he was told and kept his eyes on Bob, who was still entering data on his clipboard as he walked along the materials outside of the trailer. "I'm watching, I'm watching," he insisted. "But how the hell do you know how to do that?"

Louise continued making small moves with her metal pick as she replied. "My parents used to keep their liquor cabinet padlocked."

Stanley's eyes squinted. "So you learned to pick locks just to get to your parents' booze?" he questioned. "Who does that?"

Louise froze for a moment and looked up at Stanley. "Is that judgment coming from a guy impersonating an EPA officer?"

Stanley looked down at Louise. He let that question roll around for a moment before responding, "Yeah, that's a fair point."

Louise returned to her business as Stanley continued to watch Bob outside. "It wasn't my idea, actually. My brother is the one who wanted the booze. He learned how to pick the lock, and I got him to show me how to do it. You'd be amazed how often it can come in handy."

Stanley nodded. "Clearly."

Then, after a few more twists of her tool, the lock popped open. "Got it!" Louise quietly exclaimed as she pulled open the drawer.

"What do we have?" Stanley asked, still watching to make sure the coast was clear.

"Hold on," Louise said as she rifled through the contents of the drawer. A few odds and ends, nothing spectacular. Then she came across a small metal box towards the back. "Wait, I've got something." She pulled the box out, showing it to Stanley.

Stanley took a quick look at the metal box, recognizing it in half a second. "That's a money box. Probably petty cash for Bob."

Louise let out a breath. "I guess that explains why it was locked."

Stanley sighed. "Well, that was really disappointing," he

mumbled. Then he looked back up to check on Bob the *'earth mover.'* And good thing he did, as Bob had turned and was starting back towards the trailer. "Oh shit, he's coming back. He's coming back!"

Louise quickly tossed the money box back into the drawer, snapped the lock in place, and looked out the window. "Oh my shit!" she blurted, seeing that Bob was about halfway back.

Stanley crouched down and pulled Louise along with him. He led the way back to their makeshift workroom, carefully ducking below the windows as he rushed them across the trailer. They had just made it through the threshold of the little office door when they heard Bob turning the entry handle. They both grabbed hold of the nearest set of folders and whipped them open, doing their best to act natural as Bob stepped in. Stanley looked up and waved.

Bob awkwardly waved back. "Sorry to bother you guys. I just needed my measuring tape."

Stanley smiled. "No bother, Bob," he said, doing his best to maintain his composure as his heart pounded in his chest.

Bob spotted his measuring tape on a nearby table, grabbed it, and headed back outside. Stanley and Louise watched silently, waiting until the door closed behind him before they let out a unified breath.

"Holy crap," Louise said. "I thought we were toast."

Stanley nodded his head in agreement. "Yeah, me too." Then he let his eyes drift down the stacks of papers Bob had brought for them. "But no easy answers for us today," he quipped. He picked up one of the binders and handed another to Louise. "Well, let's dig in."

With that, Stanley and Louise started poring over the documents, their eyes scanning for signatures and details within the technical jargon and detailed charts. After a few minutes, Stanley pointed to a section in the hydrogeological survey, his finger tracing a line of data.

"Look at this, Louise. The depth of the water table is recorded as thirty feet below ground level, and the foundational supports are set at twenty-five feet. That's a five-foot margin for error. Legal, technically. But way, *way* too close."

Louise nodded, her eyes wide as she examined the data. "And look at this," she said, pointing to another section. "The materials used for the foundational supports are listed as reinforced concrete, but there's no mention of any additional waterproofing measures. If there's any compromise in the concrete's integrity..."

"We're looking at potential contamination," Stanley finished, his voice grim. "This is exactly what we talked about. It's one thing after another. Risk on top of risk. But I'm still not seeing any signatures. Are you seeing anything?"

Louise shook her head. "Yes, but only on manifests or financial reports. No waivers or liability forms. Nothing like that."

Just like when they were at the diner, minutes started drifting into hours. Page after page. Report after report. Lots of information. Some of it, good. Some of it, not so good. But no waivers. No signatures. No smoking guns.

Stanley rubbed his eyes. "It's not here," he said, exhausted and defeated.

"I know," Louise agreed. "There's a lot here, a lot worthy of attention. But you're right. Without something showing knowledge of the risk, it's just dry data. Just '*words*,' like you said."

At the far end of the trailer, Bob was turning off the last of his lights and closing the last cabinet. He had been in and out of the trailer the whole time Stanley and Louise searched and reviewed the records, working his daily grind to prepare for breaking ground. But this was it. He stepped over to the little office that Stanley and Louise had been plugging away in.

"I'm afraid that's the end of the day, folks," Bob said.

Stanley exchanged a look with Louise before replying. "You're quite right, Bob," he said. "We need copies of these documents. Could we run some of these through your copier before we get out of your hair?"

Bob sighed, rubbing the back of his neck. "Yeah, sure. I can make you copies."

Bob reached out, and Louise gave him a small stack of paperwork. She smiled, trying to lighten the mood. "You've been great, Bob. Thank you so much."

Bob stepped away to make the copies, and Louise took that chance to lean over to Stanley. "He obviously has no idea what's going on here in this mess of papers and charts."

Stanley nodded. "That's usually how it is. Bob here is just doing his job. He's told to dig, so he digs. He's told to put that beam here or there, and he does it. Most everyone you'll find at this level are pretty honest people, mostly just doing their jobs. But in the end, it'll come down to one person, or a few people. One signature, or a few."

Louise nodded, the reality of that fact sinking in, and the difficulty of their task even more real. She reached over and knocked her fist against Stanley's shoulder. "Thanks for having my back here. I couldn't—wouldn't—have been able to do this without you."

Stanley returned the smile. "You're stuck with me, kid."

When Bob returned with the copies, Stanley and Louise

thanked him and left the office. As they walked back to the car, the weight of their discoveries settled on them, weighing them both down. They may not have found all the information they needed, but they found some of it. It was real now.

Louise took hold of the car door handle and looked up at Stanley. "What's next?" she asked. "Where do we go now?"

Stanley took a deep breath and contemplated the various ins and outs for a moment. "We found a lot here that corroborates our theory. But if what we really need isn't at this level, we have to go up."

Louise looked back at Stanley, not following his logic.

"We follow the power," he said. "Next step—city hall."

Chapter Seven

Stanley's apartment was a cluttered mess of papers, printouts, and hastily scribbled notes, all from or connected to the files gathered from the ParaWorks building site. On any other day of the week, Stanley's apartment would have been a quiet, orderly place, like Superman's fortress of solitude. But now it served as a makeshift war room. A few scattered lamps cast a warm, golden glow around the room, offering a sense of calm to the focused busyness going on.

Louise was on the couch, her face a picture of concentration as she pored over document after document. Stanley, meanwhile, was at the dining table, quietly hunched over a stack of records. He flipped through them with the practiced eye of someone who had spent years in bureaucracy.

Though unaware of it, Stanley was muttering to himself as he read, half-reading and half-talking to himself. "Oh yeah? Think you can get this one past me, ParaWorks? Think you've got what it takes to beat me? Better think again."

This habit of talking to himself was nothing new to Stanley. It was one of those little things that he had always done. When it manifested many years ago, it would normally come out as he cooked dinner, put away laundry, or did other mundane activities. He would mumble the directions to the meal he was making, or repeat the specifics of a case he was working on while he folded clothes. For the last forty years, since Chicago, Stanley's mumblings had shifted from harmless random thoughts to outright rants against Leo Vincent. The people in town often noticed it, but Stanley himself was largely unaware of it. He had spent so much time alone that his mumblings became white noise, to Stanley anyway.

Stanley was so unaware of his mumblings that he didn't realize Leo Vincent wasn't the focus of his ire. It was a momentary thing, slipped in between speaking out loud the various facts and reports in the papers he had been reviewing, but it was a change, nonetheless. Louise, while looking over a document of her own, glanced over in Stanley's direction and quietly chuckled at his amusing idiosyncrasy.

It had been like this for hours, ever since the two environmental crusaders left the ParaWorks construction site with a handful of not-so-legally obtained documents and records. The silence was broken only by the occasional rustle of paper, clicking of a computer mouse, and the ticking of Stanley's old grandfather clock in the corner.

Then, a ring of the phone broke the silence. Louise's body snapped up, startled by the sudden ringing sound. Stanley looked up, puzzled. He rarely received phone calls unless it was from Elizabeth, and almost never at a late hour. Stanley raised an eyebrow, thoroughly annoyed at having to break his concentration. He pushed the stack of papers he was looking at aside, got up, and reached for the receiver. But when he answered the phone, there was no response. Just silence on the other end.

"Wrong number?" Louise asked, glancing up curiously from her work.

"Probably," Stanley said. He shrugged it off and returned to his pile of records on the dining room table.

The two continued working in silence for a few minutes before Louise shook her head, frustrated. She tossed the pen she had been writing notes with onto the coffee table. "You know, Stanley, I still just can't get over this," she said. "How is it that so much information could be overlooked so easily? Even without an administrator's signature, so much of this begs to be questioned, at the very least."

Stanley nodded, his eyes still scanning the documents like an activity learned by rote. "It's usually like this," he said. "Little bits here. Little bits there. On their own, any of these things isn't all that important, but together they make an image. It's like a puzzle, only without a picture to use as a guide. They're counting on people not putting the pieces together, Louise."

"I know, I know," Louise agreed. "But it's all here. People have seen this. I even saw some of it pass through my office. I feel so stupid for not seeing it."

Stanley put his paperwork down and turned to Louise. "It's hidden in plain sight, kiddo. You weren't meant to see it, funny as that sounds."

"But I should have!" Louise said. "That's supposed to be my job. And you clued into it over coffee!"

Stanley shrugged off Louise's comments. "Don't beat yourself up, Louise. I'm like a thirsty bloodhound. I'm a freak. A freakazoid."

Louise let out a quick chuckle. "Freakazoid?"

"Yep," Stanley said. "That's me." Then he lifted the side of his upper lip and snarled. "Grrr."

"Let me guess," Louise replied, "another word from your daughter?"

Stanley smiled and laughed. "How'd you guess?"

Louise smiled back. "That's how my dad sounds sometimes."

Stanley chuckled. Until that moment, it hadn't occurred to him that while he didn't know Louise Talbot's actual age, she didn't seem to be that much younger than his daughter, Elizabeth. No more than five years younger, if he had to guess. That realization provided Stanley with a comfort, of sorts. Maybe that was part of the reason he felt like he could trust this local EPA representative.

Louise's face took on a disappointed look, but she pushed it away quickly. "You're not a freak, Stanley," she said. "You're dedicated, and I admire that. More people should be like you."

Stanley shook his head and waved Louise's comment off. "The world isn't big enough for two Stanley Pecks, kiddo. Besides, I'd like this one to go out on better terms."

Louise nodded in understanding. It was clear Stanley was referring to the events in Chicago. She wanted to ask. She wanted to know. What was it like? What happened? Was it really how people described it? But she didn't ask. She let the comment go. Maybe when he was ready, she thought.

Louise leaned back on the couch and stretched out her arms. "You know, I've got to tell you, Stanley," she said, "I never imagined I'd be doing this kind of thing. It feels like we're in some sort of spy movie or TV show. I feel like *Columbo*!"

"*Columbo*?" Stanley questioned.

Louise smiled wryly. "Yeah, *Columbo*. Wasn't that an old detective show? I remember my dad used to watch it."

Stanley smirked. "Yes, it's an old detective show."

Louise sat up, excited. "And that other one with the guy in

the tweed jacket who drove a brown Firebird. I feel like we're living that show too!"

Stanley contemplated for a second. "You mean *The Rockford Files?*"

Louise slid forward to the edge of the couch. "Yeah, that's it! I know we aren't getting into shootouts or being held hostage in the last act, but isn't this exciting? Looking for clues. Finding evidence. Digging around. It's—fun."

Stanley smiled and nodded. "I never really thought of it that way."

Louise looked down at the piles of papers on the coffee table. "I just wish it didn't involve so much paperwork."

Stanley chuckled. "Welcome to my world, Louise. It's not always glamorous, but it's often necessary." He contemplated for a moment and smiled. "I suppose it was even fun, in a way."

Louise regarded Stanley. "Do you ever miss it? The old job, I mean."

Stanley sighed as he leaned back in his chair, and the memories came swirling back. "Sometimes," he admitted. "I miss the sense of purpose, the feeling that I was making a difference. It felt good when I caught something or sniffed something out." Stanley's eyes welled up ever so slightly. "But it came at a cost."

Louise nodded sympathetically. "I'm sorry," she said. "I didn't mean to bring it up."

Before Stanley could respond, his stomach growled loudly, causing both of them to laugh.

"Guess we've been at this longer than I thought," Stanley said as he stood up. "How about a coffee break? I'll make a fresh pot."

"That sounds great," Louise replied, smiling.

As Stanley moved over to the kitchen to brew a new pot of coffee, Louise kept leafing through the documents she had spread across the couch and the coffee table. Within a minute, the comforting sound and smell of the coffee machine bubbling away filled the room. It reminded Stanley of his office days, and before he knew it, his thoughts started drifting to the past. He was about to share a memory with Louise, something of Chicago, when a sudden movement outside the kitchen window caught his eye.

Stanley stepped over to the window and peered out onto the darkened walkway lining the row of apartment doors. He carefully scanned the area, looking for movement or something out of place. Stanley was about to shrug it off and look away when he caught a figure standing in the shadows across the courtyard from his apartment. The mysterious person seemed to look directly at him. It was eerie. Stanley could almost feel the person's eyes touching him. He squinted his eyes, trying his best to make out the person's details, but the figure was just too far away, too well obscured by the darkness, intentional or otherwise. Stanley looked away for a moment, trying to dismiss what he was seeing and feeling as a flight of fancy of an overactive imagination. He whipped his head around to look back. The figure, however, was gone.

"Everything okay?" Louise asked.

Louise's voice brought Stanley's attention back to the inside of the apartment. "Yeah," Stanley said as he shook his head. "Just thought I saw someone outside. I could swear they were looking over here." He waved his hand in the air. "Probably just someone taking an evening walk."

Stanley pulled out the coffeepot and poured two cups of coffee, then walked over to the living room and handed one to Louise. He went back to the table, sat down, and tried his best to shake off the uneasy feeling of what he *thought* he had seen. "We'd better get back to it," Stanley said. "We have a lot more to go over."

Just as the two settled back into their work, there was a knock at the apartment door. Stanley looked over and exchanged a wary glance with Louise. A late-night phone call was definitely out of the ordinary, but a late-night visitor was outright unheard of. Louise could read Stanley's curious expression and nervously pulled her legs up onto the couch.

"This is very strange," Stanley said. "I wonder who that could be."

Stanley stood up and walked over to the door. He peered through the peephole, but it was too dark to make anything out. He let out a breath and slowly turned the lock. Stanley opened the door cautiously, peeking around the cover of the door as he pulled it his way. Then, his eyes widened in surprise.

"Elizabeth?!" Stanley exclaimed.

There in the doorway stood Stanley's daughter, Elizabeth. The welcoming smile on her face quickly transformed into a look of worry and concern. He glanced down and noticed a suitcase sitting on the ground next to Elizabeth's feet. Stanley's heart sank as he put together in a heartbeat why she was standing at his door.

"Hi, Dad," she said with an awkward smile. "Are you gonna let me in?"

Stanley stepped aside, still in shock. "Of course, honey, of course. Come in."

Elizabeth stepped inside and set her suitcase by the door. Her eyes scanned across the apartment. Papers and clutter everywhere. The smell of fresh coffee and such a late hour. Then she noticed the unfamiliar woman in business attire sitting on her father's couch. Elizabeth's scan of the environment ended as she noted both of their worried expressions.

"I knew something was off the last time we talked," Elizabeth said, shaking her head. "So I asked for some time off. I came to check on you and see what was going on."

As Stanley closed the door behind Elizabeth, he quickly took his own assessment of the messy apartment and combined it with the look on Elizabeth's face. In the space of a breath, he felt both joy in seeing his baby girl and sorrow for the worry he had obviously caused her.

"Elizabeth, this is Louise Talbot," Stanley said, gesturing the two women to each other. "She's with the EPA. Louise, this is my daughter, Elizabeth."

Louise stood and extended her hand. "It's good to meet you, Elizabeth."

Elizabeth shook Louise's hand, her look of worry deepening. "Nice to meet you, too." She wasted no time in asking, "Is my dad in some sort of trouble?"

Louise put her hand on Elizabeth's arm. "Oh, Elizabeth, no!" she said. "Quite the opposite, actually. Your dad has been helping me get to the bottom of something. He's helping me with a case."

The color came back to Elizabeth's face as her body tension eased. "Seriously?"

"Yes, seriously," Louise confirmed. "We're really just getting started, but already your dad has clued me into some real dangers of a new industrial site coming to Redmain." Elizabeth nodded and smiled affectionately at Stanley as Louise continued. "And earlier today he even helped me break into a construction site."

Elizabeth's eyes nearly bugged out of their eye sockets. "You broke in somewhere?!"

Stanley calmly shook his head as Louise realized what she had just said. "Maybe '*break in*' is too strong," she corrected. "We were kind of undercover, actually."

"Undercover?" Elizabeth questioned, still clearly concerned.

Recognizing the conversation was going downhill, Stanley diplomatically jumped in. "I think Louise is letting her excitement get the best of her," he said, easing Elizabeth further into the living room. "It's an investigation. We're doing research and combing through documents. Pretty boring stuff, really."

Elizabeth froze in place, feeling the con. "So you're telling me you didn't break into some construction site?"

"Perish the thought," Stanley said.

"And you didn't go undercover?" Elizabeth asked.

Stanley's eyes tilted up a bit as he shook his head. "Not in the strictest sense."

Elizabeth's eyes opened wider as she leaned in toward her father. "Dad..."

Stanley pulled out a chair at the dining room table and eased Elizabeth into the seat. He stepped over to the coffee machine and started pouring into a fresh cup. "I think we're getting ahead of things here," he said as he pivoted and brought the coffee over to Elizabeth. "Why don't you have something to drink, and we'll explain everything we've been up to."

Elizabeth nodded her head as she took in the collection of papers, charts, and graphs spread around the room and at the table before her. "Yeah, I think that's a really good idea."

* * *

Stanley and Louise spent the next hour filling Elizabeth in on everything: ParaWorks, the environmental risks, their investigation, and the whole of what they had suspected and had put together. Elizabeth listened intently, her mind already working through the information.

"This is pretty serious," Elizabeth said, now working on a second coffee of her own, as Stanley and Louise finished their story. "If there's even a chance that this ParaWorks facility poses a risk like you say, you have to do something. But going to City Hall might not be enough. If someone knowingly signed off on this build, they won't just hand over that evidence."

Stanley nodded. "That's what we're worried about. We need to find proof—something undeniable. We can go to City Hall, but like you said, no one is going to throw their hands up and say we've got them."

Elizabeth thought for a moment. "There's always legal leverage. I could talk to them."

Stanley smiled, trying not to seem dismissive. "Honey, you're an entertainment lawyer."

Elizabeth rolled her eyes. "A lawyer is a lawyer, Dad," she said with assurance. "I could demand access to records under the pretense of needing information for a potential lawsuit."

Stanley smiled and cocked his head. "That's not bad. But this is city stuff, building codes, public works kind of stuff. Isn't that a bit out of your usual scope?"

Elizabeth smiled confidently. "Dad, you'd be amazed at the scope of things entertainment law includes. I know how to find information and how to ask the right questions. And besides, I have a friend from law school who handles industrial law. He lives in Jersey, but I could give him a call. He might help point me in the right direction."

Louise nodded in agreement. "That would be amazing. Legal pressure might be just the thing we need to get at information we would be blocked from otherwise."

Stanley beamed at his daughter with pride as the sound of the telephone ringing again cut through the living room. Stanley checked the time. 11:13. "Everyone I know is here," he said. "It must be that damn spam caller from earlier. This is ridiculous. It's almost midnight!"

Stanley walked over to the phone and picked up the receiver. However, he proved to be one ring too late as the answering machine activated. Louise and Elizabeth could hear Stanley's recorded outgoing message play as Stanley himself tried to answer the phone and speak to the caller.

"Hello?" Stanley said, trying to speak over the recording.

"You've reached Stanley's phone. I'm not in right now..."

"Hello? Hello?" Stanley kept saying, pushing a few buttons on the machine, trying in vain to stop the recording.

"...or I'm too busy to answer. In either case, you can leave a message..."

"Hello?" Stanley said again as he frantically flipped open the answering machine's cover, still unable to stop the machine's pre-recorded voice.

Louise looked at Elizabeth. "Should I show him what to do?" she asked.

Elizabeth shook her head. "No, it'll just upset him. This isn't the first time Stanley Peck has battled technology. Just let it play out."

"*...just wait for the beep thing to happen, then leave me a message when it beeps.*"

Stanley pushed a few more buttons, but to no avail. "Hello. Hello," he continued to say over his own recording. Finally, the machine played its merciful '*beep*,' and the room went quiet. "Hello," Stanley said one last time. After a moment, he turned to Louise and Elizabeth. "They hung up. And good thing, too. I was gonna let 'em have it."

Elizabeth snickered in amusement as Louise realized the time and gathered her things. "On that note, I think I'll head back to my place and get some rest," Louise said. "We have a big day tomorrow."

Stanley walked Louise to the door. "Thanks, Louise. For everything. I can't tell you what this means to me."

Louise smiled. "See you tomorrow, Stanley."

Stanley closed the door and turned to Elizabeth, who was still sitting at the kitchen table. "I suppose we should call it a night, too," he said. "The guest room is ready for you as always. Is there anything you need?"

Elizabeth stood and stretched her arms out in front of her chest. "Thanks, Dad. And no, I'm fine." She stepped closer to her father. "I'm just glad you're okay."

Stanley smiled. "I'm really glad you're here, Lizzy."

Elizabeth returned his look. "Me too, Dad."

Chapter Eight

The drive to City Hall wasn't a long one, but it was mostly quiet in the beginning, giving Stanley plenty of time to think about the past, about Chicago. The crusade he was now on reminded him so much of what had come before, the events that led him to divorce and to Redmain. As he watched from the passenger seat as the houses and businesses passed by, his mind started to flash back to forty years ago and the drive he and a small team took as they headed to the CleanCycle BioSystems plant in the industrial outskirts of Chicago.

Forty years ago.

The air outside the CleanCycle BioSystems' facility was thick with the buzzing hum of machinery and the faint aroma of some sort of chemical processing. Stanley Peck, so young and ferocious, marched up the concrete steps, a court order wedged under his arm like a trophy. He was sporting a newly pressed suit, but the summer heat wave made him sweat, leaving stains under his arms. Two city officials flanked Stanley, along with an environmental engineer in a hard hat who carried a heavy-duty toolbox.

Stanley's lips curled into a defiant grin as he skipped

knocking altogether and walked right in. He had warned them, warned Leo Vincent, and now he would prove it. Vincent's fancy tech was a sham, Stanley knew, and a cover for toxins he was probably dumping God only knew where. But today, he would expose it all.

The inside of the CleanCycle BioSystems plant buzzed with activity. Workers in yellow safety vests moved between massive, gleaming steel tanks, their chatter a product of routine. Until they saw Stanley Peck, that is. The workers in the reconfigured warehouse stiffened at the sight of him, their eyes tracking Stanley and his team as he led them toward the control room.

Leo Vincent raced out of his office at the other end of the facility. "Peck!" he shouted, his voice echoing against the giant tanks and storage units in the warehouse. "Stay outta there!"

Stanley paid Leo Vincent no mind as he threw open the control room door and began letting his entourage inside.

Leo looked over at a group of men standing by a console as he darted across the space. "Hey, you guys!" he yelled. "Get in here with me!"

Stanley and his men were looking over the monitors, dials, and levers in the control room when Vincent barreled in behind them, his lead technicians trailing in seconds later.

"Peck!" Vincent called out, his voice cracking. "Why don't you and your men come with me back to my office?"

"It's too late for that, Vincent," Stanley said. "You had your chance." Stanley thrust the court order forward, a scowl forming on his face. "This is a cease and desist order for you, your operations, the premises, and its equipment. It's also a cease and desist for the use of all city utilities and a general inspection order. This order, signed by a circuit court judge, says that we are to shut down your processing units immediately, pending a full legal and technical review."

"This is bullshit, Peck!" Vincent blasted back.

Stanley stepped up to Vincent. "I convinced the judge that you could be falsifying data and that you've violated your provisional permit by not submitting the required checklists and reports. We're shutting you down and taking a look, and you're not going to stop us." Each word dripped with certainty.

"You're out of your mind, Peck!" Leo exclaimed. "This is private property! Our permit is still valid, and our systems are safe. A few missing reports don't change that!"

"You may have the city of Chicago fooled, Vincent," Stanley said sternly, "but not me. For the last time, we're shutting you down. Now." Stanley looked at the environmental engineer and waved his finger around the room. "Find whatever power taps you need to and turn all of this off. Every bit of it."

Leo Vincent couldn't mask his heavy breathing or the sweat forming on his brow. "Peck, if you shut this plant down mid-cycle, you'll regret it."

Stanley pointed his finger at Vincent. "And you'll regret thinking you could pull one over on me. Now, stand aside and let me do my job."

"Damn it, Peck," Vincent stammered, "this system is under intense pressure. You can't just flip a switch on it. The results could be catastrophic."

"You had your chance, Vincent," Stanley said as he looked at his engineer technician. "Let's get started."

The engineer hesitated. "Sir, their setup looks pretty delicate. High pressure, extreme heat. It might need a slow shutdown. If we cut the power abruptly…"

"Delicate?" Stanley snapped, cutting him off. "It's a cover-up, not a science project!" He waved the court order around like a flag. "I don't want to hear anything else. Just shut it down."

The officials exchanged looks but ultimately signaled to the engineering technician, who obeyed and moved to the control panel. He took everything in and brought Stanley's attention to one large lever. "This one here looks like the power supply to the main equipment out there. Pull this, and it all stops."

Stanley stepped forward and placed his hand on the large master power switch. Vincent looked to his lead technicians, who shook their heads at what was coming.

Leo shouted. "You'll blow the seals!"

But Stanley ignored him. Watching the dials spin, hearing the hum of the system slowing, he pictured the headlines: "EPA Hero Exposes CleanCycle BioSystems' Fraud." Stanley's chest swelled with victory as he gripped the power lever—and pulled down.

At first, there was silence. Then the first spark flew. A loud cracking sound split the air, followed by a deep roar as the pressure tanks buckled. Red warning lights flashed at each of the control stations, and the control room filled with the acrid smell of burning insulation. Stanley froze, his grin faltering, as a fire erupted from behind the main electrical hub, and a wall of flame started crawling up the circuit board wall. Smoke billowed into the room, thick and choking, carrying a putrid haze that stung everyone's eyes and throats. In the main room, workers scattered as control units started sparking and the sirens started wailing.

Leo's voice cut through the chaos. "Are you happy, Peck? Look what you've done!"

Smoke seeped out of the large, floor-to-ceiling steel tanks that lined the main floor as the plant erupted into an inferno.

Stanley and his men, as well as Leo Vincent and his lead engineers, rushed out of the control room and towards the exit. Just before reaching the outside, the men were all able to see the flames climbing the walls and the giant steel tanks starting to shake as the pressure inside them mounted.

Once they made it outside, Stanley and his team took refuge behind his car. The court order almost slipped from Stanley's fingers, but he didn't notice as the unfolding chaos around him consumed his focus. Stanley had meant to stop a crime, but he'd unleashed a catastrophe instead. Everyone waited quietly as the low rumbling coming from inside the plant grew louder and louder.

Leo Vincent, who was crouching for safety with his men behind a nearby wall, pointed to the huge grey smokestacks just within view at the top of the building. "It's only a matter of time now!"

Sadly, Vincent was all too correct. Within a few moments, the rumbling and turning within the plant succumbed with a series of massive booming sounds, followed by a forceful spray of yellowish gas from the giant smokestacks. Stanley, Vincent, and all the other men could do nothing but watch as the erupting smoke cloud coming from the smokestacks grew larger and larger, drifting its way into the Chicago skies.

"This," Leo Vincent yelled to Stanley, pointing at the wreckage, "is what happens when bureaucrats play God." His eyes locked on Stanley, daring him to disagree.

Stanley watched from beside his car, his face pale, as the weight of his failure settled onto him like the ash settling on his face.

He thought he was right.

Stanley shook his head of the forty-year-old memory and

refocused his attention on the present. What could he have done differently? What million other ways could he have tried to prove his point? Did it really matter anymore, Stanley wondered? Maybe. Maybe not. He looked in the rearview mirror at Elizabeth in the backseat, who was scribbling notes on a legal pad, then over to Louise, who was focusing on driving.

"You know, it's funny," he said, looking out the window as they drove through the quiet streets of Redmain. "I used to be the guy everyone avoided. The '*bad guy*' who shut things down. It's strange to feel like I'm on the other side of that somehow, that I'm the '*good guy*' this time, even though I'm basically doing the same thing."

Louise looked at Stanley from the driver's seat. "Circumstances change, Stanley," she said. "And sometimes, the role we play changes with them. You're doing the right thing, and that's what matters."

"I suppose you're right," Stanley said before turning in his seat to face Elizabeth. "We didn't have much time to talk this morning, did we, Lizzy?" he continued. "How are things at work, besides taking time off to be here?"

Elizabeth took a breath. "Well, entertainment law is not as glamorous as you might think," she said. "We rarely deal directly with the '*talent*.' Most of the time, it's just with other lawyers. Lots of contracts, lots of late nights. No undercover work," she snickered. "But I like it." She twirled her pen in her fingers, a trick she had perfected over years of tedious law school lectures. "Usually it's minor disputes, rights holder stuff, negotiations, that sort of thing. But once in a while, we get one where some company is trying to muscle its way into taking something from someone new, a writer, or a producer.

I like those. I enjoy fighting the big dogs." She smirked. "It's kinda fun."

Louise chuckled. "I guess the apple doesn't fall far from the tree."

"No," Stanley said, smiling. "I guess it doesn't."

* * *

A few minutes later, the trio arrived at the Redmain City Hall. Louise found an open spot off to the side and tucked her Buick in. The City Hall building itself was a grand old building that stood as a testament to Redmain's history, brick and stone from top to bottom. It was three stories high, which in a town like Redmain was almost illegal. It was really quite beautiful, Stanley thought, despite the bureaucratic machinery it contained inside.

Stanley, Louise, and Elizabeth met the familiar look of office busyness as they stepped into the main foyer. Clerks and assistants moved about with purpose, and the steady chatter of conversations filled the space. With Stanley in the lead, the group approached the front desk. A young receptionist with long blonde hair pulled back into a ponytail looked up and greeted them with a polite smile. Her badge identified her as *'Christine.'*

"Good morning," Christine said. "How can I help you?" She had a slight Southern accent that seemed somehow out of place in the bustling government building.

Elizabeth stepped forward, her lawyerly demeanor on full intentional display. "Good morning, Christine," she said, noting the receptionist's name. "I'm an attorney representing..." Elizabeth choked for a moment, realizing she hadn't planned on who to say she represented. "Representing—a client," she said in a save. "These are my associates. We're here for a review of the public records related to the ParaWorks industrial project."

Christine swallowed as she turned to her computer. "Let me just check to see who to direct you to." As she typed a series of commands into her computer, Christine looked up at Stanley, Louise, and Elizabeth. A peek more than a look, really. Stanley and Elizabeth were front and center, giving their best impression of people with authority. Louise, however, was quietly observing Christine. She saw the receptionist's stolen glance, and she didn't look away when Christine's eyes fell across her own. Christine nervously looked away, like a child afraid to look at something scary, just as a digital *'ding'* sound came from her computer speakers. "I have someone for you," she said. "Ms. Chapman will see you now."

Christine stood from her desk and stepped out into the lobby, gesturing the group in her direction. "If you'll follow me, it's just down the hall."

As Christine led the trio into the innards of the building, Louise took a few steps ahead of Stanley and Elizabeth, bringing herself side-by-side with Christine. "How long have you worked for City Hall?" Louise asked.

Stanley and Elizabeth flashed each other quick looks, both curious about Louise's sudden curiosity in the city hall receptionist. Neither said anything, though, instead letting Louise have the moment.

Christine tucked a loose strand of hair behind her ear. "Oh, about two years now."

Louise kept her gaze fixed on Christine, who kept her focus forward. "Is that right? You must like it here."

Christine nodded. "I do. It's a nice place."

Louise refused to look away, waiting for Christine to look back at her. It didn't happen. "The people here must be good to work with."

Christine nodded again. "Mmm hmm. They're nice."

Stanley and Elizabeth watched Louise in curiosity as Christine navigated them through a few different hallways until finally reaching the *'public relations'* office. A middle-aged woman with graying hair and a perpetual scowl on her face saw them coming and started over from her desk. Christine stepped aside and was quietly walking away when Louise caught her passing eye.

"Thank you for showing us in," Louise said.

Christine offered a polite nod as she went on her way, heading back down the hallway. Stanley took advantage of the brief moment of transition to lean over to Louise. "What was that about?"

Louise shook her head, nibbling on the edge of her lower lip. "I'm not really sure."

Stanley was about to press Louise more when Ms. Chapman arrived in the doorway. "How may I help you?" she asked.

Stanley stepped forward and took the lead. "Yes, we're here for a review of the public records for the ParaWorks industrial project. We need to see all the documents related to its approval and any environmental assessments and building code documentation." She nervously pulled out a small bottle of hand sanitizer and used it liberally.

Ms. Chapman smiled a fake smile and shook her head. "Oh, I'm afraid those files *are* indeed public, but not accessible without legal representation, ma'am. You would need authorization to access them."

Elizabeth stepped forward and pulled her bar card from her purse and held it up to Ms. Chapman. "You'll see that I am an officially licensed attorney, and as such, I have full clearance to access these records."

Ms. Chapman gestured to a small table at one end of the room, doing her best to ignore Elizabeth's statement. "I have plenty of preprinted literature and information that you might find useful."

Stanley looked over the various pamphlets and documents on the table and scoffed. He stepped forward, trying his best to channel his old authoritative and condescending self. "We aren't interested in press kits or documents from your media department, Ms. Chapman. This is a public project, and we have every right to see those records. We're here on the authority of the Environmental Protection Agency, and we would appreciate your cooperation, not generic media spin." He adjusted his tie with unease.

Ms. Chapman did her best to maintain her demeanor, which she was obviously used to being effective. "Sir, I'm just telling you the process," she said, visibly rattled. "If you want to see those records, you'll need to speak with Mr. Hargrove, the head of our planning department. He's the only one who..."

Elizabeth cut Ms. Chapman off, her tone firm. "Then direct us to Mr. Hargrove." She held a hard look at Ms. Chapman. "Now," Elizabeth said sternly.

Ms. Chapman cleared her throat, stepped over to her desk, and picked up the phone, mumbling something into the receiver.

Stanley took advantage of this momentary distraction to

lean over to his daughter. "I'm glad you're on our side," he whispered.

After a moment, Ms. Chapman looked back up at the group. "Mr. Hargrove will see you," she said as she pointed down the hall. "It's the third door on the left."

At that point, the group quietly made their way down to Mr. Hargrove's office. As they moved down the hall, Stanley looked past the third door on the left and followed the corridor with his eyes until he landed on the last door at the back. He scanned the nameplate: *Mayor Jim Mass.* Stanley wondered if he was in his office and how it would play out if he simply marched over and knocked on the door. Would the politician he had seen in the newspaper, on the posters, and in the commercials welcome him in and dazzle him with bullshit? Or would it go like his last visit to a mayor's office—badly? Stanley shook the question from his mind as he realized that moment hadn't yet come. Maybe eventually, but not yet.

The door to the third office on the left was open, revealing a large office with a mahogany desk facing toward them. A tall, thin man with a meticulously trimmed mustache and an air of self-importance rose from the desk to greet them at the door. As he approached, Stanley noticed how immediately put off both Elizabeth and Louise were at the sight of Mr. Hargrove. Stanley, however, found the man strangely familiar. Not unlike the presence he gave off 40 years ago. Stanley had to fight a look of admiration as he found the man instantly strong and authoritative.

Mr. Hargrove extended a hand to each of the trio. He was a towering man, easily six-foot-two, slender, but imposing. His hair was salt and pepper, matching his mustache. His suit was expensive, Stanley noticed. Definitely not off the rack. Hargrove straightened his posture as he twisted his cufflinks. "Good morning," he said, his tone polished. "I'm Alan Hargrove. How can I assist you today?"

Louise spoke up first. "We're here to review the public records for the ParaWorks project." She fiddled with her bracelet, but thankfully, no one noticed. "We believe there may be some missing paperwork at the corporate office, so we need to see all of your recorded files."

Hargrove's smile faltered slightly for half a second, but he quickly recovered. "I see. Well, those records are indeed public, as I'm sure Ms. Chapman no doubt told you, but they're also considered sensitive documents." He looked the group up and down. "And what corporate office do you represent?"

"The Environmental Protection Agency," Louise said.

Elizabeth stepped forward and displayed her bar card again. "And I'm here to ensure these two have full access to whatever they need."

Hargrove nodded, his expression unfazed. "I see," he said. "You understand that we already completed the approval process, and the EPA cleared the project. We're all set to sign the final go-ahead to break ground at next week's town hall meeting." He paused. "What records are you looking for exactly?"

Stanley leaned forward, smiling with authoritative assurance. "Listen, Alan, we just need to see the environmental assessments and any documentation related to the approval process. It's a bit of a dot the 'I's' and cross the 'T's' thing. Typical management BS, you know what I mean? I'd really appreciate your helping us out here."

Hargrove raised an eyebrow. "Well then, I really don't appreciate the..." he glanced at Louise and Elizabeth, "the show of force. As I've said, the EPA has already given its approval. We've signed the contracts. Payments made. We're set to break ground after the final signing next week, and we won't have that interrupted." His tone was firm, forceful, yet measured. One hundred years ago, a man such as Alan Hargrove would have been considered a gentleman by way of his appearance and language, but this wasn't one-hundred years ago.

"We're just double-checking everything, Mr. Hargrove," Elizabeth said confidently. She flipped open her notepad and got herself ready. "But if you have some sort of objection to transparency, I'd be glad to add your comments to the official records."

Hargrove's eyes widened. He looked ready to pounce. Recognizing that Mr. Hargrove just might be at his limit, Stanley stepped to the side and gestured for Mr. Hargrove to meet him closer. Hargrove scowled a bit at Louise and Elizabeth, then stepped over to Stanley, who leaned in close, all but whispering. "The girls here can be a bit much, I know. But if you can get us what we need here, we can put this thing to bed, and we'll be out of your hair."

Hargrove's eyes quivered with irritation and just the smallest hint of trepidation, but he maintained his composure. He raised his voice for all to hear, "Of course, transparency is always of utmost importance to this office and to our city officials. That said, I must remind you again that without proper authorization, I cannot simply hand over those documents." He looked directly at Louise and Elizabeth. "Do you have such a letter of authorization from our city mayor, Mr. Jim Mass?"

Elizabeth held Hargrove's gaze, but Louise dropped her head, easing her approach to something less confrontational.

"Mr. Hargrove," Louise said, "we're not asking for much here. Just a quick look at a few documents. If everything is in order, we'll be on our way. No fuss, no trouble." She toyed with a loose thread on her jacket, trying to stay calm.

Hargrove stood silent, weighing his options. His face tightened with indignation. And just as Hargrove was about to reply, the phone at his desk rang. He excused himself and stepped over to answer it. After a couple of 'yeses' and a few 'very wells,' Hargrove stepped back over to the group, his back stiffer than before, and the smallest curl of his upper lip barely hidden under his mustache.

"The records room is across the hall," he said curtly. "Please follow me, and I'll direct you to what you're looking for."

With that, Hargrove led them to a room across the hall from his office. He reached into his pocket, removed a small set of keys, and unlocked the door to admit Stanley, Louise, and Elizabeth. Hargrove moved out of their way, revealing a cramped storage room filled with file cabinets. He unlocked one of them, pulled out a drawer, and brought a stack of document folders over to a small desk in the corner of the room.

"These are the files you're looking for," Hargrove said. "I'm sure you'll find everything is in order." He moved back to the door and gestured to his office. "I'll be right across the hall if you need anything." He stepped out and swung his head around one last time. "Please don't remove anything from this room. These are official records and cannot leave this office."

Hargrove headed back to his office, leaving both the records room door and his office door wide open. He took his seat at his desk in full view of Stanley, Louise, and Elizabeth, who sat down and began poring over the papers.

As they sifted through the documents, Stanley noticed something odd in one of the environmental assessments. He nudged Louise and pointed it out. "Look at this," he said. "This report here. It's the same data we saw in the other documents from your office."

Louise's eyes narrowed. "Yes, but look at these numbers here. They're not quite the same. Someone manipulated the data."

Elizabeth leaned in, scanning the page. "How so?"

"They adjusted projected environmental impact numbers," Stanley explained quietly. "It's subtle, but they're making it look like the project has less of an impact than it actually does. The real numbers are higher."

Elizabeth squinted at the document again, trying to make sense of it. "What's the point of changing the numbers here? Wouldn't everything here have copies at the EPA?"

"Welcome to the world of bureaucratic spin," Louise said. "If anything were to happen because of ParaWorks, the city administration, or whoever signed off on the plans, could deny all knowledge of the risk factors and blame any discrepancies on the EPA."

"The overzealous EPA," Stanley said.

Elizabeth nodded. "So we're looking at plausible deniability. Not only is something dirty, but someone or some people are trying to cover their tracks, too."

"Exactly," Stanley said. "Looks like someone's already ahead of us here."

Louise glanced over to check on Hargrove, who was on his phone and not too discreetly watching the group. "This puts us right back to square one," she said. "They've covered the evidence here, and they've made whatever we could recover at EPA headquarters questionable." Louise took a thoughtful breath. "We've got a big, fat, nothing burger here."

Elizabeth leaned in closer as she whispered, "Not necessarily. We could bring all of this to court or even just an open forum. We may not be able to prove our entire case, but we have enough to at least make people question it. There's no way the project would go through."

"You're right," Louise said. "By covering their tracks, the person or people who did this created a genuine conspiracy."

Elizabeth nodded. "And people have a funny way of believing a conspiracy."

"We can stop ParaWorks with what we've got right here," Louise said. "Let's get copies of this stuff and get out of here."

Stanley, who had been quietly listening to the back-and-forth between Elizabeth and Louise, seemed lost in thought. Then, as if on cue, he broke into the discussion. "And then what?" he said, almost in a daze.

Louise and Elizabeth stopped mid-discussion and looked at Stanley, who looked straight ahead at both of them, more serious than he had looked the whole time.

"And then what?" he repeated. "We could bring all of this out into the open, and you're right, it would probably stop the build. But then what? Whoever did this just gets away with it? We uncovered something here that proves someone or some people in power, who are supposed to be representing the people, put all of them at risk, put the whole town at risk. And for what? A vote? A kickback?" Stanley shook his head. "I'm not going back home and forgetting about that. You don't climb Everest and stop halfway. You go all the way to the top." He looked stone-faced at Louise and Elizabeth. "We're not done climbing here."

Louise smiled and took hold of Stanley's hand. "You're absolutely right."

Elizabeth nodded. "Alright, then we'll keep digging. We'll keep looking. We still need that signature, that consent form, assuming it exists," Elizabeth followed. "It's obviously not here with this stuff, and they sure aren't going to just hand it to us. So, where is it? Where could it be?"

Louise and Elizabeth looked at Stanley. He wasn't just a father slowly turning frail. Nor was he just a cautionary tale memorialized on a disrespectful poster. He was young again, strong, smart, and cunning. Stanley Peck, the man who stood up and dared to fight when no one else even knew there was a battle to be fought.

"Ladies," he said. "I have absolutely no idea."

Elizabeth frowned. "Well, that's not very helpful, Dad."

"Even if we keep trying to find the tip of the iceberg," Louise said, "we're going to need some of this paperwork to back up the story. But we won't get far with our friend out there watching the door."

Stanley glanced across the hall. "You're right," he said as he looked back at Elizabeth, giving her a go-ahead nod. "Go get 'em, Tiger."

Elizabeth stood abruptly and marched across the hall to Mr. Hargrove's office. "Mr. Hargrove," she said. "I need—some—water."

Hargrove looked up and made no effort to mask his annoyance. He maintained his best ironic smile. "Of course." He pointed down the hall. "There's a water cooler just over there. It's in the conference room."

Elizabeth fired her own annoyed expression back at Hargrove. "You don't want me wandering around this place by myself, do you?" she asked. "Could you please show me where it is?"

Hargrove sighed and stood up, leading her out of the room as he adjusted his cufflinks. "Very well. Follow me."

He led Elizabeth out of his office and down the hall, out of sight of the records room. Knowing they had only moments, Stanley and Louise worked fast.

"We need these data sheets," Stanley whispered, folding a few papers and shoving them into the inside pocket of his suit jacket. "And look for anything else that conflicts with what you showed me from your files. But keep your eyes peeled for anything else—meetings, people, that sort of thing."

Louise nodded, flipping through the documents at lightning speed. "Here," she said, pulling out a file. "Look at this. It's a memo. It mentions a meeting with the zoning board. That could be where they pushed this through." She shuffled through the papers a bit more. "And look who was the head of that meeting—our friend out there, Mr. Hargrove."

Stanley's eyes widened. "That's great!" he said. "Grab it. We'll need to find out who else was at that meeting, too. But this is obviously more than just one person."

Just as Louise slipped the memo into her briefcase, a shadow passed by the door. She was back to the papers on the desk just as Elizabeth returned with Alan Hargrove in tow.

"Is everything all right here?" Hargrove asked with a hint of suspicion in his voice.

Stanley quickly stepped forward, allowing Louise to close her briefcase unnoticed. "Yes, we're just about done here, Mr. Hargrove. Everything looks good. Thank you for your cooperation."

Hargrove nodded impatiently. "Yes, yes. If you have any

further questions, please feel free to contact me." He gestured for them to follow him down the hall. "If you'll allow me to show you out."

The group gathered their things and followed Hargrove as he guided the trio to the front lobby. He offered them a curt "good day" and turned back down the hall.

"Friendly guy," Stanley said as he watched Hargrove walk away.

Elizabeth chuckled ironically. "Yeah, a real charmer."

As they made their way to the exit, Louise looked towards the receptionist's desk. She saw Christine toiling away at her computer, and Christine saw her, too. Just as before, the receptionist looked up and immediately glanced away. That's all it took for Louise to break away from Stanley and Elizabeth and make a slight detour to the front lobby desk. She reached into her bag and pulled something out as she reached her target. Christine silently looked up, and without a word, Louise placed her business card at the front of the desk. She smiled, a gesture Christine eyed with curiosity as the EPA representative walked away and rejoined Stanley and Louise, who had made it to the front door.

As they passed through the doorway, Stanley raised his eyebrow. "Are you going to tell us what that was about?"

Louise shook her head. "I'm honestly not sure. Just a feeling, I guess."

Down at the opposite end of the building, Alan Hargrove was about to turn the corner when he looked back towards the front. He watched as Stanley, Louise, and Elizabeth disappeared down the steps, then turned his attention towards the reception desk. Had he looked just a minute earlier, he would have seen Louise approach Christine, and had he looked just a second earlier, he would have seen Christine snap up Louise's business card and tuck it away.

Mr. Hargrove caught Christine trying not to look at him. He fired a dirty scowl her way, then disappeared down the hall.

* * *

Once outside, Stanley, Louise, and Elizabeth hurried back to the car as the sound of rolling thunder boomed in the distance. Louise unlocked the doors, and everyone got in. Once inside, they let out a collective sigh of relief.

"We did it," Elizabeth said triumphantly. "We actually did it!"

Stanley nodded, with a renewed sense of determination on his face. "We did well. But now we need to follow up on this memo Louise found. That could lead us to who might have signed off on this thing."

"Yes," Louise agreed. "But let's get a drink first."

Stanley and Elizabeth looked wearily at their compatriot.

"Oh, like you weren't sweating through your shirts too," Louise said. "Now let's get out of here before that thunder up there turns into rain."

Stanley chuckled. "Sounds good to me. *Everett's Place* ought to be open by now. Let's go."

Chapter Nine

The rain drummed against the windows of *Everett's Bar*, creating a cozy cocoon of dry warmth inside. Steady conversation filled the establishment, punctuated by the clink of glasses and the occasional burst of laughter from the bar. The casual setting provided a comforting backdrop for the trio of intrepid investigators huddled in a corner booth. Stanley, Elizabeth, and Louise had commandeered the table, and the remnants of a few drinks gone by were on full display.

Stanley, looking more like his old self in his neatly pressed suit, stood peering over the song list of a jukebox in the corner. The machine's soft neon glow cast a kaleidoscope of colors across the worn wooden floor of the bar. Stanley's brow furrowed as he scanned the song selections. His fingers hovered over the buttons as he struggled to make a choice.

"Stan, you gonna pick something or just stare at that thing all night?" Everett, the bar owner, said as he walked along the bar towards Stanley at the jukebox, his limp still ever-present.

Stanley didn't look up, keeping his focus locked on the jukebox's display. "I'm looking for something with soul and some story to it, Everett. You know, real music. Franklin or Dylan. Maybe some Mamas and Papas. None of this autotuned noise you've got clogging up the list of this beautiful machine."

Everett snorted, setting the glass he was cleaning down with a deliberate clunk. "Clogging? Stan, this isn't 1965. My customers want something they can dance to, not something to cry into their beer over. Pick some Dua Lipa or Post Malone, will ya? Keep the vibe alive."

Stanley shot Everett a mocking glare. "Vibe?" Stanley questioned. "Everett, the only vibe this place needs is a little Creedence! Something with some heart! You want your customers to feel something, not just twitch like they're at some rave."

Elizabeth, sitting next to Louise at their nearby half-round table, scooted to the edge as she looked over to Stanley. "Dad, there's a time and place for all of that. The '60s don't belong in here. Nobody here's trying to relive Woodstock. Give us something from this century."

Stanley turned, feigning betrayal. "Et tu, my beautiful Lizzy?" He slapped his hand across his heart. "My own daughter, siding with the enemy! I raised you better than that. You used to fall asleep to '*Rumours*' when you were a kid. Don't you remember?"

Elizabeth laughed and tossed her pen at Stanley playfully. It bounced off his shoulder and clattered to the floor. "Yeah, I remember," she said. "I also listened to The Clash and Duran Duran, and I still turned out fine despite listening to that devil's music. Come on, Dad, pick something fun." Elizabeth looked over to Louise and poked her in the arm. "Even Louise agrees with me, don't you?"

Louise, sitting next to Elizabeth with a half-drunk glass of Long Island Iced Tea, looked up from her drink, her eyes twinkling. "Oh, I'm staying out of this one! But I will say, Stanley, your taste in music is about as dated as your..." She looked at Stanley's 1980s suit, then quickly darted her eyes away. "The man's got a point," Louise recovered. "Let's hear something that doesn't sound like it came with a side of bell-bottoms."

The bar erupted in a few chuckles from nearby patrons, and Stanley threw his arms up in offense. "This is a conspiracy, I tell you! You're all ganging up on me. Fine, I'll pick something," he turned back to the jukebox, "but don't blame me when your '*modern*' customers beg for some Dylan."

Everett leaned over the counter, his grin wide. "Dylan? Stan, if you play *Blowin' in the Wind,* I'm unplugging that jukebox myself. Give me some Lizzo garbage, something the younger crowd will like, something with a beat. My bar, my rules."

Stanley shook his head, playfully imitating Everett under his breath as he punched in a selection. "*Your bar,* my soul." A few seconds later, the opening chords of Jackson Browne's "Fountain of Sorrow" filled the tavern, in all of its raw and thoughtful complexity. Stanley turned, spreading his arms triumphantly. "There we go. Compromise! It's the '70s, not the '60s, and it's got more heart than anything your pop stars are churning out."

Everett groaned, but a smile tugged at his lips. "You're impossible, Stan. But I'll give you this one. It's not half bad."

Elizabeth clapped, laughing. "Nice save, Dad! But next time, I'm picking. You're not ready for my playlist."

Louise raised her glass in a toast. "To Stanley, the unexpected defender of vinyl in a streaming world."

Elizabeth laughed as Stanley smirked and slid onto the seat next to Louise. "Laugh all you want," he said, "but you'll thank me when this song gets stuck in your head." Louise giggled as Stanley arched back and pointed his finger at Louise. "Hey, are you going to fill us in on what was up with you and that receptionist from city hall?"

Louise rubbed her forehead for a moment. "I don't know. It's hard to explain, really. I just got the feeling that she knew something. I mean, I don't know what or anything, but the way she avoided eye contact and... I just felt like there was something there, something under the surface."

"Like she's in on it somehow?" Elizabeth asked.

"No," Louise said. "Not that. I feel like she wanted to tell us something, but couldn't."

Stanley took a sip of his drink. "It's not a crazy thought. She's in that office every day. She could know anything. Did I see you give her your card?"

Louise nodded. "Yeah. I didn't want to draw any attention to her. I just hope she uses it—if she knows something."

"Who knows," Stanley said. "Maybe you should try reaching out to her discreetly somehow."

Elizabeth leaned in. "Yeah, that's a good idea. We could track her down on social media or find her contact information. If she really is holding on to something, she might just be needing a little push in the right direction."

"I hope you're right," Louise said.

"Hey, Louise," Elizabeth said after looking at her empty glass and raising her hand for the waitress, "fun fact about Stanley Peck. Did you know he tried to use his detective skills on me when I was a kid? Can you picture that?"

Louise laughed as the waitress replaced the trio's table with fresh drinks. "You know, I can *actually* imagine that. Were you any good at getting out of things?"

Stanley smiled and jumped in. "Good?! She's a Peck! She was damn good! Better than most of the greenhorns I had to deal with way back when."

Louise raised an eyebrow, intrigued by the hint of the former family dynamic in the Peck household. "Oh, there must be some stories there. Do tell."

Elizabeth laughed as she tucked a few loose strands of hair behind her ear. "Well, there *was* the great '*Sneak-Out Caper*' of 1995."

Stanley leaned back, crossed his arms, and chuckled, a nostalgic twinkle in his eye. "Oh boy. You're bringing up ancient history now, Lizzy!"

Louise smiled, leaning in close as Elizabeth started her story. "I was sixteen," Elizabeth said as she took another sip of her drink, "and Detective Peck over here was convinced I'd been slipping out at night to meet my friends at an old arcade in town. He turned our kitchen into a courtroom." She looked at Stanley. "Remember that, Dad? You had your '*evidence*' all lined up like you were Perry Mason or something."

"Perry Mason?" Louise questioned.

Stanley rolled his eyes and shook his head, then downed some of his drink. "Forget it."

Louise laughed at the obvious reference she had missed. "Go on," she insisted.

Stanley chuckled, the memory flooding back. "Oh, you were a slippery one, Lizzy." He turned to face Louise. "I had her dead to rights. Mud on her sneakers, an arcade token in her jacket pocket, and one of our neighbors, Mrs. Callahan, swearing she saw her near the arcade at midnight. An airtight case!"

Elizabeth's grin widened, her eyes glinting with the same sharp cunning she'd shown all those years ago. "Airtight, huh?

He sat me down at the kitchen table, pacing like a detective, asking me where I was at 11:47 p.m. on a Tuesday. He even had a notepad with timestamps. Timestamps, Louise!"

Stanley leaned back, a playful smirk tugging at his lips. "What do you want? I was thorough! You've gotta be thorough when you're dealing with a mastermind like teenage Elizabeth Peck. So go on, tell us all how you wiggled out of that one."

Elizabeth sat up straighter, relishing the story. "Oh, I didn't just wiggle out, Dad. I *schooled* you." She looked back at Louise, who was grinning from ear to ear. "He laid out his evidence—mud on the sneakers, the token, Mrs. Callahan's story. He was so proud of his case, the whole time demanding that I explain myself."

"Oh, I had her pinned down," Stanley added with a smile.

"And I just sat there, calm as could be," Elizabeth said. "Then I said, 'Dad, let's talk about the mud.'"

Stanley playfully furrowed his brow. "The mud? What about it?"

Elizabeth lowered her voice into a mock-serious tone, mimicking a courtroom drama as she continued to spin her story to Louise. "He said the mud on my sneakers came from the alley behind the arcade. He even brought out a little baggie of dirt from the backyard to compare it, like he was a CSI before CSI was a thing." Louise laughed as Elizabeth continued. "But I pointed out something he missed. The mud on my shoes wasn't just any mud. It was mud with red clay. The kind you could only find at an old quarry on the edge of town, not in some city alley. I told him I'd been hiking with my science club that weekend and that he'd seen me come home with those same muddy shoes on Sunday." She turned her attention to Stanley. "But you conveniently forgot about that."

Stanley shook his head. "Yep, you sure turned it around on me."

"Oh, I wasn't done," Elizabeth said, her grin turning wicked with delight. "Then there was the arcade token. He held it up like it was the smoking gun, saying I must've been at the arcade because where else would I get it? But I asked him to look closer. That token wasn't from the arcade. It was from the pizza place next door. Turns out they used the same tokens for their claw machines."

Stanley let out a low whistle, shaking his head. "You were a menace, Lizzy."

"Wait for it..." Elizabeth said, holding up a finger. "And then, just to seal the deal, I turned the tables. I said, 'Dad, if you're so good at spotting sneaks, how come you didn't notice *your* car keys were missing last weekend when I borrowed the station wagon to get ice cream with Jenny?'"

"You admitted to another crime?!" Louise blurted out.

Elizabeth laughed. "Yeah, I got a little full of myself." She winked at Stanley. "I can't imagine where I got *that* from."

Stanley's laughter faded, replaced with a warm chuckle. "I should've known you'd be a lawyer someday."

Elizabeth laughed at the memory. "I remember that like it was yesterday. You were so mad at me for finding the loophole you missed."

Stanley shook his head, smiling. "Proud, Elizabeth. Not mad. Proud."

Elizabeth smiled warmly at Stanley. "Most of the kids my age were brought up on *Full House* or *Mr. Rogers*," she said, refocusing her attention back to Louise. "But not me. Not in the Peck household. I was raised on a steady diet of legalese and code violations."

"I guess it's no wonder you went into law," Louise said. "You certainly have the pedigree for it."

Elizabeth fired back quickly. "Oh, I wanted nothing to do with it! After growing up with it, the last thing I ever wanted was to open a law book professionally."

Stanley leaned back confidently, adding, "But…"

Elizabeth smiled. "But… after spending about a week working as a tech in the hospital my mom worked at, I knew I didn't have a taste for anything but law."

Stanley cleared his throat jokingly. "I do believe the exact count was four days."

"Four days!" Elizabeth said. "And my dad made sure I remembered that every time I complained about the long hours or tough assignments during law school."

"I'm sure all those late nights you spent helping your dad gave you an edge, though," Louise said.

Elizabeth put up her hands in resignation. "I can't deny that."

As the rain continued to pour outside, Stanley leaned back in his seat, looking at his daughter and Louise. "It's been a long time since I've done something like this. It feels like old times. We just switched chocolate milk for some Jack Daniels."

Elizabeth smiled. "And we added a new member to the team." She glanced at Louise. "We're all in this together."

Louise raised her glass. "To unexpected team-ups and bringing down corrupt officials!" She leaned back, her glass still raised, a thoughtful look forming on her face. "You know, it's funny how we all ended up here, fighting this fight. I never thought I'd be sitting in a bar, plotting against corrupt officials with a lawyer and…" she looked at Stanley, "no offense intended—Stanley Peck."

Stanley held up his glass and fired Louise a playful wink.

"None taken," he said as the trio clinked their glasses together in the air.

Elizabeth tilted her head, curious. "Okay, Louise, you've heard about my childhood cross-examinations, and Dad's story is famous. But what about you? How did *you* end up at the Environmental Protection Agency, digging through data and faking out city officials?"

Louise giggled, setting her glass down. "Oh, it's not exactly a glamorous story. I didn't grow up dreaming of spreadsheets and environmental regulations, I'll tell you that much. In college, I was a biology major. I thought I'd be out in the field, saving endangered species or something noble like that."

Stanley raised an eyebrow, intrigued. "So what happened? How do you go from saving whales to wrestling with government red tape?"

Louise sighed. "It started with a summer internship at a wildlife refuge. I was young and idealistic and thought I could change the world one panda at a time. After some coursework, I found myself in the Congo, working with the locals to help move a troop of gorillas as part of an intern project with the Humane Society. Their land was being cut into by developers, and I wanted to help."

"That sounds amazing," Elizabeth said.

Louise nodded her head. "It does. But I hated it."

Stanley laughed out loud. "Heavens, why?"

"It turns out there are a lot of bugs and insects in the Congo," Louise said. "And it's hot. It's humid." She shook her head. "I grew up in Oxnard. The jungle wasn't..."

"Wasn't for you?" Elizabeth finished with a question.

"No, ma'am!" Louise said with a laugh as she took another sip.

Stanley leaned in. "So, how on Earth did you end up at the EPA?"

"Well," Louise said, "I may not have liked the Congo, but I still wanted to help. The entire issue with the gorillas was because developers bought the land and were going to displace the indigenous animals. And the locals didn't have the legal know-how to stop them."

Elizabeth leaned forward, resting her chin on her hand. "Sounds like you got a crash course in humanity's tricky morality."

"You could say that," Louise said, her eyes glazing over in the memories. "I got mad, really mad. That's when I realized I couldn't just sit on the sidelines. I wanted to fight."

Stanley nodded. "So that's when you found the EPA?"

"As soon as I got home," Louise said. "I applied to the EPA because I figured if I was going to fight, I needed to be where the rules get enforced. Or at least, where they were *supposed* to be enforced. I thought I could make a difference from the inside. I thought I could fight for the underdogs." She shook her head. "It hasn't been easy, though. Half the time, I'm drowning in paperwork or fighting with people who'd rather look the other way. But every once in a while, you get a win. You stop a dangerous project, or you catch someone dirty, and it feels like it's worth it, like a win. You know?"

Elizabeth smiled, impressed. "That's some serious grit, girl. Most people would've given up after that first brush with bureaucracy."

Louise cocked her head. "Oh, I thought about it. Plenty of times. But I'm stubborn. And I grew up in a small town, kinda like Redmain. I saw what happened when people didn't speak up when the water got dirty or the air got bad, and when no one did anything because it was easier to stay quiet. I couldn't be that person."

Stanley raised his glass, respect in his eyes. He held his glass in the air. "To stubbornness, then. And to fighting the good fight, no matter how much paperwork it takes."

Louise laughed. "I'll drink to that! But let's be honest, sometimes I think the paperwork is the *real* enemy."

The trio clinked their glasses just as Louise's phone, which was sitting on the table, rang and buzzed. She pulled in close, focusing through the alcoholic haze in her eyes. She cocked her head. "Don't know this number. Probably spam." She brought her finger to the '*accept*' button. "Okay, spam, let's see what you're selling."

Louise hit the button, accepting the call. "Yes, this is Louise Talbot," she said in response to whatever the person on the other end of the line said. There was silence for a long moment, and Louise's face took on the appearance of seriousness. Stanley and Elizabeth saw Louise's tone shift and leaned in curiously. "I understand," she finally said. "Is now possible." Another pause. "Okay, that's fine. We're not far from there. We'll meet you there in fifteen minutes." She hit the digital button and ended the call.

Stanley leaned in. "Is everything all right?"

"Yeah," Elizabeth said. "And did you mean 'we' as in all of *us*?"

Louise shook off the surprise at the call. "You're never going to believe it. That was Christine, the receptionist from City Hall."

"The one you left your card with?" Stanley asked.

"Yep," Louise said. "She said she wants to meet with us—and that she has something that might help us with the case."

Elizabeth let out a puff of air. "Wow! Okay. Didn't see that coming."

"Looks like your instincts were right about her," Stanley said to Louise. "She didn't say what she had?"

Louise shook her head. "No, just that she had something and wanted to meet right away. She asked to meet in the post office parking lot."

Elizabeth started gathering her things. "Well, let's not keep Christine waiting. Let's go!"

The group stood and started for the door. They didn't get more than a few feet when Everett leaned over the bar and called out to them. "Hey Stan, I don't know about your girls there, but you sure aren't good to drive. Why don't you let me call you an Uber?"

Stanley looked over to Elizabeth and Louise. Without a word spoken between them, the trio all nodded in agreement.

"That's probably a good idea," Stanley said.

* * *

Good to his word, Everett called for an Uber, and luckily for the trio of Stanley, Louise, and Elizabeth, it didn't take long to arrive. They made it to the parking lot of the Redmain post office a minute after the fifteen minutes Louise had told Christine. They had just stepped out when another car pulled into the lot, its lights illuminating the empty asphalt. Christine left her car running as she walked over. She was already dripping wet and looked around hesitantly.

Stanley raised an eyebrow as she approached. "Well, if it

isn't our favorite City Hall receptionist. Fancy meeting you here?"

Christine looked around nervously before speaking. "I… I know what you were looking into at City Hall today—the whole ParaWorks thing, I mean. I wondered if someone was going to show up asking questions like you were today. It's none of my business, but…" Christine let her words fade away as if caught in a mental loop of doubt.

Louise stepped over and put her hand on Christine's forearm. "It's okay. You're safe here. Whatever you want to say, we'll leave your name out of it."

Christine nodded thankfully as she regarded Louise. "I don't know if I ever could have said anything, but when you looked at me today, I felt like I had to, like I had to do something. I looked at your card all day, then I started thinking about what you might be at City Hall for." She looked around, as if scanning the empty lot for someone familiar. "I don't know exactly what you know right now, but I thought you might be able to use this." Christine pulled an envelope out from under her coat and handed it to Stanley, her hands trembling slightly.

Stanley exchanged a curious glance with Elizabeth and Louise as he pulled the envelope close, thumbing the edges of the manila paper as he looked up at Christine. "Whatever this is, thank you?" He took a quick breath, then looked down at the envelope, opened it, and pulled out the contents. His eyes widened as he processed what he was looking at—the signed ParaWorks building consent form, bearing the unmistakable signatures of Mayor Jim Mass and head of the planning commission, Alan Hargrove.

Stanley held the paper for Elizabeth and Louise to see. "This is the consent form we've been looking for! I knew it had to exist."

Elizabeth's jaw dropped. "How'd you get this?"

Christine looked down. "Mr. Hargrove started making a lot of calls after you left. He ended up on the phone with Mayor Mass for over an hour. I don't know what you said to him, but you scared him." She fidgeted with a loose string on her jacket for a moment. "Anyway, what Hargrove didn't tell you is that there's another records room, locked away, for protected files. So, I waited for everyone to leave for the day, and I looked up the ParaWorks file."

Stanley leaned forward. "If the protected records are locked, how did you get into them?"

Christine couldn't resist a coy smirk as she held up a ring of keys. "I'm the chief secretary there. I have the keys to everything."

Elizabeth chuckled. "I love it."

Christine smiled, then quickly wiped it away. "I didn't really know what you might be looking for, but it turned out that form was all that was in the file. So, I took it."

"Thank you for doing that, Christine," Louise said. "That's very brave of you."

Christine took a breath. "I couldn't just stand by and do nothing. The mayor—he's been getting away with too much for too long. And he's not alone. Hargrove, he's got something to do with this, too. But I don't know what."

Louise leaned forward, her expression serious. "Not that I'm complaining, but why would you risk doing this for us? You could get in a lot of trouble for this."

Christine swallowed hard. "I know. And I need this job. I do. But I've lived here my whole life. My son goes to elementary school here. I couldn't be part of this town if I knew someone got hurt or sick because of something I could have helped to stop. I just couldn't."

Stanley reached out and placed a reassuring hand on her arm. "You did the right thing, Christine." He smiled. "This is exactly what we needed."

Christine sighed, relief washing over her face. "Just promise me you'll use it. Make sure they don't get away with whatever they've got going."

Elizabeth nodded firmly. "We will, we promise. You've given us exactly what we need to kick this thing forward. We can't thank you enough."

Christine glanced nervously. "I should go. I don't want anyone to see me here." She turned and climbed back into her car, pausing before closing the door. "Good luck."

As Christine drove away, Stanley, Elizabeth, and Louise stared at the form in Stanley's hands. The paper had next to no heft to it, weighing in at only a few grams. But with the black ink signatures at the bottom, it somehow felt like a piece of solid gold, weighing pounds instead of grams.

"Louise," Stanley said, "this is all you. You gave Christine the push she needed."

Elizabeth nodded in agreement. "Yeah, great instincts, Louise."

Louise smiled. "I just hope it gets us where we need to go."

Chapter Ten

The Uber driver's tires crunched against the pavement as it pulled up to Stanley's apartment building. The smell of wet asphalt mingled with Stanley's not-so-faint scent of whiskey as he stumbled out of the door, his tie askew and jacket dangling from one hand. Louise followed, her heels wobbling underneath her as she giggled, clutching Elizabeth's arm for balance. Elizabeth, slightly steadier but her face flushed from her multiple Bloody Marys and Vodka Mules, shoved the Uber door shut. Somehow, she managed to keep the envelope containing the signed ParaWorks consent form tucked securely under her arm.

"Stanley Peck, *O father of mine*," Elizabeth slurred, "I do believe you're quite drunk!" She burst into laughter, nearly tripping over the curb as her dark hair fell into her face.

Stanley spun around, his own cheeks flushed from one too many whiskeys. His grin was wide, almost boyish, as he struggled to point his finger at Elizabeth. "Oh, you're one to talk, *O daughter of mine*! You looked like a fish out of water when you were trying to keep up with that jukebox song!" Stanley mimicked her wild arm movements, nearly dropping his jacket, which sent Louise snorting into her sleeve.

"Both of you were a disaster," Louise said, working to keep herself steady. "*Are* a disaster! Obviously, I'm the only one holding it together here. I was waiting for Stanley to start singing 'Fountain of Sorrow' to the bartender!" She reached into her purse, pulled out a twenty, and paid the Uber driver. The man shook his head at the inebriated group before driving away.

Stanley swayed slightly as he pointed a wobbly finger at Louise. "Don't you dare diss my song choices, Talbot! That's a classic, and you'll be humming it by morning, I guarantee it!" He tripped over a crack in the sidewalk, catching himself on the building's door frame with a theatrical '*Oof*!' that set Elizabeth off again, her laughter ringing like a bell down the empty street.

"Dad, you're gonna wake the whole damn town!" Elizabeth said, wiping tears of laughter from her eyes. "Let's get inside before someone calls the sheriff on us for being a public nuisance!"

The trio staggered into the narrow stairwell of Stanley's apartment complex that led upstairs. Their footsteps clattered on the concrete steps, and their laughter echoed up and down the stairs. It was chilly in the open stairwell, but the invisible alcohol overcoat they all wore kept them from noticing.

Stanley and Elizabeth were holding each other up, and Louise trailed behind them. "If I'd known I was signing up for babysitting duty," Louise said, "I'd have stayed in the Congo with the bugs."

After a wrong turn and Stanley's battle to find the right key, the trio stumbled into Stanley's apartment. A single lamp left on illuminated the cluttered living room. The trio had left piles of papers strewn all over the dining room table. The impromptu meeting place had become a war room, and the apartment very much looked the part.

Stanley tossed his jacket at one of the dining room chairs, missing entirely, and flopped onto the couch with a groan. "Home sweet chaos," he declared, kicking off his shoes, one sailing perilously close to a plant beside the TV.

Elizabeth placed the envelope containing the signed consent form on the coffee table and collapsed beside Stanley, her head rolling back. "Dad, his place smells like a library," she teased, nudging his arm. "When's the last time you vacuumed, anyway?"

"Vacuumed?" Stanley scoffed as he feigned offense. "This is the aroma of *wisdom*, Lizzy! As my daughter, I would expect you to know the difference."

Louise perched herself on the couch's arm. "You two are ridiculous! Remind me never to let you two drink together again." She pushed her glasses up, giggling with amusement.

Their laughter bounced off the walls. Louise and Elizabeth continued joking and laughing as Stanley leaned back, his gaze drifting to the window. The blinds were half-open to the dark street below, allowing Stanley just enough of an opening to see through. A flicker of movement caught his attention. His eyes followed the movement to the glint of chrome under a streetlight. The water droplets on the bumper seemed to shine under the street lamp. Stanley's smile vanished, and the whiskey buzz evaporated as he sat up, his body taut like a coiled spring.

"Hold on," Stanley said, all traces of drunken mirth gone. He stood and crossed to the window with measured steps. Parting the blinds, Stanley peered out. A black sedan sat across the street, its engine purring softly. The driver's window, cracked just slightly, revealed a silent watcher inside. A faint red glow, a cigarette, flared briefly in the darkness.

Elizabeth noticed Stanley's shift in tone, her own alcohol buzz fading as she joined him at the window. "What's wrong, Dad?" she asked, her eyes narrowing as she followed his gaze down to the street.

Louise was already up at this point. She pushed her glass up and squinted through the blinds. "That doesn't look right," she said.

"No, it doesn't," Elizabeth agreed. "Did either of you notice it out there when the Uber guy dropped us off?"

Louise shook her head. "I didn't. But I wasn't really looking either."

Stanley's jaw tightened. "We've got a tail, kids," he said, his voice a low growl. "Someone knows we're onto things. Someone might even know we've got the consent form." His eyes squinted in thought. "It could be Hargrove or Mass, maybe both."

Elizabeth's breath caught, but her eyes blazed with defiance. "Then we don't sit here like sitting ducks. We go out there. Now. And we find out who that is and who's behind this."

Louise nodded, slipping her phone into her pocket. "I agree. We can catch them off guard. Maybe we can sneak up on them."

Stanley hesitated, but the fire on Elizabeth's face and Louise's steady resolve grounded him. "Alright," he said, grabbing his jacket from the floor. "We can get out near the side entrance."

As they stepped towards the door, Elizabeth stopped and grabbed Stanley by the arm. "Dad, maybe you should stay here."

Stanley scowled. "Not a chance, Lizzy. I'm not letting you girls go out there alone."

"Maybe she's right, Stanley," Louise countered. "You could stay up here and..."

Stanley cut Louise off mid-word. "I get it, girls, I do. But I'm going out there with you."

Elizabeth took a deep breath. "Okay, Dad. Just be careful, alright?"

Stanley nodded. "I promise."

With that, the trio slipped out of the apartment's side exit into the alley. The back of the complex was thick with the scent of rain-soaked garbage. Their footsteps were quiet as they all but tiptoed, but their breaths came quicker and quicker as adrenaline sliced through their bloodstreams. The alley was a narrow gauntlet of overflowing dumpsters, but they made it through without knocking anything over. The distant idling of the sedan's engine grew louder as they crept further toward the street.

Stanley peered around the corner, his pulse hammering in his chest. The taillights of the sedan glowed like malevolent eyes. The driver's silhouette shifted in their seat, a cigarette's glow pulsing from the window. Stanley stepped forward as he continued his approach, but Elizabeth overtook him and maneuvered herself into the lead. Stanley reached out for her in vain as she deftly moved the group out into the open. She looked back and signaled for the others to follow. Stanley kept up, though his movements were slow and awkward, but he pressed forward anyway.

As they reached the midpoint between the hidden safety of the apartment corner and the mysterious car, Elizabeth yelled, "Now!" The group broke into a sprint, cutting across the street toward the idling car. Inside, the driver's silhouette whipped around, the cigarette falling out of the window. The engine shifted into gear, and the tires screeched against the wet pavement as the car pulled forward. But the trio was faster, blocking the sedan's path.

"Hey, you!" Elizabeth shouted as she raced to plant herself in front of the car and slammed her hands against the hood. The headlights illuminated her from below, casting her defiance in perfect form.

The driver, a bulky man in a dark jacket and baseball cap, swore under his breath and threw open the door. He stumbled out with a clipboard clutched tightly in his fist. He was older than expected. His face was pale under the streetlight, and his eyes darted around like a trapped animal. "Get out of my way!" he yelled. His voice was rough but unsteady, betraying his nerves.

Stanley stepped forward, putting the car door behind himself and the man. "Who are you, and why are you watching us?!" he demanded, each word deliberate.

"Did Hargrove send you?" Louise said, backing Stanley up beside the door. "Mass? ParaWorks?"

The man backed toward the car, raising his hands, but a look of worry crossed his face. "I'm just a P.I., doing my job, Peck," he said, spitting Stanley's name like a jab.

Stanley shook his head. "You're a P.I.?"

"Yeah, yeah," the man stammered. "I'm just doin' a job here. So all you crazy drunks can slow down, alright!"

Stanley shot a look at Elizabeth, who pointed her finger at the man like it was the tip of a sword. "If you're a P.I., show us your license!"

The man backed up and reached into his back pocket.

Stanley and Louise took a slight step back in fear as the man pulled his hand back out. He flashed the trio a small, laminated card. Elizabeth squinted at it from the front of the car, but Stanley snatched it from the man before he could respond. His eyes darted across its contents.

"His name's Reese," Stanley said, loud enough for Elizabeth to hear. "It's a P.I. license. It looks real enough."

"I'm real enough, Peck," Reese said. "And I'm not here to hurt anyone. Just watchin'."

Stanley tossed the ID card back to P.I. He missed it, and it fell to the ground. Stanley, Elizabeth, and Louise shot each other looks as the man leaned down and picked the ID up and slipped it back into his pocket.

"And just who are you working for, Mr. Reese?" Elizabeth demanded.

"Look," Reese said. "I can't tell you that. But trust me, you all are stirrin' up trouble you can't handle."

Louise moved around the car. Her phone flashed as she snapped a photo of the man and his license plate. "Just doing your job, huh?" she said. "Stalking us in the middle of the night? Why don't you cut the shit and tell us who's paying you?"

"All it'll take is one phone call, and we've got you on harassment," Elizabeth said.

The investigator's eyes narrowed. His fear faded as he assessed the trio. For a moment, he seemed ready to talk, his shoulders slumping. Then, in a flash, he turned and jumped back into his car, slamming the door shut behind him.

"Hey, get back here!" Stanley barked as the investigator quickly shifted into reverse, sending the car screeching backward down the street.

Elizabeth, fueled by adrenaline and fury, immediately started after him, her bare feet slapping the ground after she kicked off her heels. Louise took off next, keeping pace with Elizabeth. Her glasses were fogging up, but her focus was razor sharp as she scanned for shortcuts, her phone still in hand. Stanley made it to the nearest corner before coming to a stop, breathing hard as he fought to catch his breath.

Halfway down the street, Elizabeth reached out for Louise's arm, bringing the women to a slow stop as they watched the private investigator's car turn a corner in the distance. "Forget it, he's gone," she said. "We can't catch him now."

Stanley stood, wincing, his hand on his chest as he took a few deep breaths, slowing his heart down. He slammed his hand onto the corner stop sign as Elizabeth and Louise made their way back to him.

"Are you okay, Dad?" Elizabeth asked, visibly worried.

Stanley waved his hand in the air. "I'm fine, I'm fine," he said through catching breaths.

Louise dropped to the grass at the corner near Stanley's feet. "I can't believe that just happened. It's like something out of a movie."

"It's no movie," Elizabeth said. "That was a real P.I., and we're really being watched."

"He knew my name," Stanley said as he moved to the ground next to Louise. "This isn't just about the form. Someone's scared. This is real."

Louise looked up to Elizabeth. "Can we report that guy?" she asked. "I mean, can we go to the police or something?"

Elizabeth shook her head. "We could. But it wouldn't really matter." She took a deep breath, steadying her breathing as she leaned against the stop sign. "A licensed private investigator has protections under California law. And he doesn't have to give up his client."

Stanley harrumphed. "Well, isn't that great?"

Elizabeth's eyes burned with resolve. "One thing's for sure. Someone's scared. So scared that they're watching our every move."

"I wonder if there's a connection between those empty phone calls I've been getting and this P.I. guy," Stanley questioned.

Elizabeth nodded. "Could be. Probably a scare tactic."

"Well, it's working," Louise said. "I'm scared." She stood back up. "If whoever is behind this is willing to go this far, who knows what could be next?"

"Then we can't stop," Stanley said, pulling on the stop sign to bring himself to his feet. "We've got to connect all the pieces."

Chapter Eleven

Forty years ago.

Chicago Mayor Harold Washington sat behind his desk, tie loosened, his face lined with the weight of a suburb near Leo Vincent's burning waste disposal plant, now choking on a toxic smoke cloud. Stanley Peck stood rigid by the window. Through everything, he still held on to the court order, which was crumpled up in his fist. Ash from the CleanCycle blaze still smeared his suit. Cracks of doubt were breaking through his hardened expression. Across the room from Stanley, Leo Vincent sat lounging in a chair, his face still covered in arrogance, and his suit still mostly pristine, despite a dusting of soot on his shoulders. The room buzzed with tension, the walls practically vibrating with the city's anger outside as a large crowd of reporters, activists, and the general populace gathered, demanding answers about this cloud of toxic gas that now threatened homes near the melting plant.

"Gentlemen," the mayor said, slamming a hand on his desk. "We've got a disaster on our hands, and I'm stuck between you two like a damn referee. I've got a waste management plant burning on the edge of my city, spewing a cloud of toxic vapor so bad that the National Guard has to help evacuate the nearby suburbs, suburbs filled with homes, filled with people. Voters!"

Leo Vincent tried to cut in. "Mr. Mayor, I tried to..."

Mayor Washington cut Vincent off with the wave of his hand. He shifted his weight as he sat perched on the edge of his desk. "The phones have been ringing off the hook. Everyone wants answers. Everyone wants someone to blame." Mayor Washington looked at the row of experts and political advisors lining the back of his office wall. "And everyone is looking to this office to figure it out." He turned his attention to Stanley. "Peck, you got yourself a court order and shut down CleanCycle BioSystem." The mayor stepped closer and bore his gaze into Stanley's eyes. "Tell me why."

Stanley straightened as he clung to his righteousness. "Mister Mayor, I had no choice. Leo Vincent's operation was a ticking bomb. Their provisional permit was a sham. No filed reports, no real oversight. I acted to protect the city. That fire and the smoke cloud? It's not my fault."

Stanley glared viciously at Leo, daring him to disagree, but his confidence wavered under the mayor's unyielding stare. Vincent chuckled, a low, arrogant sound that made Stanley's fists clench in fury. He leaned forward, eyes locked on the mayor, ignoring Stanley entirely. "Negligence? Please. Peck here panicked and shut down a system he didn't understand, and now half of Chicago's suburbs are coughing up toxic smoke. We were weeks from final approval, doing exactly what the state and city asked." Vincent side-eyed Stanley as he said to the mayor with dripping venomous disdain, "Everything would have been fine if it weren't for the human *ball sack* here."

The mayor rolled his eyes at Vincent's last comment and

rubbed his temples, glancing at the stack of news clippings on his desk. Early headlines were screaming "EPA Sabotage!" and "CleanCycle BioSystems Crisis!"

"Vincent, your plant's a mess," the mayor said. "But Peck, you escalated this. You made this happen. The public's ready to lynch someone, and right now, I'm seriously considering feeding both of you to them." Vincent shot Stanley a dirty look as the mayor continued, "What am I supposed to tell them? Sorry, our EPA guy thought he was Sherlock Holmes?"

Stanley's face flushed, his sureness cracking. "I followed protocols, sir! Vincent's been dodging inspections, playing fast and loose with safety inspections. This man and his company are a scam, a fraud. I know it looks bad right now, but I saved this city from a worse fate." He pointed at Leo, voice rising. "He's the liar here, Mr. Mayor. Check his books! Check is tech!"

Leo stood towering over Stanley, his smirk widening into something predatory. "Check my books? You wouldn't know a balance sheet from a dumpster, Peck. My tech is revolutionary, and you killed it. Now look outside—smoke, panic, lawsuits. You're not a hero. You're a hazard. A public menace." He turned to the mayor, voice dropping to a conspiratorial purr. "Harry, let me handle the press. I'll spin this as CleanCycle's triumph over uninformed stupidity. Peck's your problem here, sir, not me. Ship him out, and I'll save face for both of us."

The mayor's eyes darted between them, sweat beading on his forehead. "Save face? Vincent, your plant's still smoldering." He turned to Stanley. "And Peck, your '*protocols*' just cost us millions, probably more. I've got calls from the governor, the press, and even the damn sanitation union is waiting for answers. The both of you are a pair of wildfires, and I'm the one getting burned!" He slammed a fist down, causing papers to fly.

Stanley opened his mouth to retort, but the noise from a television playing in the background caught everyone's attention. On the screen, a TV crew played footage of a yellowish cloud hanging over part of the city. Citizens had to be masked. And a scrolling text on the screen that read, "*Who Is At Fault*?"

The mayor pointed at the screen. "That's your legacy, gentlemen." He waved his hand at the two men. "Get outta here, the both of you."

Leo adjusted his tie, unfazed, and shot Stanley a parting glance. "See you on the news, Peck. Hope you like infamy."

But before he could leave, the mayor raised a hand, stopping Leo Vincent in his tracks. "Wait," he said, the wheels turning in his eyes. "Vincent. Swear to me now your shit is real."

Leo took a breath, looked at Stanley, then back to the mayor, stone-faced. "It's real."

Mayor Washington contemplated for a long moment, then said, "I need you out there, Vincent, spinning this, cleaning up the mess. The city's counting on CleanCycle to recover, to fix this. You've got my support, but you better deliver." He turned to Stanley, eyes hard as steel. "Peck. You're done here. Get out and don't come back. This is Vincent's show now."

Stanley's mouth opened, but no words came out. He choked on a gasp as the weight of defeat crushed his righteous expression. Leo's smirk widened as Stanley stiffened his back and walked to the large white door, opened it, and stepped out into the outer office, which was full of people silently waiting to see who would emerge defeated. Stanley Peck is who they saw.

Forty years later, the late morning sun barely cracked through the faded curtains of Stanley's apartment. Louise lay snoring on the living room couch, covered by a large blanket, with a soft pillow tucked under her head. She didn't flinch as the clock on the wall sounded, calling attention to the hour change, which in this case was eleven o'clock. Louise did flinch, however, when the guest room door opened and Elizabeth slowly emerged.

Elizabeth's hair, which she pulled up into a ragged bun, had dozens of hairs falling to the side that refused to cooperate. She had a thick blanket draped over her shoulders as she walked to the kitchen and started the coffee machine brewing. She shuffled over to a recliner in the living room and slid into it, curling her legs up under her body.

"Good morning," Louise said.

Elizabeth's eyes popped open. "Oh my gosh, Louise. I'm sorry I woke you up."

Louise shifted and sat herself up, rubbing some of the sleep from her eyes. "No, no, you're fine," she assured Elizabeth. "Eleven o'clock should be my limit, anyway. But thanks for letting me stay here. I really didn't want to go home alone last night."

Elizabeth ran her fingers through her hair. "I wouldn't have wanted to either. I just can't believe how real this got."

"And how fast, too," Louise continued.

Elizabeth and Louise continued to talk. Stanley, on the other hand, was nowhere to be seen. Much as he tried to deny it, he wasn't quite the same Stanley Peck he used to be. Age, the final villain anyone must face, won the battle late last night and forced Stanley to surrender when Elizabeth and Louise were still up talking, but not until the wee hours of the morning, something he silently took pride in. The smell of the coffee pot filling had just filled the room as Stanley emerged from his bedroom in his robe and slippers, still groggy from his few hours of restless sleep.

With only a quiet wave to his two compatriots, Stanley grabbed his coffee cup and filled it to the brim. Straight black, a method few others could stand, but Stanley preferred it that way. He stood silently in the kitchen and let the next few sips drip down his throat until some of the caffeine entered his bloodstream and cleared his foggy vision. He glanced out the window and noticed the mail truck pulling away from his building. As with so many retirees, mail time was something of a ritual.

"I'll be right back," Stanley said as he took the mail key off the hook and stepped out.

He made his way down the flight of stairs leading to the first floor, where the mailboxes for the apartment complex sat in a massive metal structure. As he descended the stairs, Stanley unconsciously started mumbling to himself. And just like he had done a few nights ago while reviewing records with Louise, Stanley's focus had shifted.

"Better watch out, Mass. Stanley Peck is on the case."

"What's that? Who am I? I'm Peck, Stanley Peck."

"Those chains feelin' tight, Hargrove? Shoulda thought about that before messing with me!"

Stanley rounded the corner leading to the front of the apartment complex and unlocked the mailbox, expecting the typical bills or junk mail. But Stanley's stomach dropped when he pulled out a crisp, cream-colored envelope bearing the Redmain city seal. His fingers hesitated over the flap, and a chill crept up his spine as he gripped the edge and tore it open. For a moment, Stanley hesitated to pull the contents out, but just for a moment. Like ripping a Band-Aid off quickly, Stanley reached into the envelope and pulled out his life's newest surprise.

Inside the envelope was a cease and desist letter, typed on heavy letterhead, signed by Alan Hargrove himself. It demanded that he and his "*associates*" halt their "*unauthorized and defamatory investigation*" into ParaWorks and the mayor's decisions regarding said company, threatening legal action for harassment and slander if he didn't comply. The words blurred as Stanley's pulse quickened, the paper trembling slightly in his hands.

Stanley raced as fast as his aging body would allow back to the apartment. The letter felt heavier with each step. He burst into the apartment and slammed the letter onto the kitchen table. Louise and Elizabeth were standing in the kitchen, sipping their coffee as Stanley sat down.

Elizabeth looked up from her mug, her dark eyes narrowing at Stanley's expression. "What's that?" she asked, sensing trouble.

Louise paused mid-sip, her glasses fogging slightly from the coffee's steam, her gaze fixing on the letter.

"Trouble," Stanley said. "Hargrove's trying to shut me down." He sank into his chair, rubbing his temples. "They're coming for us, just like they did in Chicago. I should've seen this coming."

Elizabeth walked over to the dining room table and snatched the letter. Her lawyer instincts kicked in as she scanned the text and absorbed the formal language. "This is another scare tactic, Dad," she said. "It's not as bad as it looks, though. They can't stop us from speaking as private citizens, especially if we stick to the facts, like the consent form. All the data Louise has pulled, all the pieces, are good. But..."

She paused, her brow furrowing as she flipped the page. Stanley knew that look. He had seen it on the faces of so many people when he had served them with similar unwanted letters in the past.

"They *could* drag us into court," Elizabeth said. She set the letter down, her hands fidgeting with her mug. "We're looking at possible defamation suits. Even frivolous ones cost time and money we don't have. It's not horrible, but it's bad. Simply put, they're trying to scare us into going away."

Louise stepped over and took a seat at the table with Stanley, her skepticism etched into the lines of her face. "Another scare tactic, like the phone calls and the P.I. last night. Well, this clinches it for Hargrove, doesn't it? I'd bet my career on it. He's not just protecting himself. He's potentially protecting everyone involved in this thing, which could *still* be—anyone! And now this kind of move? It's what you do when you're desperate."

Elizabeth took a sip of her coffee. "If he's this panicked, there's got to be something bigger he's hiding, or someone, like the mayor. It could even be kickbacks from ParaWorks, maybe, or some sort of financial stake. We need to dig into Hargrove's history—campaign funds, property holdings, bank transactions, and anything that could directly tie him or them to this thing. Same with the mayor. We've got to dig into everything."

Stanley had stood up and was pacing the small kitchen, his frustration boiling over. "They're cornering me, cornering us, just like they did back in '85. I pushed too hard in Chicago, thought I could take on the system single-handedly, and they crushed me for it. I lost my job, my reputation, and nearly lost Elizabeth." He looked over at his daughter. "I can't let that happen again. Maybe we should back down. I know that's letting them win, letting Redmain choke on ParaWorks' lies. I don't know how to live with that either." He stopped, staring at the letter, its cold black ink a challenge he couldn't ignore. "But I can't..."

Elizabeth got up and walked over to Stanley, her hand finding his. Her grip was steady despite the fear in her eyes. "You're not alone this time, Dad. We're a team, and we're smarter than they think. This letter? It's proof we're getting to them. Hargrove wouldn't bother if we weren't close to the truth." She squeezed his hand. "I'm not saying it's not scary. But I didn't come here to watch you fight alone."

Louise nodded, pushing her glasses up her nose. "Same here, Stanley. I've spent too long at the EPA playing it safe, filing reports that get ignored. This is my chance to actually make a difference, to stop a cover-up before it's too late." She leaned forward. "That private investigator last night? He wasn't just watching us. He was reporting back. Hargrove knows we're dangerous, and this letter is his first shot. But it also tells us he's vulnerable. We just need to find the crack in his armor."

Stanley looked between them, his jaw tight, the ghosts of his past failures warring with the fire their words reignited within him. He lowered his head and thought before finally replying. "Okay, okay. You're right," he said. "So what's our move?" His voice was steadier now, though his hands still trembled slightly. "We've got the consent form, Louise's data, and a pocket full of theories. But this letter means they're watching every step. One misstep, and they'll bury us in court. Or worse."

Elizabeth tapped the letter, her mind racing. "Then we take it public, but not just anywhere. When we were at City Hall, Hargrove mentioned the city council meeting is next Tuesday night."

"Yeah, that's right!" Louise remembered. "And he said they were going to be signing the last bit of documentation for ParaWorks to break ground."

Stanley nodded and contemplated out loud. "It's big. It's public. And it's on the public record. If we bring the evidence there, the form, and the data, maybe even get Christine to speak…" Stanley trailed off in thought before continuing. "They won't be able to sweep it under the rug then. They'll have to face it, and they'll have to answer for it!"

"I can prepare a statement and lay out the facts so clearly that no lawyer can twist it," Elizabeth followed. "And I'll call my friend from law school to see if we can file a preemptive motion to protect us from any kind of legal harassment." Her voice was firm now, her fear channeled into strategy, her pen already scratching notes on a legal pad.

Louise smiled, defiance in her eyes. "And I'll keep digging. If we can tie Hargrove or the mayor to ParaWorks financially, say, through a campaign donation or who knows what, we'll have an even bigger bomb to drop at that meeting."

"I've also got a contact at the state records office who owes me a favor," Elizabeth said. "Maybe we can find something in the records there that will help us point fingers in the right direction." She glanced at Stanley, her tone softening. "But we need to be ready for pushback. That P.I. wasn't working alone, and Hargrove's obviously not above playing dirty."

Stanley stopped pacing, his gaze settling on the letter, then shifting to Elizabeth and Louise. "You're right," he said. "They think they can scare us off, just like they scared me forty years ago. But not this time. Redmain deserves the truth, and we've got the evidence to back it up." He clenched his fist, the old Peck fire roaring back. "We'll go to that city council meeting, and we won't just speak up; we'll end this. We'll expose Hargrove and the whole damn conspiracy."

Elizabeth's eyes met his, a small smile breaking through the tension. "That's the dad I remember! Now go take a shower and pack a day bag. Whether or not we hear from my friend, we're going to the state records office."

Chapter Twelve

The marble floors of the State Department of Records echoed with Elizabeth's confident heel strides as she flashed her lawyer's badge at the security desk. After checking for clearance, the guard waved them through. Elizabeth passed through the metal detector with confidence. Stanley, however, trailed behind nervously. His tie was slightly askew, and he stuffed his hands in his pockets to hide the nervous energy that had dogged him since they had pulled into the parking lot. While an investigation like this was well within his wheelhouse, that wheelhouse fell apart years ago. It *was 'old hat,'* so to speak, only the hat didn't quite fit anymore. The game was familiar, but the rules were different, updated for the times.

The air inside was cool, almost sterile, with the faint buzz of fluorescent lights and the distant clatter of printers, interspersed with the occasional cough from a nearby clerk shuffling papers. That part—the smell of bureaucracy—never seemed to change.

"This way, Dad," Elizabeth said as she guided Stanley past a labyrinth of cubicles toward the records room. "The room we're looking for is over here."

As a licensed attorney, Elizabeth had the clearance to access public filings, corporate registrations, and property deeds when in the service of a client. Of course, Elizabeth had no client, not in this case anyway. But her friend had come through on the drive over and made sure that she and Stanley's names were on the "allowed" list of visitors for the day.

The rooms and files of this building housed documents Stanley could only dream of seeing without Elizabeth's help. Framed state seals and faded posters about business compliance lined the walls, their edges curling from years of neglect. Strangely, it was a setting Stanley felt very at home in.

"Are you sure they won't toss us out of here?" Stanley asked, keeping his voice low as he glanced at a security camera in the corner. "Last time I tried something like this, I ended up with a restraining order. Of course, I was sneaking into an old-age home at the time."

Elizabeth chuckled. "Oh, Dad. And people say you don't have a sense of humor."

Stanley held her gaze as he kept pace with his daughter's long strides. "I'm serious."

Elizabeth fought a laugh as she adjusted her briefcase at her side. "Well, that was Chicago, Dad. This is different. I've got the credentials, and these records are public. They won't stop us unless we break a law."

The duo reached a small, dimly lit room with a bank of computer terminals and a microfiche reader gathering dust in the corner. The space was more than a little cramped, with the walls lined with filing cabinets. A single window let in a weak amount of late afternoon sun that barely cut through the haze of dust in the air.

Elizabeth set her laptop on a table, connected to the state

database, and logged in with a series of security questions and two-factor authentication codes that made Stanley raise an eyebrow. It was all so different in his day. There were no computer files, at least none that mattered. Back in the 80s, it was all paper. No authentication passwords. No digital keys. Just people and paperwork.

"How long is this going to take?" Stanley asked, pacing.

"Depends," Elizabeth said, her fingers hovering over the keyboard. "Corporate records can be a maze. Hargrove's or Mayor Mass's name might pop up in campaign filings, property deeds, or LLC registrations, but we'll have to cross-reference everything. It's not like Googling. Mass is a public figure, so there are layers of bureaucracy to wade through. But Hargrove is different. So we're going to be looking through a lot, digital..." She gestured to the wall of filing cabinets, "and not so digital."

Stanley sighed, slumping into a chair beside her. "Bureaucratic language. Story of my life, honey."

Elizabeth chuckled. "I know it well."

"At least it used to be," Stanley said as he looked at Elizabeth's computer, then at the old dusty file cabinets. "The digital stuff is all yours, kiddo. Why don't I start with the old-school stuff?"

Elizabeth waved her dad on. "Oh, be my guest."

With that, Stanley started digging through cabinets. He started with property ownership and deed filings. This was a world Stanley understood. Paperwork. He knew exactly what he could find in a simple filing. He also knew that relevant information could come from one line in a 1,000-page text.

Elizabeth, meanwhile, started with Hargrove and Jim Mass's names, entering them into the state's online portal for connections to corporate entities. The screen loaded slowly, displaying a list of hits: campaign finance reports from two years ago, personal property declarations, supplemental tax returns, and a vague mention of a business interest tied to real estate.

This was going to take some time.

* * *

A few hours later, Stanley had accumulated a few file folders' worth of notable entries. A few connecting pieces here and there. But nothing too damning. Elizabeth was having slightly less success. Nothing was jumping out, but suddenly her brow furrowed as she scrolled.

"Look at this, Dad," she said, pointing to a line item. "So, according to the documents you and Louise came up with, the parcel of land that Paraworks is building on is owned by a small firm called Redstone Holdings, LLC., and registered five years ago as a real estate management firm. The address is a P.O. box in Delaware. Now that's a *little* suspicious. Delaware's a haven for shell companies because it doesn't require detailed owner disclosures."

Stanley leaned in, squinting at the screen. "Shell company? You mean a fake company? So someone is hiding... something?"

"Maybe," Elizabeth said, her tone cautious. "But we need more. Let's check the ownership structure. If it's a shell, there might be another layer." She navigated to the LLC filings, but the database lagged, forcing her to retry the search. "Ugh, state servers," she grumbled, tapping her foot. "They're slower than molasses."

Stanley watched, his impatience growing. "Can't you just call someone? Hack in or something like that?"

"Dad, I'm a lawyer, not a hacker," Elizabeth said. "And no, I'm afraid we can't just *'call someone.'* These are protected records, but accessible with the right credentials, which I have. It's just tedious."

Stanley harrumphed but gave in to the process as they continued to hit roadblocks. They hit barriers. They hit walls. It turned out the ownership details for Redstone Holdings were incomplete, requiring Elizabeth to request additional documents through a separate system for Delaware filings.

Elizabeth explained to Stanley, "Delaware corporations file with *their* state, not ours, so we're dealing with an interstate tangle. We might need to pull their annual reports, but those can take days to process unless we pay for expedited access."

"Days?!" Stanley groaned, running a hand through his hair. "We don't have days. ParaWorks is breaking ground in less than a week!"

Elizabeth shot him a look, half exasperation, half sympathy. "I know, Dad, but this is how it works. Legal due diligence isn't glamorous. You know that. It's paperwork, red tape, and patience. We're lucky I can even access this much. Most civilians wouldn't even be allowed in. We're lucky to have this much access."

Elizabeth persisted, finally pulling up Redstone's annual report after another fifteen minutes of waiting and refreshing the screen. The document was dense with legalese, terms like *'beneficial ownership,' 'nominal shareholders,'* and *'asset segregation,'* but Elizabeth's eyes lit up when she spotted a footnote.

"Wait a minute. Here we go!" she said. "Redstone Holdings

isn't the end of the line. Another entity serves as the parent company. It's called Parkview Enterprises, also in Delaware. Another P.O. box, no physical address. Dad, this is classic shell company structure."

"Parkview Enterprises?" Stanley questioned. "Why is that familiar?" He pondered for a second, then shook it off. "Ok. Confusing. But, okay," Stanley said. "So, who owns Parkview?"

"That's what I'm looking for right now," Elizabeth replied, her fingers flying again as she cross-referenced Parkview with Redmain property records. The system crashed once, forcing her to restart, and she muttered under her breath about '*outdated infrastructure*.' Eventually, though, the screen refreshed.

She pulled up city lease agreements, a process that took another ten minutes of navigating municipal databases filled with jargon like '*eminent domain waivers*' and '*public-private partnership disclosures*.' Finally, a lease document appeared.

"I don't know who owns Parkview yet, but look at this, Dad," Elizabeth said. "The town of Redmain is paying Redstone Holdings fifty thousand dollars a month to '*lease*' the land for ParaWork's construction." Her finger traced a line on the screen. Her eyes narrowed as she traced the financial trail, accessing bank transaction summaries available through public records. "From what I can tell, every penny of that rent, minus a few bucks for administrative fees, gets transferred to Redstone. But then, in a separate transaction, Redstone transfers that exact amount to a private account in Florida—owned by one Alan Hargrove. It's disguised as '*consulting fees*' and '*management services*,' but it's a straight funnel. Redmain's taxpayers are funding Hargrove's pocketbook while he pushes this project through as town business."

Stanley stared at the screen, his face a mix of shock and a little bit of confusion. "So he gets paid for use of the land through this shell company, but why would a real estate company seemingly unconnected to Hargrove transfer him that money?"

"Exactly," Elizabeth said, gathering the printouts. "We're still missing some things."

"Are you able to see who owns Redstone Holdings?" Stanley asked. "Could it be Hargrove himself? Or maybe even Mayor Mass?"

Elizabeth cocked her head as if she were being challenged by her dad. "Let's see." A few clicks here, a few clicks there, and a few minutes later—nothing. "I can't find anything about that. It lists a private owner, but I can't see who."

"Okay," Stanley said, visibly stumped. "But we know Redstone pays Hargrove the exact amount that the town of Redmain pays Redstone for leasing the land that ParaWorks is going to build on. So, that ties him to the deal. Of course, listing it as '*consulting fee*' does leave room to argue a break in the chain of culpability."

"That's true," Elizabeth agreed. "But Redstone lists Parkview Enterprises as a parent company. So, let's try to see who owns that." Elizabeth made a few more clicks and let out a few grunts. "Nothing. Wherever that information is, it isn't connected to this system."

The duo sat scratching their collective heads for a few moments. Stanley got up and started looking through the paper files he had accumulated from the file cabinets. A few minutes later, he held up his prize.

"Ah, I knew Parkview Enterprises was familiar," Stanley said, bringing the document over to Elizabeth. "Any corporation that makes donations to an election campaign has to submit a record of that donation to the state for public review. I pulled this particular record because it listed a campaign donation to a candidate in Redmain. Parkview Enterprises is the listed owner." Stanley gestured for Elizabeth to follow his finger as he flipped the form over and pointed at the bottom of the document. "But look who the candidate is. None other than Jim Mass. Mayor Jim Mass!"

Elizabeth dropped into the chair next to her. "Okay, okay. Let me get this straight. Redmain pays rent on the land it's building ParaWorks on to a shell company, Redstone Holdings, owned by… someone… who pays Alan Hargrove a *'consulting fee'* of the same amount." She paused for a moment in thought. "Redstone Holdings itself is owned by another apparent shell company, Parkview Enterprises, which is owned by… someone. And that company made campaign donations to Jim Mass's mayoral run." She looked to Stanley for confirmation. "Does that sound right?"

Stanley added the pieces together in his head. "Yeah, yeah, that's it exactly. So we have two companies. One seems to filter Paraworks' rental fees to Alan Hargrove, and the parent company of *that* company made campaign donations to Mayor Mass."

"Right," Elizabeth said, scratching her forehead, "but without some sort of connective tissue in the ownership records, all this amounts to is some coincidence and some dubious financing."

Stanley's back stiffened. "You don't believe that, do you, Lizzy?" Stanley asked, his face covered in dismay. "The data. The threats. These companies. This is all connected."

Elizabeth put her hand on Stanley's shoulder. "Of course it

is, Dad. I know that. But legally speaking, what seems obvious to us wouldn't mean much in court."

"But we also have the ParaWorks consent form signed by Hargrove and Mass," Stanley reminded Elizabeth as he stood up and paced.

"I know," Elizabeth said. "But technically, there's nothing illegal there. Bad business, maybe, but not illegal. The argument would be that the *'consultation fees'* and campaign donations are simply unrelated business. And any good lawyer will argue that we made all of this up in an effort to slander Hargrove and the mayor."

"But why would we do that?" Stanley asked.

Elizabeth lowered her head and let out a breath. She was afraid it would come to this, the inevitable blame that would come from this investigation. She knew, no matter how much she didn't believe it herself, that the person people would point fingers at would be her father, Stanley Peck. Elizabeth knew they would bring up his history. She knew they would try to take him apart. She knew they would call him a crackpot and dismiss him, even with her and Louise's association. Elizabeth looked up at Stanley, the pained look on her face providing just enough for Stanley to put the pieces together.

"I see," he said, nodding in acknowledgement of the inevitable that played across Elizabeth's face. "Because I'm Stanley Peck."

Elizabeth sat frozen, her heart broken.

Stanley scoffed. "So, that's it? Are we dead in the water?"

"No," Elizabeth said. "But we've hit a wall here. We've got to keep digging. We need to look into everyone's financials—Mass and Hargrove, for sure, but also Parkview and Redstone. Shell companies and silent ownerships like what we're seeing here are usually designed to hide legal control of something. Well, most of the time, anyway."

Stanley rubbed his temples. "They're both tied to those companies. Is there anything beyond a money trail that could link Mass or Hargrove to them? I mean, if they're truly hiding something here, they wouldn't just sign something with their own names."

"That's probably right," Elizabeth said, "but I still have contacts from my time in family law, people that can trace assets."

Stanley grimaced. "Would family law people really know about shell companies and hidden money?"

"Are you kidding?" Elizabeth scoffed. "You'd be amazed at the lengths people go to hide assets from a divorce attorney. People hide ownership in their parents' names, their dogs, their friends, you name it. Once I even caught a husband who hid a secret bank account in his wife's own name, thinking no one would look for something *she* owns, even if she didn't know she owned it."

"Diabolical," Stanley said.

Elizabeth nodded. "Dad, you have no idea. So, I'll poke around the public filings for Redstone and Parkview, and I'll get some of my old forensic asset friends to look around too. We'll cross-reference with the data we have, and who knows, maybe we'll find something. We need to find out who these people are who own these shell companies, so I'll make that my priority."

"You're right," Stanley said. "We followed the money. But if we can't connect those companies to Redmain illegally, it all comes down to theories."

Chapter Thirteen

The sun had dipped below the horizon by the time Stanley, Elizabeth, and Louise stepped into *Beans & Brew*. For the trio, the coffee shop's warm atmosphere was a welcome difference from the cool evening air they felt on the walk over from Stanley's apartment. The bell above the door jingled its familiar melody, announcing their arrival to a handful of late-night caffeine seekers scattered across a handful of tables and chairs. It was just after eight p.m., and the trio had a long night of work ahead of them as they continued digging deeper into the ParaWorks mess. They needed some mental fuel, and *Beans & Brew* was the perfect place.

Stanley approached the counter. He noticed the barista, a young woman with dyed black hair and a nose ring, as someone he couldn't remember seeing behind the counter before. Of course, Stanley's normal visits to Beans & Brew were usually an a.m. thing. Maybe this visit wouldn't result in the usual naming issue, he thought. He hoped.

"Black coffee, no syrup, no froth," Stanley said. "Just plain coffee."

The barista nodded and pulled out a cup, marker in hand. "Name?"

"Stanley," he said, emphasizing each syllable as if daring her to get it wrong.

Elizabeth and Louise ordered next. A chai latte for Elizabeth and an herbal tea for Louise. The trio looked around and found a small table near the window. Stanley sat with his back to the wall, his fingers tapping restlessly on the tabletop, his mind racing with thoughts of zoning laws, shell companies, and the looming town council meeting.

A few minutes passed, and the barista called out that their order was ready. Louise started up from her seat, but Stanley waved her off as he stood and shuffled to the counter. He grabbed their three cups and returned to the table. As he eased into his seat, Stanley looked down at the name scribbled in black marker on the side of his coffee cup. *'Pecker.'* His jaw tightened, the familiar sting of humiliation creeping up his spine. Stanley turned and shot a nasty look at the barista, but she was already busy with the next order. She must have noticed Stanley's scowl, though, as even with her back turned, Stanley spotted a faint smirk on her face. Stanley snorted, setting the cup down with a little more force than necessary.

Elizabeth noticed Stanley's scowl and asked, "What's wrong, Dad?"

Stanley turned the cup toward her, the word *'Pecker'* glaring under the fluorescent lights. Elizabeth's lips twitched, fighting a smile, while Louise coughed into her tea to hide a laugh.

"Real mature, you two," Stanley said, taking a sip. "Some things never change, I guess."

Louise leaned forward, still doing her best to hide her laughter. "Oh, come on, Stanley. It's almost a badge of honor at this point."

"Honor's not quite the word I'd use," he grumbled.

Stanley caught Elizabeth's eye, who covered her mouth with her hand. "I'm sorry, Dad, really," she said, fighting a laugh. "It's just been a long day, and..."

Stanley stopped her. "You know, I can handle the looks, the whispers, all of that, but this is the thing that *really* burns me."

Elizabeth shook her head as she struggled to fight the laugh about to overtake her. She glanced at Louise, then at the counter. "I'm gonna grab some sugar."

Louise nodded, barely holding back her laughter. "I think I'll join you."

Stanley snarled at the two women, sipped his coffee, and stared out the window at the quiet street. Taking their cue, Elizabeth and Louise got up and stepped over to the condiment station, which was well out of Stanley's earshot. Elizabeth stirred a packet of sugar into her latte, in no hurry to finish. She kept her voice low as she looked back at Stanley to make sure he wasn't listening.

"Louise," she started, hesitating, "I'm worried about my dad. This whole ParaWorks thing—it's consuming him. He's so sure there's a conspiracy, but what if..." She trailed off, her fingers tightening around the stirring stick.

Louise tilted her head and spoke just as quietly. "What if it's a wild-goose chase?"

Elizabeth nodded, with a worried look on her face. "Yeah. I mean, we've found some shady things for sure. Those shell companies and the zoning changes you found. But what if he's seeing more than what's there? He's been through so much, and I know how much Chicago broke him. I'm just scared he might be chasing something that isn't there again. And I don't want him to get hurt. Not like before."

Louise sipped her tea, her gaze steady. "I get it, Elizabeth,

I do. I've seen his file. Hell, that *Uncle Sam* poster was in my office. He's got a history of diving headfirst into fights he can't win. But..." She paused and looked over at Stanley, who was busy scribbling something on a napkin. "This doesn't feel like Chicago, not to me anyway. The data we've found, the water table risks, the missing reports—that stuff is real. I've cross-checked it myself. He's not imagining this."

Elizabeth sighed. "I know the data's real. It's just... I see that fire in his eyes, the same one he had when I was a kid, when he'd come home ranting about some injustice at the EPA. It scares me."

Louise squinted her eyes. "I get that, but after what the two of you brought home today, everything seems so obvious."

"Sure, to us," Elizabeth said. "But what if we're wrong? What if we're wrong about all of this and he takes the fall again? I can't watch him go through that, not again."

Louise reached out, squeezing Elizabeth's arm. "He's not alone this time. You're here. I'm here. And honestly? I think he's right about ParaWorks, Hargrove, and the mayor." She glanced over at Stanley, sipping away at his coffee. "He's made me believe in him."

Elizabeth smiled at Louise. "He *does* have a way of doing that, doesn't he?"

"He sure does," Louise said.

Elizabeth's eyes filled up with tears she wouldn't set free. "Okay. Okay. I think I just needed to say it out loud." She shifted her stance. "It's just... I love him, you know? I don't want him to lose himself again."

"He won't," Louise said. "We'll make sure of it."

The two women returned to the table, where Stanley was scribbling on a napkin, his coffee half-gone. He looked up, his brow furrowed as he examined both of their faces. "You two plotting against me?"

Elizabeth forced a smile, sliding into her seat. "Just how to keep you in line, Dad."

"Ha," he snorted, pushing the napkin aside. "Good luck with that!"

* * *

The moon had completely replaced the setting sun in the time it took the trio to reach Stanley's apartment. The streetlights flickered above as gnats bumped off the fixtures. As they turned the corner onto his street, Elizabeth stopped short, her hand grabbing Stanley's arm. "Hey, Dad," she said, gesturing up to the second floor. "Didn't we turn the lights off before we left?"

Stanley followed her gaze up to his apartment's balcony window. The lights were on, pouring light through the curtains. Then, as they watched, the lights switched off.

"Oh my God," Louise whispered. "Someone's in there."

Stanley's heart raced, his empty coffee cup nearly slipping from his hand. "Stay behind me," he said, already moving toward the apartment building.

Elizabeth moved quickly to keep up with Stanley, Louise trailing right behind her. "Wait, Dad," she said between steps. "*You* stay behind *me*!"

The group hurried up the stairs, their footsteps echoing in the quiet stairwell. Elizabeth would overtake Stanley, who would then overtake Elizabeth, both silently fighting for control. As they approached the apartment, Stanley fumbled with his keys, his hands shaking.

"The door's already open, Dad," Elizabeth said, noting the door was ajar as she pushed in front of him.

Louise clutched her phone, ready to call for help, while Elizabeth gripped her bag, her eyes scanning the shadows as she slowly opened the door. Stanley perched himself on his daughter's shoulders as they moved in. The apartment was dark, but a faint rustle came from the living room, as did the sound of a few cracks and pops that definitely didn't belong in an empty apartment.

"Who's there?!" Stanley called out, his voice as deep as he could make it.

A shadow moved near the living room table, where Stanley, Louise, and Elizabeth had left a stack of papers and their laptops. The figure was clearly male, tall, yet indistinct in the dim light sneaking in from behind the balcony window's curtains, his face hidden in shadow underneath a hood.

"Oh, my God. Oh, my God," Louise said under her breath.

"Stay back!" Stanley barked as he grabbed the four-foot-tall fake tree by the front door. He pushed ahead, pointing the shrubbery of the tree forward as the trio stepped closer to the mysterious figure.

The figure brought his hands together in front of his chest, and again the trio could hear the distinct sound of knuckles cracking. If it hadn't been so quiet, no one would have heard what the intruder quietly whispered. "I'm sorry," before darting toward the balcony window, where the fire escape waited. Elizabeth lunged, trying to reach him before he could throw open the balcony sliding door. But the figure was quicker, shoving Stanley's old recliner chair in her way.

Elizabeth nearly tripped over the chair but recovered fast. "Oh, no you don't!"

"Holy actual shit!" Louise yelled as she hit the flashlight on her phone, flooding the room with light.

The figure spared no time as he whipped the balcony door open, clutching a stack of their papers in his hand. He rushed for the fire escape ladder beside the balcony as Elizabeth grabbed a nearby broom, swinging it like a baseball bat at the fleeing intruder.

"Not so fast, pal!" Elizabeth yelled, swinging hard as she made it through the balcony sliding glass door. But the man ducked, and the broom smacked the nearby wall with a thud. "Damn it!" she cursed.

Stanley rushed to the window behind Elizabeth, fake tree in hand. But the mysterious man was already halfway down the fire escape ladder, the bundle of papers he had taken tucked firmly under his arm. "Stop!" Stanley shouted, leaning out, but the man hit the ground and sprinted into the alley beside the apartment complex, vanishing into the night.

The trio stood panting, the adrenaline still coursing through their veins. Elizabeth lowered the broom, her chest heaving, and Stanley lowered his mighty fake plant.

"Well, that was—eventful," Elizabeth said, catching her breath.

Stanley ran a hand through his gray hair. "I think he took some of our stuff, some of our papers and documents."

Louise, still frozen in place, stepped one step forward. "Is he gone now? Are we safe?"

Elizabeth doubled back into the apartment, flipped the main light switch on, and came up behind Louise, putting her arm around her. "I think so," she said as she tapped a digital button on Louise's phone, turning off its flashlight mode. "He wasn't here to hurt anyone, I don't think. I'm guessing he got what he came for—our evidence."

Stanley scanned the table, his eyes narrowing. "Not everything. The consent form and the financial records are still in Elizabeth's briefcase in her car." Stanley started sifting through various papers on the dining room table. "But he still got a lot, though. I'm not seeing a lot of the papers Louise brought from the EPA office."

Elizabeth set the broom against the wall, her hands still shaking a bit. "That was obviously no random thief," she said. "But just like with the P.I., we don't know who sent him."

Louise lowered herself to the edge of the recliner chair that the mystery thief had toppled when fleeing the apartment. "Are we gonna call the cops this time?"

Elizabeth put her hand on Louise's shoulder. "Yes. The P.I. was different, but whoever sent that guy has really stepped things up. Breaking and entering. Theft. The police will come, dust for prints, all the basics. But don't hold your breath on them getting anything useful."

Stanley rubbed his temples, the ache behind his eyes throbbing. "Then what do you suggest, Lizzy? We've still got the consent form, the meeting minutes, and some financial records, but most of what Louise pulled from her EPA office is gone. So far, it seems to be just Hargrove and Mayor Mass, but the entire city council could be in on this thing. After today, with everything we've uncovered, I'm not sure who else we can trust, even the police."

Elizabeth started pacing the length of the living room. "Then we don't wait for the town hall meeting. We go public. Now. Hit them before they hit us with some sort of trumped-up charges. If we can get the Redmain Gazette on board, or even a blog, we could force the council to face this *before* the Tuesday night town hall meeting."

Louise stood up, the adrenaline in her blood ebbing. "That's a good idea, Elizabeth. One thing's for certain. They're scared. Really scared. That must mean we're getting closer."

Stanley frowned, the memory of Chicago's headlines flashing in his mind like a warning light. "I don't know, kids. Go public? After what just happened?" Stanley started pacing. "They'll call me a lunatic again, Lizzy. The town already thinks I'm chasing fantasies as it is."

"So what?!" Elizabeth shot back, her hands gesturing wildly. "Let them think what they want at first. But if we lay out the facts—the consent form, the water data, Hargrove's '*consulting fees*,' and Mayor Mass's campaign contributions—they'll have to listen."

"Karl Hensley at the Gazette is the best-known reporter in town," Louise added. "We could call him and tell him we've got evidence of a cover-up. He'll bite if it's juicy."

Elizabeth registered the look of fear in her father's eyes. "You know, Dad," she said, "this doesn't *have* to be you. I could meet with Hensley. I could speak at the council meeting. There's nothing that says it has to be you."

Louise stepped closer to Stanley. "Or I could, Stanley. I believe in this as much as you do. Maybe Elizabeth and I..."

Stanley pushed his fears aside and stood up straight. "No! Absolutely not. I won't jeopardize either of you like that. Elizabeth, you're using sick time to be here. And Louise, you spend every second here when you're not in your office." Stanley shook his head, defiance in his eyes. "Helping me is one thing, but I won't let either of you take the heat if this goes south. I couldn't live with myself." Stanley hesitated, his gaze dropping to the piles of clues and evidence on the kitchen table. "You really think he'll run it?"

"Maybe," Elizabeth said, nodding her head. "Hargrove and Mass can't silence or influence everyone. We've got two days until the meeting. If we move now, we might be able to turn the tide on them."

"Alright," Stanley said, pulling out his phone. "I'll call him tomorrow morning. But if this backfires, girls, it's on me. Only me."

"Then it's settled," Louise confirmed. "Stanley will reach out to the reporter tomorrow. Elizabeth, you'll keep working on the identities of the shell company owners, right?"

Elizabeth nodded. "Oh, yes. I've been running a search on both Parkview and Redstone Holdings, trying to pull from different databases, hoping to get a name. I left it running in the background on my laptop while we went for coffee. Hold on…" She stepped over to the dining room table and woke up the computer with a shake of the mouse. The screen lit up, revealing a progress bar completed at one hundred percent. Elizabeth's eyes popped open. "Hell yes! We've got a hit, folks."

Stanley and Louise stepped over to the table. A few seconds ticked by as Elizabeth cross-referenced some data. "Here we go," she said. "It looks like Redstone Holdings is owned by someone named Lillian Gaines."

Stanley's brow furrowed. "Who the hell is that?"

Elizabeth shook her head. "I have no idea."

"But I've got more here," Elizabeth said. "The registered owner of Parkview Enterprises is someone named Mark Marietti."

Again, Stanley's brow furrowed. "Who the hell is *that*?"

Again, Elizabeth shook her head. "I still have no idea. And from what I'm seeing here, these are seemingly unconnected people. One of them lives in Ohio. The other reports to be living in Indiana." She paused, letting the information sink in. "All I've really got here are repetitive records stating that Lillian Gaines and Mark Marietti are the registered owners, but even that data is old." Elizabeth opened her email account and started typing away. "I'm reaching out to an old colleague who works at a data retrieval firm to help us run a deeper trace."

"Do you really think there's something there?" Louise asked.

Elizabeth shook her head. "I don't know, but all roads that should lead to information on these owners just lead to dead ends. I'll check the probate records too. Maybe there's something I can find that way."

"That's great. And I'll go into my office tomorrow," Louise said. "I'll check for any information my office might have on the zoning changes Hargrove and Mass may have authorized. It's something."

"That's a good idea," Stanley agreed. "Call me when you're there if you find anything."

"I will," Louise said. "And good luck with the reporter."

Chapter Fourteen

The local EPA office in Atherton buzzed with its usual energy. The rustle of papers and the indistinct murmur of familiar voices joined the sound of printers and ringing phones. Louise had spent so much time with Stanley and Elizabeth in the past few days that her office had felt like an oddity, the unusual instead of the norm. She made her way through the typical office business, notated files, sent emails, all the normal things. But it felt strangely hollow, at least these last few days.

At the moment, Louise stood by the coffee machine, stirring cream into her mug, her eyes half-focused on the morning's inbox waiting on her desk. She found her mind drifting to the conversation about the zoning changes that further allowed ParaWorks to break ground. It was a long shot, but maybe there was something more she could find through her office to help connect the dots of this little private investigation that wasn't so little anymore.

Louise crossed from her office to the front desk. The receptionist was typing away, entering data from the minor case Louise had been locking down earlier that morning.

"Janice," Louise asked the receptionist, "could you do a cross-check on any records we have regarding signing off on zoning changes?"

Janice, young and bubbly, replied, "Sure. For any specific case?"

Louise was about to say '*Redmain*,' but she froze a moment before, unsure if she should even say that much to anyone outside her investigation team of Stanley and Elizabeth. In the end, she opted to keep it close to the vest. "No," Louise said. "No specific case. Just any involvement we may have had in approving zoning changes in the last year or so."

Just as Janice was about to get up to pull the requested records, the front door to the office swung open, and a chill cut through the office like a razor blade. Three people entered, each with well-fitted suits and absolutely no smiles. Within a few steps, the apparent leader of the group, a thin man with wire-rimmed glasses, took the lead and directed the other two to follow him to the front desk. Behind the leader was a woman with a tight bun carrying a laptop case. A younger man, who hauled behind him a rolling crate stuffed with binders, followed her.

"Environmental Protection Agency, Regional Compliance Division," the lead announced, his voice flat but commanding. The man held up a memo for Louise to examine. The memo had the stamp of the regional office's seal, signed by the director.

Louise's breath caught in her lungs, and her half-smile started faltering. "May I help you?"

"We're here for an immediate audit of all your Redmain-related records," the lead said.

Louise could feel every muscle in her body suddenly lock. She did her best to play off a look of confusion. She couldn't tell if anyone could see past it, but she kept up the look just the same.

"Please direct us to the file room," the lead said. "And please ensure all staff remain at their normal workstations." His eyes swept the room, lingering on Louise for a split second. It was just long enough to make her uncomfortable. She tightened the grip on the folder she held in her hand.

"Uh, yes, of course," she said, gesturing for the group to follow her past the reception desk. "Just follow me." She gestured toward the hallway as she guided them. "May I ask what prompted..."

"It's a directive from the main office, Ms. Talbot," the female auditor cut in. Her tone and demeanor offered no argument. "We'll let you know when we're done."

Louise flipped on the light in the records room, and the three auditors immediately started getting comfortable. The lead placed his clipboard and coffee on an empty desk, while the female auditor opened her laptop on a nearby table, its screen glowing as she began typing. The younger male auditor wheeled the crate to a nearby chair and flipped open the lid.

Louise stood frozen in the doorway, unsure whether to stay or go. The lead auditor looked back at her, unaffected by Louise's uncertain look. "We'll let you know if we need anything, Ms. Talbot," he said. "You can return to your normal business."

"If you tell me what you're looking for," Louise offered, her voice steadier than she felt, "I might be able to help."

"That won't be necessary," he said, turning away, already flipping through a binder.

Louise nodded, knowing full well there was nothing routine about an audit of the Redmain-related files. Of course, these three people likely knew nothing specific, but they were there for a reason. They were looking for something. The question Louise wondered was—what, or who?

Louise's stomach twisted as she returned to her desk, the coffee turning bitter as it mixed with her churning stomach acid. The auditors' arrival was no coincidence. She had, of course, been in and out with the Redmain files, many of which were sitting on Stanley's dining room table or were in the hands of the mysterious thief from last night. Either way, she knew the rules. She knew the regulations. She was in the wrong. But Louise also knew that missing files might not be what these auditors were looking for, or at least that's what she hoped.

Louise knew the auditors weren't here on a whim. Someone called them, and there were two probable reasons for their visit. One: someone connected to the investigation, trying to obtain or destroy evidence. Two: someone in Redmain was crying foul in realizing her involvement with Stanley. Neither option, Louise knew, was good. Either way, there were going to be questions that would need answering.

Louise reached for her phone and was three numbers deep into dialing Stanley when the lead auditor approached Louise's desk, his clipboard still firmly tucked under his arm. "Ms. Talbot, we'll need your access logs for the ParaWorks files," he said. "Also, we'll need your records for any documents this office accessed within the last six months. I'll also need any correspondence from this office related to the Redmain project."

His gaze was clinical, and it pinned Louise in her place. She nodded back at him, her throat impossibly dry. Those requests could fit either of the reasons she feared. All she could do at this point was play along and hope her expressions didn't give her away.

"Of course. I'll pull them now," Louise said.

"Thank you," the auditor replied, returning to the file room.

Louise couldn't shake off the need to warn Stanley. The lead was on a phone call, and the others were unpacking files in the file room. Louise took this opportunity and slipped her phone from her blazer pocket and dialed Stanley, her pulse hammering.

Stanley answered on the first ring, his familiar voice already a comfort. "Louise? Everything ok?"

She whispered, her eyes locked on the auditors across the hall. "Stanley, listen. They're auditing my office right now. Redmain files, my logs, everything."

"Oh my God," Stanley said from the other side of the line. "Have they said what they're looking for?"

"No," Louise said. "But they're going through everything."

It took a long pause for Stanley to respond. "Louise, I'm so sorry. You shouldn't have to be dealing with this."

"There's no point in any of that right now," Louise whispered. "What am I supposed to do?"

Stanley cursed under his breath. Louise imagined him pacing around his cluttered apartment. "Don't panic. Just stay calm. They could be looking for something specific or anything at all. It might have nothing to do with you."

"What if they ask me about the missing files?" Louise asked. "What do I say? Should I lie?"

"No, don't lie," Stanley insisted. "Don't say or do anything that would land you in more hot water. If they ask you about anything missing, tell them I must have taken it when I came to your office at the start of this."

"No," she said, cutting Stanley off. "I'm not going to turn them on you or Elizabeth. I knew what I was getting into. But I wonder if some of the files that guy got away with last night gave away my involvement in this?"

"Maybe," Stanley said.

"We must be so close to something real if someone called for this audit." Louise looked again at the auditors doing their thing. "Don't worry about me. I think…"

"Ms. Talbot?" The lead auditor's voice snapped her attention away from her phone call. He stood at her door, his clipboard lowered, his eyes narrow. "Personal calls during an audit? You know that is not proper protocol."

Louise tapped the drop button and ended the call with Stanley, her face burning as she slipped the phone into her pocket. "Sorry, sir. It was urgent. My mother's been sick. I just needed to check on her." Her voice wavered, but she met his gaze as her heart pounded away.

Before the auditor could respond, another man's deep voice cut through the room. "That'll be enough of that."

Mr. Jeramy Grayson, regional director of Louise's EPA office, strode into the office with all the swagger of a man in power. His tall frame commanded the space. His dark hair was slicked back, and his face was a mask of cold authority. The auditor stepped back, deferring control to Grayson as he fixed his gaze on Louise.

"Ms. Talbot," Grayson said, "a word, please." His tone was icy. He gestured to a glass-walled conference room down the hall, its blinds half-drawn. Louise rose, her legs unsteady, and followed Mr. Grayson as he led her to the more private room. Louise could feel the weight of everyone's eyes on her, but she kept her eyes forward.

Once inside, Mr. Grayson shut the door. The click of the latch seemed like the drum roll of an old-time hanging, at least to Louise. Grayson didn't sit, instead choosing to loom over the table as Louise sat down at the other end. She kept her hands clasped in her lap, doing her best to hide their trembling.

"Ms. Talbot, do you have any idea the trouble you might be in?" Grayson began, his voice low and terrifying. "The main office received a formal complaint from Redmain officials, accusing you of colluding with Stanley Peck. They claim you're sharing confidential EPA documents with him. Our files. ParaWorks files. Compliance reports. Please tell me this isn't true, Ms. Talbot."

Louise's stomach dropped, but she forced a reply out. "Sir, I've been doing my job. I have legitimate concerns about ParaWorks and the potential impact it could have on the town of Redmain. I would think that this agency..."

"Don't play noble with me," Grayson snapped, slamming a hand on the table, making Louise flinch. "Stanley Peck is a known troublemaker, a disgrace to this agency. If you're feeding him information about anything, you're not just insubordinate, you're a liability. The Environmental Protection Agency doesn't tolerate leaks, Ms. Talbot. You know that."

Louise swallowed, her mind racing. "Sir, if people from Redmain are complaining, maybe they're scared of something. ParaWorks *is* a risk. I've seen the gaps in their reports."

Grayson's eyes narrowed. "You're out of your depth, Ms. Talbot. I don't know how you're involved in this, but this audit *will* turn over every stone, and if I find one shred of evidence that you've leaked documents, you're finished here. No severance, no references, nothing." He leaned closer and spoke in a menacing whisper. "Back off, Talbot. Stop talking to Peck, stop digging into things that aren't your business, or you'll lose everything. Am I clear?"

A lump formed and caught in Louise's throat. Her fists clenched. She wanted to argue, to throw everything she knew right into his smug face, but Grayson's glare silenced her. This wasn't the time. For the same reasons she, Stanley, and Elizabeth hadn't gone public yet, Louise didn't think this was the time to lay it all on the table. Grayson was a jerk, but he wasn't wrong. She *did* leak information. But her investigation with Stanley was so close to bearing fruit, she couldn't surrender now and confess. The truth, she hoped, would vindicate her. But not here. Not now.

"Yes, sir," she managed.

"Good." Grayson straightened, adjusting his tie with an almost violent tug. "Now return to your desk. Cooperate with the auditors. And pray they don't find what I think they will."

He opened the door, dismissing her with a curt nod. Louise walked back to her desk, her legs shaking, the office's busyness deafening. The auditors' eyes followed her, their laptops glowing with data that could end her career.

Louise could only hope that Stanley would be successful in his meeting with the reporter and get their investigation safely out into the open.

Chapter Fifteen

Stanley sat at his kitchen table, the consent form and Louise's email printouts spread out like a battlefield map. The apartment was quiet. Too quiet, Stanley thought. The police, who had come in response to their call late last night, were long gone. Dust left from their fingerprinting attempts still covered the living room. The only sounds were the faint ticking of the wall clock and the occasional creak of the floorboards as Stanley shifted in his chair. Elizabeth was out trying to gather information about the shell company owners. Louise, fresh off their tense phone call, was facing a team of auditors who could very well end her EPA career. Stanley felt the pressure of inaction squeezing his chest.

He looked around the room until his eyes landed on an old newspaper clipping pinned to the corkboard on the wall. It was from the *Redmain Gazette*, with a byline from Karl Hensley. Stanley's gut twisted. Hensley could be their shot to go public, to force Hargrove and Mayor Mass's hand. It was time, he decided. Stanley grabbed the phone, his fingers trembling as he dialed the *Gazette*'s number. After a few rings, the receptionist answered.

"This is Stanley Peck. I need to speak to Karl Hensley. It's urgent."

After a brief pause, the receptionist connected him to another line. Hensley's voice came on, skeptical but curious. "Stanley Peck? Name rings a bell. What've you got for me?"

Stanley knew he had to dangle the carrot a bit. He leaned in, choosing his words carefully. "Hensley, I've got evidence of a cover-up at the ParaWorks facility. It goes high, all the way to Mayor Mass, maybe further. I need you to hear me out."

Hensley's silence stretched, heavy with calculation. "That's a bold claim, Peck. You got proof of this, or are you just talk?"

"Proof?" Stanley said, knowing his case was weaker than it would have been 12 hours ago, thanks to the break-in. "I've got documents, signatures, emails—enough to shake things up." Stanley began to sweat, knowing his evidence was weaker now.

Another pause, then Hensley gave his answer. "Alright, you've got my attention. Meet me at the diner on the boulevard. Thirty minutes. Don't be late." Then the line went dead.

That was it, Stanley thought. He exhaled, his heart racing. It was all much easier than he'd expected. Maybe too easy. He closed his eyes and took a deep breath. That's all it took for Stanley's mind to flash back to events forty years ago, to events and circumstances so similar to what he was facing in his present.

The City Hall plaza in late 1985 was a stage for redemption, or so the mayor hoped. A crowd gathered around a large stage. To the left and right of the stage were tall poles with torches at the top, blowing flames about a foot in the air for added visual flair. Just behind that stage stood a large object, at least twenty feet tall, covered by a massive drape that concealed it from the onlookers on the other side of the stage. News crews stood poised, cameras were rolling, and the people were ready for the event to start.

Mayor Harold Washington stepped onto the stage and grabbed the microphone off its stand, taking the center position on the empty stage. "Good evening and welcome to everyone who has come to this joyous event!"

The crowd below erupted in cheers as the mayor flashed his best smile. But there was one person in the crowd who was not smiling, one person who was not looking forward to this '*joyous*' event. Stanley Peck was just another nameless face in a sea of people. He had heard about this special event the day of its announcement, which itself was only a few days after the week-long, highly publicized cleanup of the CleanCycle BioSystems site. Stanley was far from looking his best. He had dark circles under his eyes, and he was days past needing a shave. Even his suit looked like it needed a wash. But he wasn't about to let any of those details stop him from attending this public event.

"A little over a week ago," Mayor Washington continued, "we faced a disaster that could have been far worse if not for the tireless work of one man. This terrible calamity may have been man-made, but we're not here to talk about *that* man."

Stanley grimaced at the mayor on the stage, knowing he was *that* man.

"Today," the mayor continued again after a short laugh from the crowd, "today, we're here to celebrate a man with passion. We're here to honor the man who had the vision not only to see another way to clean up some of our world's messes but who also cleaned up a terrible mess in Chicago's own backyard."

He gestured to the corner of the stage, where a large box lay waiting. "We've also brought everyone some fireworks to celebrate the occasion."

Stanley rolled his eyes, and the crowd cheered again. He didn't know how, but Stanley still believed that Leo Vincent had somehow gotten away with everything, and now he was being held up on the shoulders of Chicago for it. This was it, Stanley knew. This was the last chance to show the mayor, to show everyone, that his suspicions were true. The cameras were here. The mayor was here. *HE* was here. This was his last chance, Stanley knew.

Mayor Washington stretched his arms out wide. "So please help me in welcoming our man of the evening, our very own '*eco hero*,' Mr. Leonardo Vincent!"

The cheers and claps built to a fever pitch as Leo Vincent bounded up onto the stage with Mayor Washington. He brought his open hands to his mouth, kissed them, then turned his hands back to the crowd, waving his kisses onto them. Tucked into the sea of chanting onlookers, Stanley stuck his tongue out in a mock gesture like he was going to vomit, which he very well may have done if the mayor's adulation had continued for one more word.

Mayor Washington handed the microphone over to Leo Vincent, who took it from the mayor after a very ceremonial bow. "Thank you so much for that extremely kind introduction, Mayor Washington." He turned to face the audience of reporters, journalists, and varied Chicago citizens. "But I must, however, object to the use of the word '*hero*.' I'm no hero, ladies and gentlemen. I'm just a guy who wouldn't stand being bullied, just a guy who stood up and fought for all of us when the skies darkened with all that ugliness."

Stanley had heard enough. He started stepping closer to the stage, waiting for his moment to come.

"I used my new technology to clean up the hazardous explosion at my facility," Vincent said. "I worked with the National Guard and FEMA to help create an airborne mixture that cleaned and dissipated the toxic cloud that threatened the lives and homes of hundreds of people in our precious city." He nodded ceremoniously. "Yes, I did that. But I'm no hero. I'm no savior. I did what any of you would have done if you were in my shoes, because I *am* one of you!"

The crowd exploded with applause. This was it, Stanley knew. It was now or never. He pushed his way through a few rows of people and reporters until he was mere feet from Leo Vincent at the front of the stage. Stanley pointed his finger at his enemy and shouted as loudly as he could.

"This man is a fraud!"

Vincent and Mayor Washington looked down, quickly picking out Stanley in the standing audience. "Oh, shit," Leo Vincent mumbled into the microphone without thinking.

The mayor instinctively covered the microphone after Vincent's vulgar word slipped out. The crowd hemmed and hawed, then openly gasped as Stanley crawled up onto the stage. Before Vincent or the mayor could react, Stanley ran up to both of them and snapped the microphone from Leo's hand and turned to the sea of people before the stage. He turned to the crowd, a wild-eyed expression on his face.

"People of Chicago!" Stanley yelled. The reporters started scribbling, and the video cameras focused in. "This man, Leo Vincent, is a fake, a sham! His technology is a lie! He's pulling the wool over all of your eyes!"

The mayor stepped forward and tried to take the microphone from Stanley's grip, but Stanley quickly pulled away and stepped further to the side of the stage.

"No, I won't be silenced!" Stanley said, his volume going higher. "This man is corrupt! This mayor is corrupt!" He looked down at the front of the stage and saw a news camera inching closer. Stanley dropped to one knee and leaned into the lens, his face taking up the frame. "I won't stand for this mockery! My name is Stanley Peck, and I know the truth! I tell you, I know the truth!"

At the other end of the stage, Mayor Washington leaned over to Leo Vincent and said, "There's no security here. Should we do something?"

Vincent smirked and quietly said, "No, no. Let it happen."

Both the mayor and Vincent backed slowly off the stage, leaving Stanley alone to continue his rant, which he most certainly did.

"I did what I did to save the people, to save all of you!" Stanley yelled to the crowd as he turned and pointed at the twenty-foot-tall object covered in a massive drape. "And *he's* getting an award?!" He stepped closer to the object, taking hold of a chunk of the drape in his hand. "I won't allow it! I won't let this happen!" Stanley pulled hard on the drape, pulling it free and exposing a giant, twenty-foot bronze statue—of Leo Vincent. Stanley's face sank as the color drained from his skin.

The crowd went silent for a moment as they took in the beautifully crafted representation of the CleanCycle BioSystems' owner and operator. The statue stood tall, depicting Leonardo Vincent with one hand at his side and the other hand reaching out to the heavens, a smile the size of a burrito carved on his face. Stanley stood in horror at the figure before him, the drape he had yanked off still clutched in his white-knuckled hand. The reporters feverishly scribbled in their notepads as the cameras followed Stanley and the unfolding action.

"I tell you, everyone, this man is a menace!" Stanley barked as he threw the drape carelessly behind him. So focused Stanley was, in fact, that he didn't notice he had thrown the drape at the pole holding the torch at the end of the stage. So focused was his rage that he didn't see the drape shake the pole, sending a small flame down into the box of fireworks intended for the end-of-celebration event.

"He's got all of you fooled!" Stanley continued as the flame took hold in the fireworks box. "I'm the only one who sees it! I'll show you! I'll show *all* of you!"

Stanley started pulling on the arm of the statue as the spark inside the fireworks box reached what it needed, igniting the box in flames. Sparklers and fountains of fire and light exploded from the box. Roman candles and strobes ignited, sending a shower of aerial spectacle across the length of the stage and over the crowd. The people fled, running away wildly to avoid the pyrotechnic disaster show Stanley had unintentionally unleashed. The newscasters, however, cameras at their side, did not flinch in the madness. They moved in closer, sure to catch every moment of the chaos.

"I won't stand for it!" Stanley continued to rage as he yanked harder on the bronze arm. "I won't let this mockery of a statue stand!" He centered all of his anger in his chest and summoned his strength, giving the statue a last pull, sending the twenty-foot monument off its base. A collective gasp rippled across the remaining audience as the statue wobbled, finally giving way to gravity as it fell and collided with the ground and part of the stage with a thunderous crash on its way down.

The box of hundreds of fireworks continued to ignite and launch across the stage in all directions. The box itself was being consumed in fire as the explosions of light and color fired away. Stanley stood in the back corner of the stage, the fallen bronze Leo Vincent lying precariously against the dais next to him as the whizzes, pops, and bangs whirled around him.

This was it, Stanley thought. This was the moment he had been waiting for, his chance to expose Vincent and the whole CleanCycle BioSystems scam. Instead, however, he stood at the forefront of a public disaster with flaming fireworks going off all around him in celebration of his inability to stop and walk away. Stanley lowered his head, and his shoulders dropped. This was it, alright. This was truly it.

Cameras and news crews captured every second as the statue lay fallen on its back, its head caught by the edge of the stage, leaving it propped up at an angle, flames and fireworks surrounding its tortured glory. Leo Vincent's bronze hand, which would have been reaching for the heavens, now seemed to point straight at Stanley Peck, who stood defeated near the statue's midsection. In fact, Stanley's position and shrunken pose were so imperfectly positioned that from the view of the recording video and photographers' cameras, an obscene illusion was being created. From just the right angle, the angle all of the news people were in, Stanley's perfectly positioned, hunched-over head and body looked like the fallen statue's half-erect penis.

"Look at the Pecker!" a voice from the crowd shouted, and the word spread like wildfire.

"Pecker!"

"Pecker!"

"Pecker!" the crowd chanted, cameras recording as Stanley tried to wipe his eyes, only smearing more filth across his face.

About fifty feet away from the scene, a newscaster with a camera squared up on his shoulder, perfectly captured Leo Vincent live as the insanity devolved behind him. His voice cut through the noise and explosions. "Well, folks," Vincent said with a crooked smile, "looks like Stanley Peck's found his true monument—right where he belongs."

The footage went national that night. News reports plastered Stanley's face across every television screen in America, the *'Pecker'* taunt immortalized in the minds of anyone with a TV screen or a newspaper. And to add insult to Stanley's injury, when the smoke cleared and the facts came to light, Leo Vincent's secret waste treatment and disposal technology had proven to be very much real. He had been cryptic and vague in order to keep the rest of the industry from replicating his methods before he could patent them. Stanley was wrong. He was wrong, and the entire world watched his outrageous downfall on live TV.

This was it. And it was over.

Back in his apartment, Stanley took another breath and forced the memories from his mind, returning his focus to the present. Stanley pushed his doubt and his questions down deep, grabbed his suit jacket, and headed out, the remaining evidence stuffed into his briefcase.

* * *

The diner on Redmain's central boulevard was the oldest in

town. Its neon "*Open*" sign swung faintly in the gentle morning breeze. It was nowhere near as nice as the one Stanley and Louise ate breakfast at with the gum-smacking waitress, but it would serve its purpose well enough. Inside, a few locals hunched over counter stools, their eyes occasionally darting toward the corner booth where Stanley sat. He had decided to present himself more formally, wearing his wrinkled suit with his tie loosened. Stanley's briefcase was open in the seat next to him, and spread out on the table before him lay the evidence he had left—the signed consent form, email printouts, and notes scrawled in Louise's neat hand.

Stanley's knee was bobbing up and down as his pulse quickened. He gripped his coffee mug, *'Pecker'* typically scrawled on the side, its warmth doing little to steady his nerves. The voices started in his mind, the ever-present reminders of doubt and doom, but Stanley did his best to push them away as he mumbled under his breath.

"You're not gonna see me comin', Mass."

"What's that, Hargrove? Underestimated me, did ya?"

"I'm Stanley Peck, that's who."

Stanley took a breath as the diner's door opened with a creak, and in walked Karl Hensley. He was slightly heavyset, looking a bit disheveled in a rumpled shirt, and wore thick glasses perched low on his nose and carried a notepad and pen in his hand. He slid into the booth opposite Stanley, flashing a fake smile that didn't quite reach his eyes.

"Stanley Peck, right? The man with the big story," Hensley said, booming and raw, leaning in as if they were old pals. "So, spill it. What's this about ParaWorks and the mayor?"

Stanley straightened, his pulse quickening. He slid the consent form across the table, Mayor Mass's signature glaring under the light. "Here's your proof," he said as he pushed forward a folder with papers spilling out. "Mayor Mass signed off on the ParaWorks project, knowing full well that it posed a substantial risk to the town. And the city planner, Alan Hargrove, he's in on it too, pushing deals and taking kickbacks. I've got emails, financial statements, the works!" Stanley shifted in his seat. "And someone is harassing me, too, Hensley. I even had a break-in at my apartment last night! This whole thing is about to explode, and I'm telling you, I'm right in the middle of it. I just need you to put the story out there before any of those weasels can make some sort of legal move against me."

Hensley's eyes narrowed as he opened the folder and scanned through the various papers, his pen scratching notes. His lips puckered with interest. "Hot damn, that's a hell of a claim, Peck! You're saying Mass and Hargrove are dirty? What's tying them to ParaWorks?"

Stanley grabbed the printouts, flipping through the pages with frantic speed. "Look here!" Stanley said. "I've got meeting minutes and correspondence between Hargrove and ParaWorks, dated last year. And I've got evidence of shell companies linked to Mass and Hargrove. Then there's the water table data itself. ParaWorks' reports claim it's safe, but independent tests show contamination risks."

Hensley's eyes perked up. "You have proof that ParaWorks poses a contamination risk?"

Stanley froze for a second. "Well, not exactly."

"Why not?" Hensley scoffed. "Where is it?"

Stanley flushed in embarrassment. "The robber got it from my apartment last night."

"The break-in you mentioned?" Hensley said.

Stanley nodded. "Yeah, he got a lot. But he didn't get everything. The EPA has copies of the data, too, but it was all carefully hidden from anyone who went looking for it."

Hensley looked up, his pen pausing. "You mean the EPA's involved? You got a name, a contact at the EPA?"

"Of course. Her name is…" Stanley hesitated, stopping before giving away Louise's name. "Let's just say someone in the EPA has been helping to gather data. But let's keep her out of it for now. Focus on this." He tapped the consent form. "This is concrete, Hensley. You see, the water table in Redmain is far too high for a project like ParaWorks. The mayor knows that. Hargrove knows that. But it doesn't end there. It's so much bigger. We just need someone to run with the story and force the council's hand."

Hensley sat back. "Okay, but why come to me?" he asked. "Why not file a civil suit against these guys and let the courts string them up?"

Stanley rubbed his temples, the tension mounting in his head. "That would've been the plan. But after being followed, and after the break-in, we lost a lot of what we had."

Hensley nodded, his pen flying. "Smart move then, Peck, trying to go public. Some people around here are nervous about ParaWorks, but they also love the promise of new, high-paying jobs, too." He leaned in closer. "You've got guts, Peck. But how'd you get all of this? What's your angle? You some kind of crusader or something?"

Stanley hesitated, then pressed on, the hope bubbling up inside him. "It started as a feeling, really. Then the consent form proved it was real, and everything just started piling up." Stanley straightened up in his seat. "And I don't have an angle. I've been chasing this kind of corruption my entire career, Mr.

Hensley. Back in Chicago, I made mistakes. I know that. But this isn't about me. It's about the truth." He tapped the pile of forms and documents, his fingers trembling. "This could hurt people."

Hensley leaned back, studying Stanley. His expression was unreadable. "You're passionate, I'll give you that. But tell me some more. How'd you dig up this stuff? Who's your source?"

"It doesn't matter," Stanley said. "What matters is what's in front of you. Dirty campaign contributions, maybe money laundering. We just need you to force the council's hand and get this information out there for the public to see."

Hensley's lips curled into a grin. "You're sitting on a powder keg here, Peck. If this breaks right, it could be big, career-making, even." He paused, scribbling a final note. "What's next? You planning a showdown at the town hall meeting?"

Stanley nodded, his hope rising. "Yeah! Tuesday's meeting. I'm going to push for a public review of ParaWorks' permits. With your story, we can..."

"Hold up," Hensley interrupted, his smile widening, too wide, his tone shifting to something colder. "Let's get real, Peck. You think I'm running *this*?" He tapped the consent form dismissively. "This is a story, alright, but it ain't about ParaWorks or Mass. It's about *you*, Peck." He leaned back, folding his arms, notepad open, but ignored. "'*Crackpot from Chicago Stirs Trouble in Redmain: Stanley Peck's Latest Fiasco*.' That's the headline. Folks here still talk about that statue stunt. Half this shop's whispering it already." Hensley gestured toward the counter, where a couple of regulars were stealing quiet looks, sneers on their faces.

Stanley's stomach plummeted, his hands clenching his coffee mug with '*Pecker*' written on the side. "What the hell are you talking about, Hensley? This isn't about me!" His voice rose, drawing eyes from the counter. "The evidence is right here!"

Hensley chuckled, closing his notepad with a snap. "Evidence? What you've got here is a form and some emails, and a bag full of theories. You're no whistleblower. You're a has-been with a grudge. Redmain wants ParaWorks' jobs, not your drama. You're a story, Peck, not a savior."

"That's a lie!" Stanley snapped, his face flushing red. "People are in danger, Hensley. Don't bury this, not because of me!"

Hensley shrugged, unfazed by Stanley's emotional plea. "I'm a journalist, not your personal PR guy. The town doesn't trust you, Peck. Never has." He raised his voice so that everyone in the room could hear. "Why don't you take some friendly advice? Quit while you're ahead, before you drag Redmain down into the mud with you."

The shop fell silent, then a voice from the counter cut through. "Hey, ain't that the guy who caused that explosion in Chicago?" He was a large, bearded man, his coffee cup raised in the air like a toast.

Laughter erupted. A waitress wiping the counter shook her head. "Thought he'd learned his lesson back in Chicago," she said, loud enough for the room to hear.

A burly regular in a trucker hat leaned forward, his voice booming. "What's it now, *Pecker*? You hunting aliens now, or just stirring up things for fun?"

The laughter swelled like waves pounding the shore. A younger guy at the counter joined in, a sickly grin stretching from ear to ear. "Go back to Chicago! We don't need your crazy here."

Stanley's face burned. His hands tightened around his coffee mug until his knuckles went white. The laughter in the coffee shop grew louder, a cruel onslaught that pounded in Stanley's ears. "You'll see! This town's in danger, and you're all too blind to see it!"

Hensley stood, slipping his notepad into his pocket. "Good luck with your little detective case, *Pecker*. My story's already written." He turned to the counter, raising his voice. "Let's toast to Redmain's *real* heroes, the ones bringing jobs, not fairytales!"

The crowd cheered as Hensley sauntered to the door, which squeaked as he walked out. Stanley quickly shoved the documents into his briefcase, his movements jerky from the adrenaline dump in his veins.

"You'll see," Stanley muttered, barely audible over the laughter. He stood, his chair scraping loudly, drawing more smirks as he stumbled out, the creaky door mocking his exit. The laughter continued and chased him into the street as he walked away, defeated.

Chapter Sixteen

That night, Stanley stood on the balcony of his second-floor apartment. The sky above was a collection of purples, oranges, and rich indigo. The last slivers of daylight were fading into the jagged silhouettes of rooftops and of the ParaWorks building site on the horizon in the distance. While the day had come and gone, the morning's painful reality check by Karl Hensley still echoed in Stanley's mind, as did the phone call from Louise and her showdown with the EPA auditors. Like a house of cards, it had all come crashing down at Stanley's feet.

In Stanley's hand, a glass of bourbon trembled slightly as he raised it to his lips. The burn was powerful as it went down his throat, a welcome sting against the ache that had settled into his chest since he fled the diner in humiliating disgrace. Hensley's words, *'You're a has-been with a grudge,'* echoed in Stanley's mind, each syllable acting like a hammer strike against the fragile walls of his battered ego. He felt like a fool. That, for a moment, he thought someone might have taken him seriously, made Stanley cringe.

He leaned against the railing, his free hand gripping it so tightly that his fingernails started digging into the wood. The town sprawled out before him, a patchwork of buildings, small houses, and businesses. It was normally a sight as familiar as the back of his aged hand, but tonight it felt strangely alien, like it had never truly been his home. Thirty years ago, he'd fled Chicago, with its towering indifference and its laughter at his public failures, only to land here in Redmain. Out here, the air was clean of the familiar Chicago smog, and the only meanness the people showed was their indifference to issues outside of the city limits. He thought he could start over here and redeem himself with a quiet life of vigilance. But now that dream lay in tatters, scattered like the dozens of documents Hensley had dismissed with a sneer.

The bourbon did its thankful job and burned again as Stanley took another sip, his thoughts spiraling to the mistakes that continued to haunt him all these years later. The fiasco with Vincent in '85 started it all. That joke of a CEO mocked him, made fun of him, and dismissed him. Even when Stanley brought the police and the power to shut down Vincent's facility, the smug would-be politician still managed to taunt and disparage him. Stanley cringed at the fool he thought he had been, charging into the Chicago mayor's office with his theories about illegal dumpings and fake technology, only to be thrown out by that same mayor and later mocked on live television. CleanCycle BioSystems, more specifically Leo Vincent, had turned him into a punchline, and as a result, the EPA had buried him under paperwork and sideways glances until he was finally let go in disgrace.

Stanley had told himself that Redmain would be different, that his experiences *there* wouldn't matter *here*. But that's not what happened. Here he was again, a man out of step with the world, clutching at straws while the town turned its back. The consent form, the EPA emails, and the financial corruption were all such clear evidence of ParaWorks' potential danger. But to Hensley, to the townsfolk of Redmain, it was just *'a bag full of theories,'* and Stanley was the deluded *'has-been'* he always was, a deluded man just trying to play hero.

Doubt gnawed at Stanley, a relentless tidal wave in his mind. What if he was wrong? What if ParaWorks would never cause any problems, and what if all the evidence he had piled into his briefcase amounted to nothing? Could he have been dragging Elizabeth and Louise into a hailstorm of personal and professional destruction for nothing? He had heard the fear in Louise's tone when she had called during her surprise audit, her voice overflowing with worry.

After his run-in with Hensley, Elizabeth had called on her way back into town after a day of detective work. The sound of worry in her voice differed from that of Louise's, but it was worry just the same, the kind of worry a child should never have for their parent. Elizabeth believed in him, his daughter, and his anchor. But what if he had failed her, too? The memory of her law school graduation flashed in his mind, her proud smile as he hugged her, whispering, *'I'm so proud of you.'* He had wanted to be a father she could look up to, not a broken man stumbling through a losing battle. Yet here he was, his face still burning with the shame of Hensley's public dismissal, the diner's crowd calling him *'Pecker'* still ringing in his ears.

Stanley knew the data. He knew the risks. But what if Redmain's leadership was right to choose jobs over his warnings? The town needed the factory's payroll, the stability it promised. Who was he, Stanley Peck, to pose such a question for the people of Redmain? No one asked him. Was he the villain here? Was he clinging to a past glory that never existed, risking the livelihoods of so many people for his own self-redemption? The thought twisted in his gut, souring the bourbon.

He had failed before, failed to protect Chicago from Vincent's chaos, failed to rise in the EPA, and failed to keep his marriage intact after the stress of it all. Now, with the town hall meeting looming, Stanley feared he would fail Redmain, too, dragging Elizabeth and Louise down with him into the mud as Hensley had so gleefully predicted.

A chilly breeze swept across the balcony, carrying with it the faint scent of incoming rain. Stanley shivered and set his glass down on the railing. Stanley ran his hands down his face, his hands scratching against the rough stubble he'd let grow over the last few days. Maybe Hensley was right, he wondered. He was no savior. Maybe he should quit while he was ahead, like Hensley suggested. Maybe he should just slink back to his apartment and let the town move on without him. The weight of his doubts continued to press down like a suffocating blanket of self-recrimination. He had wanted to prove he wasn't the joke they all thought of him to be, to show Elizabeth he could still matter, that he still had something to offer, and that the rumors weren't true. But what if all he had done was prove them right?

The sound of the apartment door opening behind him broke Stanley from his self-reflection. He turned, his heart lifting slightly as Elizabeth stepped through his front door. He watched as she set her things down and stepped out onto the balcony. Disappointment marred Elizabeth's face, but her eyes softened when they met Stanley's.

Elizabeth glanced down at the glass in Stanley's hand, then

at the bottle that filled it. "I think I'm going to need one of those, too," she said.

Stanley smiled and reached down to the small table next to him. He brought his hand back up with an empty glass. "I thought you might," he said as he took the bourbon bottle and poured Elizabeth a generous serving. She took the glass from Stanley's hand and dropped the entire pour down her throat. Stanley's eyes popped open with surprise.

"I'll be accepting no judgment tonight," Elizabeth said with a smirk.

Stanley held his glass up as he cocked his head. "And I won't be giving any."

They tapped their glasses together in a mock toast. The air carried a faint scent of moisture. It served as an ironic moment of calm in a week that had felt like a storm brewing, which now seemed to be literally about to fall on Redmain. Stanley cradled his bourbon glass as Elizabeth took a seat in one of the rickety lawn chairs Stanley had set up on the balcony. She tucked her legs under her body and draped the folded blanket that was on the chair over her shoulders. The balcony light flickered above them, and the distant sound of traffic was the only sound coming from Redmain.

Stanley stared out at the street as he came to rest in the other ragged lawn chair. He looked at Elizabeth, her profile softened in the dim light, and felt a familiar ache in his chest. He closed his eyes for a moment, as if gathering the strength to speak, to say anything about the events of the day that wouldn't bring more defeat than they both already felt.

Elizabeth read the struggle in Stanley's eyes and quickly jumped in, saving him from trying to find something positive to say. "Any news from Louise?"

Grateful for the reprieve, Stanley nodded his head. "She called when the auditors left her office. They took a lot of things with them. They asked for a lot that was missing, which of course she didn't have. Her boss made it pretty clear what would happen if she'd been helping us, helping me. The final word hasn't come down yet, but the writing seems to be on the wall. She was going to come over tonight, but I told her to just go home and get some rest. She deserves it."

Elizabeth shook her head. "It's not fair. None of this is fair. If things go south for her, I'll help her anyway I can. Legally, I mean."

Stanley smiled. "I know you will." He shifted his focus. "Any luck today on your end?"

Elizabeth took a quick sip of her drink. "Well, yes and no. My friend at the data retrieval firm came through with some information on those mysterious shell company owners—Gaines and Marietti."

"That's great!" Stanley said.

Elizabeth frowned. "Not entirely. Turns out they're both deceased. They died in a car crash about twenty years ago."

"They both died?" Stanley questioned. "You mean they knew each other?"

Elizabeth nodded. "They more than just knew each other. Get this—they had a daughter, Lorraine. My friend had found out they were both killed in the same accident, so I searched birth records and found that."

"Okay," Stanley said, "so the shell company owners not only knew each other, but they had a daughter, and they're both dead. That doesn't seem to connect to anything here."

Elizabeth shook her head. "No, it doesn't."

"So what now?" Stanley asked.

"I'll keep looking into Marietti and Gaines," Elizabeth said. "I'll even dig into this daughter of theirs. There's got to be a connection."

Stanley let his gaze fall back upon the landscape of Redmain. "You know, kiddo, I never thought I'd be back in a fight like this. Not at my age, not after everything that happened. And I sure as hell didn't think you'd be right here with me, staring down Hargrove, the mayor, and whoever else." He shook his head, a twitch tugging at his cheek. "You could've stayed out of it, you know, stayed at your fancy job and kept your reputation safe. Why'd you stick around for an old man's silly crusade?"

Elizabeth turned to him, amusement and affection in her expression. "*Fancy job*?" she said. "Dad, I'm here because of you. Growing up, I watched you take on every case, every fight, no matter how much the odds were stacked against you. You think I'd let you do this one alone?" She pulled the blanket tighter around her shoulders. "Besides, it's not just your crusade. You sold me on this fight, just like you sold Louise. My '*fancy job*' doesn't mean a damn thing if the man who taught me how to fight in that job finally needs my help and I don't give it."

Stanley took a sip of his bourbon, the bitter warmth grounding him. His brow furrowed. "I'm proud of you, Elizabeth, don't get me wrong. Prouder than I've got words for. But I'm scared, too." He reached out and set the glass down on the porch railing, his hands gripping the edge of his chair. "That letter from Hargrove, the P.I. watching us, the intimidation, the break-in, and now Louise getting heat from her bosses at the EPA—it's all so much bigger than I thought. Back in Chicago, I lost everything because I didn't see the traps. I didn't pay attention to friends and colleagues telling me to back off. My job, my name, smeared and ruined. And your mom—I lost her, too." His voice cracked, and he looked away. "I could have so easily lost you, too. That reporter made me feel like it was Chicago all over again. And the worst part is, I'm afraid he's right."

Elizabeth leaned forward, resting a hand on his arm. "You would never have lost me, Dad. We're in this together, and we're smarter than they think. We're going to expose this thing. *You* are going to expose this thing. And that damn reporter is going to eat his words when you're proven right." Elizabeth's eyes softened with memory. "I remember when I was little, you'd come home late, still in your suit, your briefcase full of papers. You'd tell me stories about standing up to the big shots, making sure the rules mattered. That always stuck with me. It's why I became a lawyer. It's why I'm here now." She squeezed his arm, a small smile returning. "We're not just fighting for Redmain. We're fighting for us, for what you taught me."

Stanley looked at his daughter, a lump firmly in his throat. "You're tougher than I ever was, Lizzy," he said, managing a chuckle. "I just hope I can get this across at the town hall meeting tomorrow. I hope they'll listen. Hargrove, the mayor, maybe even ParaWorks. They'll do everything they can to dismiss me."

Elizabeth nodded. "We won't let them, Dad." She took a deep breath. "But I'm not gonna lie, Dad, I'm nervous. We still don't know who these people are who own the shell companies, and that's a huge piece of the puzzle. But what worries me is that they'll come at you, at Stanley Peck. I still think maybe I should be the one to talk at that meeting."

Stanley reached over, covering her hand with his. "They

probably will. I'd be surprised if they didn't. But I've got something they don't, Lizzy. The truth. And people deserve to know it." Stanley stood, leaning back against the balcony railing. "Its gotta be me, kiddo. It always had to be me. I won't back down. Not for Hargrove, not for the mayor, not for anyone."

Elizabeth smiled, her eyes bright as she stood next to Stanley. "I love you, Dad," she said, leaning her head against his shoulder.

"I love you, too, Lizzy."

Chapter Seventeen

The following evening, the night air in Redmain hung heavy with moisture as a light mist covered the town. The sun was setting, blanketing the landscape in a beautiful glow. Dark clouds overhead released occasional rolls of thunder. Stanley stepped out of the apartment first, his briefcase clutched tightly in one hand. Elizabeth followed close behind him. Louise brought up the rear, her EPA folder held over her head like a shield from the falling rain. Stanley scanned the sky as the misting rain threatened to unleash a full downpour. This *would* be the atmosphere tonight, Stanley thought.

The trio had spent the last few hours in Stanley's cramped living room, rehearsing their strategy for the town hall meeting. They reviewed every chart, every highlighted line in the ParaWorks reports, and every damning email until their voices were hoarse. Now, with the meeting only 30 minutes away, the pressure of what they were hoping to do sank in. With the missing reports in the hands of the home invader from the other night, and with Karl Hensley's complete lack of support, this meeting was all Stanley thought they had left.

Stanley locked the door behind them and led the group

down the stairs towards Louise's Buick. The street was mostly empty and quiet, leaving just enough silence for Stanley to hear the voices of doubt in his mind. He shook his head, trying to drive them away. "We've got this," he said, more to himself than the others as they aimed for their respective doors of Louise's car. "We stick to the plan. Facts first, then the emails."

Elizabeth nodded as Louise forced a smile, though her eyes betrayed her nerves. "Let's just hope they don't try something before you have a chance to talk."

The town hall itself was only a ten-minute drive away, but every second felt like it was ticking by far too fast. Stanley's mind raced, replaying the documents, the numbers, the risks, VOCs in the air, corruption, everything. He was so lost in thought he almost missed the sound—a pop and a snap somewhere in the distance, then the sound of a boot catching on pavement, coming from the alley to their right.

Stanley froze, his hand tightening on his briefcase. "You hear that?"

Elizabeth turned. "Hear what?"

Louise stopped. "Stanley, what's..."

Before Louise could finish, a large male figure stepped out of the alley's shadows, clad in a heavy jacket and hood, moving with the deliberate pace of a predator. The light from the streetlamp above reflected the metal in his hand—a gun, its barrel pointed directly at Stanley, Louise, and Elizabeth. He was tall, his face hidden by the brim of a dark cap under a hood. Despite the man's attempts to hide his identity, Stanley recognized the silhouette instantly. And the sound of knuckles cracking was further proof it was the same man who'd broken into his apartment a few days ago and stolen some of their critical documents.

"Please don't move," the man said. "And keep your hands where I can see them."

Stanley's heart slammed against the walls of his chest, and his mouth went dry. He raised his hands slowly, his briefcase dangling from his fingers. Elizabeth and Louise followed Stanley's lead and raised their hands too, their faces pale. The street was silent—no cars, no passersby, just the four of them and the threatening stranger.

Louise was the first to let out a sound. "Oh shit. Oh shit. Oh shit," she said uncontrollably.

"What do you want?" Stanley asked the man as he stepped slightly forward, angling himself in front of Elizabeth and Louise. "If it's about the documents, you're too late," he told the man. "We've got copies, and I've talked to the press."

"I don't want anything from you, Mr. Peck," the man said, his voice cracking slightly in the moment's pressure. "I'm not here for any of your things." He gestured with the gun, directing their attention toward the alley. "Would you all step over to my van?"

Elizabeth's eyes flashed with fury. "You think you can just wave a gun and we'll follow you into a van? Who the hell are you?"

The man tilted his head, locking his gaze onto her. "I don't want to hurt you, Ma'am." He stepped closer, the gun steady, its barrel catching the light. "But I need you and your friends to walk quietly over to my van." His eyes drifted down to the gun in his hands. "Please."

Louise's breath hitched. "Oh my actual shit," she said, her voice trembling.

The man ignored Louise, jerking his head toward the alley. "Let's get going."

Stanley's mind raced. He looked over at Elizabeth, then Louise, their eyes meeting in silent agreement. They had no choice, the trio quietly agreed. "Alright," Stanley said, his voice calm and deliberate. "We're moving. Just stay calm." Stanley started moving towards the alley, his hands still raised. Elizabeth and Louise followed close behind, also keeping their hands in the air. The man trailed them, his gun trained on their backs.

The alley was narrow and dark, and it had a curious smell of damp concrete and garbage. A stock white van waited at the far end, its engine idling, its rear doors open like a gaping mouth. The man moved to the side, giving the trio a clear path through the back doors. As they stepped closer, Stanley, Elizabeth, and Louise could finally get a better look under the man's hood. He was young, in his late twenties at the latest. He was big, and although he was brandishing a gun, his eyes weren't as cold as they expected.

"Get in," the man ordered, stopping a few feet behind them. "Wait, hold on," the man said. "I'm gonna need your phones."

Elizabeth and Louise both gave each other a look, as if acknowledging they were both hoping their kidnapper would have forgotten them. They frowned and handed them over. The man turned to Stanley. "You too."

Stanley hesitated but handed his phone over as he scanned the alley for anything they could use—a weapon, an escape, a chance. But the man's gun was unwavering, and the van was too close. Stanley climbed in first, helping Elizabeth and Louise up, their hands brushing briefly in a fleeting moment of reassurance. The man slammed the doors shut and headed for the driver's door.

Inside, the back of the van was completely empty. It didn't

even have seats. It was dark, thanks to the front windows being heavily tinted. The man climbed into the driver's seat and set the gun in the cup holder next to him. He brought his hands together in front of his chest and snapped the knuckles of his fingers, then shifted into gear. As the van lurched forward, Stanley, Elizabeth, and Louise quickly fell to the floor. They pushed themselves up and rested their backs against the cold metal walls.

Stanley leaned close to Elizabeth and Louise, keeping his voice low. "We'll get out of this. Just stay calm."

* * *

The van's engine growled as it wound its way through Redmain's quiet streets. Stanley, Louise, and Elizabeth sat shoulder-to-shoulder, with Stanley in the middle, as they suffered every bump in the road thanks to the van's uncomfortable metal floor. Stanley's briefcase and Louise's file folder were haphazardly thrown into the corner. The man who forced them into the van said nothing to them as he drove. And while he didn't specifically forbid the three of them from talking, no one wanted to be the one to test their kidnappers' patience, despite his curiously polite nature and habit of saying please.

Stanley looked over to Elizabeth and Louise. They were terrified. Who wouldn't be, after all? Where were they going? What fate awaited them when they arrived? On Stanley's left, Elizabeth had wrapped her arm around his, her hand gripping his knee. On Stanley's right, Louise sat with her knees up and her arms wrapped around them. She was shivering from head to toe.

Stanley was scared too, more scared than he had ever been in his whole life, but all he could think of was Elizabeth and Louise, and that he had brought this terrible situation upon them. Whatever was going to happen was ultimately of his doing, or so Stanley thought. He felt helpless. He was hardly a physical match for their kidnapper, even if he didn't have a gun, which he did. Stanley knew he would say anything, do anything, to see that Elizabeth and Louise got freed. But would he have that chance, Stanley wondered? Or was there no changing whatever was supposed to happen?

Thinking about what might happen wasn't going to help, Stanley realized. He knew he had to be strong for both Elizabeth and Louise. He gripped Elizabeth's hand as she fought against digging her nails into Stanley's knee out of fear. She looked at him and smiled. He smiled back. Stanley was going to tell her that he loved her and that he always would, no matter what. But Stanley knew that would sound like a goodbye, and that would not show Elizabeth the strength he hoped to show in that moment. But when their eyes connected, they both knew it anyway.

Stanley reached around Louise with his other arm and pulled her close. His body warmth and proximity helped Louise slow her breathing. Stanley gave Louise's shoulder a good squeeze, letting her know he was with her. She didn't look over. But that small act on Stanley's part calmed Louise's body, and the shaking eased. If all Stanley could be was their rock, then that's what he would be.

The drive itself wasn't all that long. Maybe about five minutes, from what Stanley could tell, but it felt like an eternity, no matter what the actual drive time. As the van slowed, Stanley could make out the sound of gravel crunching under the tires. They were off the road. That much was certain. Stanley leaned forward and tried not to be too obvious as he looked out the front window of the van. His stomach dropped as he recognized a familiar sight. The ParaWorks building location. It was the same place he and Louise had come when they met Bob, the self-proclaimed "earth-mover," and made off with copies of paperwork in that dusty old double-wide portable trailer.

The van came to a sudden stop, causing Stanley, Louise, and Elizabeth to slide to their sides and fall over. They were just sitting up and readjusting as their kidnapper cracked his knuckles again before grabbing his gun and jumping out, making his way around to the back. He unlocked the back doors and opened them wide, the gun still in his hand. The trio tensed up, not sure if something was going to happen. Stanley moved forward, in front of Elizabeth and Louise.

"It's time to get out," the man said. "Go slow and, please, no funny business."

Though his bones were killing him from the short yet very uncomfortable ride, Stanley shuffled his way out first. Elizabeth and Louise stood up as much as they could in the van, and Stanley offered a hand to them both as they jumped onto the dirt below. It was dark now, and the ParaWorks construction site was almost completely pitch black, save for a single light above the main entry door of the double-wide office.

The kidnapper gestured with his gun towards the office door. "Come on," he said. "Let's go."

As they started for the door, Stanley looked at the man's

other hand. He had a set of keys in his balled-up fist. Keys to the double-wide, no doubt. Interesting, Stanley thought as he filed the detail away in his mind, instead focusing his attention on the area and a possible escape. Now that they were out of the van and at their final destination, Stanley started wondering if their location was a clue as to what the kidnapper was going to do next. Kill them? Okay, Stanley thought, but why here? That didn't quite add up. He looked over at Elizabeth, who seemed to have the same question on her face. Louise, however, was back to shaking as terror gripped her nervous system again. Poor Louise, Stanley thought. He felt so guilty for involving her.

The kidnapper flipped through the keychain. It looked to Stanley like he wasn't familiar with the keys and was looking for a specific marker of some kind to identify the right one. After a few misses, the man found what he was looking for. He unlocked the door and swung it wide with a hard push.

"Inside, please," the man said.

The interior of the trailer was just as it had been before. Scattered across multiple desks were papers and construction sheets. Coffee cups and various odds and ends were all over the main room. And it was dark, very dark. The only light was from the overhead light outside that slipped in through the blinds.

The kidnapper directed Stanley, Elizabeth, and Louise down the hall. The first room they passed was the one Stanley and Elizabeth used to sort through the paperwork that Bob had given them a few days ago. But the mysterious man gestured them further down the hall to the last remaining room. It wasn't big by room-size standards, but it was plenty big enough to hold the giant metal desk that was pushed up against the wall. It had scratches and dents, like it had been through several construction builds in its time. The massive desk was also, Stanley noted, bolted to the floor, likely so it wouldn't move when the trailer had to be moved to the next job.

There was also something else Stanley noticed. More specifically, what *wasn't* there in the room. Plastic. Stanley had seen enough movies and television to know that a *"kill room"* called for plastic to cover the walls and floor from any mess. And there were none to be found. Stanley exhaled quietly as he hoped that was a sign of what was *not* to come.

The kidnapper pointed to the floor. "Sit down," he said as he reached into his pocket and pulled out 3 sets of handcuffs. "Put your backs against the desk and give me your hands."

Elizabeth and Louise started moving to sit on the floor against the desk. Stanley, however, hesitated as he looked at the gun, then back up at the kidnapper. "You don't have to do this," Stanley said. "Whatever they're paying you, it's not worth this."

The man stayed icy cold. "Give me your hand, please," he said.

Stanley offered his right hand. The man locked one end of the handcuffs around Stanley's wrist and guided him down to sit next to Elizabeth and Louise. The kidnapper then linked the other end of the handcuffs to Elizabeth's left hand, binding her and Stanley together. Elizabeth watched the man closely as he reached for the next pair of restraints. Even in the darkened room, she could still make out the beads of sweat forming on his brow.

"I get the feeling this isn't a normal thing for you," Elizabeth dared to say.

The man linked Stanley's other hand to Louise's right hand, leaving Stanley in the middle, as he side-eyed Elizabeth. "It isn't. I needed the money. It's not personal."

He then took his last pair of handcuffs and snapped them around Elizabeth's right hand and locked the other side around one foot of the giant metal desk, anchoring the trio together and firmly stuck where they were. The man tossed Stanley's briefcase and Louise's paperwork folder into the corner of the room.

Still shaking, Louise broke the silence and asked, "Are you going to kill us?"

The man paused and tilted his head as if the question amused him, then brought the gun closer to his face as if examining it. He looked back at the handcuffed hostages, his expression unreadable. Stanley, Louise, and Elizabeth watched the man as his thumb moved just above the handle and flicked a small latch on the side of the gun. The gun made a *'click,'* and the magazine ejected. He pulled it out and showed it to the trio as they sat transfixed on the floor. Even in the limited light, they could see there were no bullets. The man smirked as he pulled the trigger three times in quick succession. Nothing but empty clicks.

"Kill you? With an empty gun?" he said, twirling the gun in his hand like a cowboy in a cheap Western. "I'm not a killer, lady."

Elizabeth's jaw dropped. "Oh, you've got to be kidding me!"

Stanley blinked fast as his mind caught up with the absurdity. An empty gun. The fear that had gripped him moments ago now twisted into something else—anger, mixed with a heavy dose of relief. "What the hell is this?" Stanley demanded. "You dragged us all the way out here with an empty gun, for what?"

The man shrugged, tucking the gun into his pocket. “Like I said, I’m no killer. It’s just a job.” He leaned against the wall, his posture relaxed. “You three are staying put right here until the morning. The construction crew’ll find you and get you out when they clock in. Simple as that.”

Stanley’s eyes narrowed as the pieces clicked together in his brain. “This is so we’ll miss the town hall meeting, isn’t it?” he said. “That’s what this is about! Keeping us from stopping the last ParaWorks signing.”

The kidnapper’s grin faded. “I wouldn’t know anything about that. I’m just doing what I was told.”

The kidnapper turned and headed for the door. His heavy boots pounded through the trailer like a dinosaur. Stanley pulled at his handcuffs, yanking Elizabeth and Louise’s arms. Both women let out a quick sound of pain as the metal handcuffs rattled between them.

The man stepped into the threshold of the door, then stopped and looked back at Stanley, Elizabeth, and Louise. “I’m sorry,” he said, echoing what he had mumbled under his breath before being chased out of Stanley’s apartment the other night. He continued out the door, then shut and locked it behind him. The trio watched through the window as the man got back into the van and drove away, leaving nothing but empty blackness outside.

Elizabeth started pulling on the handcuffs securing her to the leg of the massive metal desk. “This is unbelievable! A friggin’ empty gun?! I swear if I get my hands on that guy after this, I’m gonna kill him!”

Louise stared at the wet spot on the floor as her breathing finally slowed. “Did either of you notice that guy had the keys to this place?” she said. “That must mean Mayor Mass or

Hargrove is behind this. They're so desperate to keep us quiet that they did this, knowing we couldn't link it to them in the morning."

Stanley nodded, his mind racing despite the cold metal handcuffs digging into his wrists. "They're scared, alright," he said. "They know we've got them." He looked over at the locked door up front, then back at the desk anchoring them to the floor. "I can't believe we're going to miss that meeting. After everything we've done. And all because of a bulletless gun." Stanley sighed. "This is really embarrassing."

Chapter Eighteen

The double-wide trailer's windowless room felt like a tomb as Stanley, Louise, and Elizabeth sat on the floor, handcuffed to the massive metal desk in the room. Light from the floor lamp outside provided just enough light for each of the kidnappees to see their desperate situation. The handcuffs linking their wrists bit into their skin, and the final connection to the leg of the metal table was holding firm.

"We're not staying here," Stanley said, his eyes scanning the room for anything of use. "Not when we're this close to everything we've been working for. We've gotta get out of here."

Elizabeth tugged at the handcuffs, the metal chain clanking against the leg of the desk. "That's a brilliant plan, Dad," she said sarcastically. "Got any ideas how?"

At the end of the handcuff chain, Louise craned her neck to peer around into the corners of the cramped portable office space. "There's got to be something in here we can use. A tool, a pipe, anything."

The trio's eyes darted wildly around the room, taking in every detail, not that there was all that much to see. The walls were bare, save for a faded safety poster hung up with thumbtacks. A trash can in the corner overflowed with crumpled papers and coffee cups. A stack of blueprints sat on a shelf, too far to reach, though it didn't look to have anything useful on it, anyway. The desk itself was a hulking beast, the kind you would find serving as a teacher's desk in the '60s or '70s. It had a scratched and dented surface, with each leg bolted to the floor. The whole thing looked like it was meant to outlast them all.

Stanley tested pulling on the handcuffs again, but the metal was absolutely unyielding. "These cuffs are the real deal. We aren't going to be breaking these."

Elizabeth nodded. "Let's try breaking the leg of this thing," she said. "Something's got to give." She braced her feet against the floor, gripping the chain attached to the foot of the desk. "On three," she said, everyone grabbing the handcuff link closest to the metal leg. "One, two, three!"

They pulled hard in unison. Their muscles strained, and the handcuffs dug into their soft wrists. The desk's metal groaned like it was fighting back, but it didn't budge, every bit of its metal body holding firm.

Stanley shifted his weight, hoping for a bend in the desk's leg. "Again!"

All three prisoners yanked harder. The chain rattled, and the desk shuddered, but refused to yield to their combined show of strength.

Louise's face flushed with effort until she stopped pulling and dropped back down, shaking her head. "It's no use. It's not even bending. We'd need a sledgehammer to break this thing."

Panting, they all slumped back to the floor, resting their backs against the desk. Stanley's eyes drifted around the room until he came upon their belongings that the kidnapper had thrown into the corner of the room.

"My briefcase," he said, gesturing toward it with his chin. "Louise, can you grab it?"

Elizabeth and Stanley got onto their knees and spread their arms, giving Louise more slack to reach her target. Louise stretched out with her free hand, straining against the chain's limit, until her fingers brushed the leather handle. All three of them let out painful grunts as their handcuff links tore into their wrists. Louise took a breath and strained her arm a little more until she finally hooked the handle with her fingers and dragged it closer, the briefcase scraping across the floor.

"Got it!" Louise yelled, pulling the briefcase over and setting it in Stanley's lap.

Stanley popped the latches and began rifling through its contents. Reports, charts, highlighted emails, and damning evidence against ParaWorks. All great material for their fight at the town hall, but useless for breaking out of handcuffs.

"Anything sharp?" Elizabeth asked. "A pen, a letter opener?"

Stanley sifted through the papers, his fingers quick but careful. "Just documents. Your notes. A pencil, but it's dull as dirt."

"Come on, Dad," Elizabeth said. "You're the EPA guy. Don't you carry a Swiss Army knife or something?"

Stanley snorted. "Left it at home with my cape and tights, kid."

Louise, using her free hand to dig through the briefcase, paused, her fingers brushing something small and metallic caught in the briefcase's lining. She tugged it free and held it up to the light coming in through the window. A single paperclip, bent slightly at one end.

"Well, well, well, look at what I found," Louise said, a hint of mischief in her voice as her eyes met Stanley's with a knowing twinkle.

Stanley's smile widened. He remembered how, about a week ago at this very site, in the room down the hall, Louise had deftly picked the lock on a file cabinet that they needed access to. "You and your little surprises," Stanley said. "Think you can work your magic again?"

Louise straightened the paperclip with her fingers, her expression focused. "Handcuffs aren't much different from a padlock," she said, leaning toward the handcuffs linking her wrist to Stanley's. "Just takes patience. And a little luck." She bent the paperclip's end into a makeshift pick and began probing the lock.

Elizabeth watched, her eyes wide and inquisitive. "You've done this before, I take it?"

Louise didn't look up, her focus locked on the handcuffs. "Once or twice. EPA fieldwork isn't all paperwork, you know. Sometimes you've got to get creative."

Stanley smiled. "I never learned how to pick a lock in my day, kiddo," he said with a smirk. "They're lucky to have you."

Still working the lock, Louise closed her eyes, the start of a tear forming in her eyes. Elizabeth noticed and asked, "Louise, what's wrong?"

Louise stopped working on the lock for a moment, her attention dropping to the floor. "They… They fired me today," she said.

"The EPA?" Stanley questioned.

Louise nodded her head, wiping away the tear that had finally released and fallen down her cheek. "Yeah," she said.

Elizabeth's jaw dropped. "Oh my God, Louise. I'm so sorry."

Stanley shook his head, sadly expecting this turn of events. "What happened?"

"It was this morning," Louise said, "right after I walked into the office. Grayson, my boss, was already there. He called me in to where he'd set up shop and said I'd violated EPA protocols and endangered the agency's reputation by sharing private files with…"

Stanley cut her off. "With me," he said, unable to mask his regret. "Oh, Louise, I'm so sorry. It's all my fault."

Louise shook her head. "It's not your fault, Stanley. I'm a big girl. I went in with my eyes open. He warned me what would happen if they could prove it. And it was all too easy to do that. Missing files, sharing of sensitive information. They had everything they needed."

"Did you try to explain it to them?" Elizabeth asked.

"I tried," Louise said. "But they wouldn't hear it." She shook her head, trying in vain to stop the emotions from brewing to the surface. "It's all bullshit. They had my desk cleared out before I even walked in the door." She swallowed hard. "I'm done at the EPA. Everything I worked for, gone."

Elizabeth's expression fell. She instinctively tried to reach her arm around Louise, but the handcuffs brought Stanley's hand up too. Elizabeth frowned, unable to embrace her friend. "Oh, Louise," she said, leaning closer in place of a hug, her voice soft and comforting. "I promise you that's not the end of this. They fired you because you found something they can't bury." She placed a hand on Louise's hand. "I'll help you fight this. We'll file a wrongful termination suit, whistleblower protections, whatever it takes. You're not alone, okay? We're in this together. I promise."

Louise managed a weak nod and smile, her shoulders

sagging but her jaw tightening with a flicker of resolve. "Thanks, Elizabeth. I just didn't expect something to happen this fast." She held up her and Stanley's handcuffed hands. "Or that I'd end up like this. But now I'm really pissed off. If I'm going down, I'm taking Hargrove and the mayor with me."

Stanley looked at her, pride and pain building in his chest. "You're tougher than they know, Louise. And you're not done, not by a long shot."

Louise smiled at Stanley as she continued to work the lock with the paperclip. Elizabeth and Stanley both swung their heads up as the lock suddenly clicked under Louise's fingers.

Stanley's eyes shot down. "Was that...?"

Louise smiled and held up her hand, which was now free of the handcuff binding her and Stanley. "It was," she said, smiling. "Sit back, both of you. I'll have you out in a jiff!"

* * *

The night stretched wide above the ParaWorks site, stars shining bright against the dark desert sky. The lot was empty, the white van gone, the single overhead light casting harsh shadows across piles of dirt and building materials. Everything was quiet when Stanley, Louise, and Elizabeth emerged from the construction building, free of their handcuff restraints.

Stanley looked down at his watch and scowled when he read its display. "We're almost out of time," he said. "The town hall meeting's already started. We've got maybe twenty minutes before it's over."

Elizabeth's eyes widened. "That guy still has our phones.

We can't call for help." She broke into a jog, turning mid-run to Stanley and Louise. "Come on! We'll make a run for it back to Dad's and get Louise's car!"

Louise hesitated as she looked around the ParaWorks lot, still shaken from the kidnapping. "He could still be out there, you know," she said as she fell into step beside Stanley, clutching his hand for emotional survival.

They ran, weaving past construction barriers toward the main road. Redmain's quiet streets loomed ahead, the familiar streets leading to Stanley's apartment building just a mile away. The night air was cool, carrying the scent of wet asphalt as the misting of rain slowly turned into an actual pour, but there was no time to savor it.

Stanley's lungs burned, and his legs protested, but the thought of ParaWorks' lies going unchallenged drove him forward. Elizabeth led the charge, her determination like a beacon, while Louise kept pace, her nerves pushed down as she focused on running and carrying Stanley's briefcase. The falling rain, which normally would have been a torment to be in, was a relief to the trio as they made their way down street after street.

They reached Stanley's apartment in under ten minutes, sweat beading on their foreheads, which mixed pleasantly with the raindrops. Louise's beat-up sedan sat parked across the street, right where she'd left it before the kidnapping. She fumbled for her keys as she headed for the driver's side. Recognizing Louise's nerves were still in full gear, Stanley snatched the keys from her and confidently stated, "I'll drive!"

Elizabeth beat Stanley to the driver's side door and grabbed his arm, her eyes wide open. "No way, Dad. You drive like you're delivering mail on a Sunday. We've got no time." She turned to Louise, who was leaning against the car, her face pale, her hands still shaking. "Louise, hop in!"

Elizabeth snatched the keys from Stanley and slid into the driver's seat before he had a chance to reply. Stanley grunted but climbed into the passenger seat anyway, his briefcase on his lap, while Louise took the back seat. The engine roared to life, and Elizabeth peeled out of the parking lot, the tires squealing. Redmain's streets blurred by as they passed empty storefronts, flickering street lamps, and business after business at breakneck speed.

Stanley gripped the dashboard, digging his nails into the imitation leather. "Take Main to Fourth," he said. "Cuts through downtown faster."

"I know the way," Elizabeth said. "You just hold on to your evidence, Dad."

Louise leaned forward, her voice steadier now. "That guy didn't take any of the evidence we had left. We can still do this. We just need to get there!"

The dashboard clock glowed '*9:50*' as Elizabeth floored it, weaving through a stop sign with a lawyer's disregard for minor infractions. The town hall building loomed ahead, its brick facade lit by floodlights. Dozens and dozens of cars still lined the lot, a good sign the meeting hadn't ended yet, or so they all hoped. Elizabeth skidded into a parking spot, the car jerking to a stop.

Stanley was out first, briefcase in hand. Elizabeth flew out next, her eyes blazing with purpose. Louise followed, her nerves still slowing her down.

"I hope we're not too late," Stanley said as they sprinted toward the town hall's double doors.

Chapter Nineteen

The Redmain town hall was a sea of busy energy. Townsfolk packed its high-ceilinged chamber, squeezed shoulder-to-shoulder on folding chairs set up for the occasion. Half a dozen ceiling fans churned lazily overhead, adding a brief reprieve to the humidity caused by the light fall of rain outside. A small table set up in the back of the room offered water and coffee to the attendees.

Most towns still hold town hall meetings like this one, but few have the turnout that Redmain usually does. Being further away from any major counties or districts, the people of Redmain relied much more heavily on town hall meetings for updates that would affect their daily lives. After the initial signing of the ParaWorks project and the promise of jobs it offered, many of the recent town hall meetings had covered employment start times and other similar information that the people wanted to know. And this meeting was no different.

The overhead lights cast a gentle glow on the crowd, mostly small families of the nuclear variety and various retirees with a vested interest in the town. Also in the crowd, curiously waiting with a notepad in hand, was the reporter, Karl Hensley. He had not yet published his article on Stanley Peck, instead waiting and hoping that tonight's meeting would provide a natural punchline to what he already planned as a scathing deconstruction of one of Redmain's most notorious citizens. Christine, the front desk receptionist from City Hall, was there too, tucked quietly into the back row of seats.

At the front of the hall was an elevated dais on which sat a long, polished wooden table, stretching about fifteen feet from end to end. A series of microphones lined the table, accounting for the five members of the city council. The American and Redmain flags flanked the table. Banners on the walls proclaimed *'Community First.'*

Stanley, Elizabeth, and Louise pushed through the heavy double doors, the squeak of hinges quietly announcing their arrival. The trio immediately looked to the dais and noted that no one was sitting at the presentation table.

"Oh no," Stanley said. "We missed it."

Just then, the lights dimmed briefly, and a small woman with grey hair walked up the side of the dais and spoke into one of the microphones. "Thank you for your patience, everyone. The break is almost over, and the council will be returning shortly to conclude the proceedings."

Louise let out a quick breath. "Oh, thank goodness," she said.

Stanley nodded in relief, his collar tight as he took in the crowd at their seats. It didn't take him long to spot Christine from City Hall sitting in the back, quietly twisting a tissue in her hands. A few rows ahead, Stanley also noted Karl Hensley, who had already observed the trio arrive and had the gall to flash Stanley a smile and a half-hearted wave.

Stanley fired a dirty look at Hensley as he squeezed Elizabeth's shoulder, a silent call for strength. "This is it," he said, shaking his head. "I wish we could have figured out the connection between those shell companies, though. That's such an important piece of this."

Elizabeth nodded in agreement. "Yeah, I know. The friend I had looking into it hadn't turned anything up. Marietti, Gaines, their daughter—I couldn't find the connection. If only we had more time to fit the pieces together."

Stanley grimaced. "Too late now, I guess. We'll have to shoot from the hip."

The lights dimmed again as the council members filed in from a room just to the left of the dais. Alan Hargrove was the first one out, his posture immaculate, his smile polished but cold. Stanley, Elizabeth, and Louise watched as the other council members walked in after Hargrove. Councilman Daniels followed the city planner, but the room's energy shifted noticeably as Mayor Mass entered next, his gray hair neatly combed, his stride carrying the arrogance of a man accustomed to control. Mass avoided the crowd's gaze, his face a mask of practiced calm as he took his seat at the center of the presentation table. The final two council members, Councilwoman Hayes and Councilman Farmer, took up the rear, their expressions a mix of boredom and obligation.

Stanley's grip tightened on his briefcase. "There he is, Mayor Mass."

"You know, it's funny," Elizabeth said. "With everything we've been doing, everything we've been digging up, it never occurred to me until just now that we hadn't come face-to-face with the mayor himself."

Stanley hunched his shoulders, almost embarrassed. "Yeah, maybe that's for the best. I haven't had very good luck in a mayor's office before."

On the dais, Hargrove silently observed the room. It looked as if he was scanning the crowd of seated attendees. Then his eyes reached the entrance at the back of the hall, and, for a moment, he locked onto Stanley. The city planner's smile faltered for a moment, a flash of recognition, or perhaps unease, crossing his face before he slowly looked away, busying himself with a stack of papers.

Stanley leaned toward Elizabeth. "He knows we're here."

Elizabeth sneered. "Good. Let him sweat."

"We'd better find a seat," Louise said, gesturing to a few open spots.

Elizabeth led the way, weaving through the crowd. Stanley followed, his heart pounding, while Louise trailed behind, her steps slower, as if each one required a conscious effort on her part. They settled into a row near the front, close enough to the public comment podium to feel the weight of their impending moment.

At the end of the dais, Hargrove's gaze found the trio again, lingering longer this time. Now he looked genuinely uneasy. As he got ready to speak, Mayor Mass noticed Hargrove's expression and followed his gaze over to the trio of Stanley, Elizabeth, and Louise. The mayor also locked his eyes on the group, though he kept his own expression cold and passive. Stanley met his stare, unflinching.

Mayor Mass cleared his throat and began the meeting again with a hard rap of his gavel. His voice boomed through the microphone and connected loudspeakers. "I hope you all enjoyed that short break and helped yourselves to some donuts and coffee. Now let's move on to the final business of the night, the signing of the final permits for the ParaWorks facility to break ground on construction."

Stanley flashed a concerned look at Elizabeth and Louise. "We must have missed the open mic," he whispered to both of them.

Elizabeth looked him dead in the eye. "Would that stop Stanley Peck?"

Stanley froze for a moment, then smiled and raised his hand for all to see. The gesture caught the attention of Councilman Farmer, who spoke for the council. "Pardon me, sir, but the open public mic part of the meeting ended before the break. I'm afraid you'll have to..."

Stanley stood up before Councilman Farmer could finish his sentence. "I do sincerely apologize for missing that part of the meeting, councilman." Stanley drew his attention to Mr. Hargrove. "My friends and I encountered a bit of car trouble getting over here. But since we *are* here now, I would appreciate the chance to speak to the council."

Hargrove leaned in closer to his microphone and answered Stanley's statement before Councilman Farmer could respond. "I'm afraid that time has passed, sir."

Stanley looked at the other members of the council. "Surely the members of this council wouldn't begrudge an old man a few words at a town hall meeting, even if he *was* late."

"Sir," Councilman Hayes said, speaking this time for the council. Her no-nonsense look gave a pretty clear forewarning of what she was about to say, but she stopped as she noticed a chatter begin amongst the crowd of attendees. Suddenly, she felt every eye in the hall drawn to her as she was about to deny this elderly man a chance to speak. She looked to her right, the rest of the council within her view. She could just make out Mr. Hargrove on the other end of the table subtly shaking his head, but as she turned back to the microphone, she noticed even more whispers had started within the crowd. "While that time of the evening *has* indeed passed," she finally continued, "let it be known that this city council never turns its ear on one of its citizens." She gestured to the public podium, which stood at the front of the center aisle of the crowd. "It's all yours, sir."

Stanley nodded his thanks to Councilwoman Hayes and approached the public podium, holding the folder he had pulled from his briefcase in his hands. The hall bustled with low chatter as Stanley stepped up to the microphone. Normally, most people paid little attention to someone at the public podium, dismissive or bored, including the council members themselves, who often avoided eye contact with the speaker as they flipped through documents or checked their watches. But not now. The people of Redmain knew who Stanley Peck was, and he had the attention of every eye in the room.

This was it. This is what it all had come down to. Louise and Elizabeth sat quietly in their seats. Elizabeth gripped her notebook. Louise had to remember to breathe as she rubbed the red marks around her wrists made from the tight kidnappers' handcuffs.

Stanley cleared his throat and started. "Members of the council, my name is Stanley Peck. I'm a former EPA officer for the city of Chicago. With the help of my..." he looked over at Elizabeth and Louise, "friends—I've spent the last week or so reviewing and analyzing the construction plans and the materials being used for the new ParaWorks construction site on the east side of town." He paused, scanning the room, meeting cold eyes and crossed arms. "It gives me no pleasure to report that I have found considerable evidence that suggests the ParaWorks facility could represent a definite health risk to the people of Redmain."

Councilwoman Hayes, who sat next to Mayor Mass, took advantage of Stanley's brief pause to jump in, her voice loaded with skepticism. "Mr. Peck, with all due respect, the contractors passed every safety inspection. They've met every legal requirement."

"Yes, I know that," Stanley said. "But if you'll let me explain, I'll show you how someone carefully structured the data in those reports to make things look less risky than they really are."

Councilman Farmer joined in next. "Mr. Peck, you do understand that all the members of this council have approved the ParaWorks project. We're all set to sign off tonight on the final paperwork for the build to begin."

Stanley nodded. "I'm aware of that, councilman," he said. "That's why my friends and I are here. If the ParaWorks build breaks ground, it would take who knows how long to stop it, and by then the damage could be done."

This time, it was Councilman Daniels who countered Stanley's statement. "You're speaking in riddles, Mr. Peck. We have business to conduct here. If you would kindly take a seat and let us proceed."

Frustrated, Stanley slammed his hand on the podium. "I'm just trying to explain the details, councilman! I'm trying to..." He froze, taking a deep breath before continuing. "People of the council, I have evidence that shows conflicting data and independent reports that clearly illustrate the environmental risk."

"What evidence do you have, sir?" Councilwoman Hayes asked. "Please bring it forward."

Stanley stammered. "Well, I don't have that particular data right now."

Hayes threw up her hands. "And why is that?"

"It was stolen, councilwoman," Stanley said, "from my apartment a few nights ago."

"This is ridiculous!" Councilman Farmer said. "Mr. Peck, the goodness of this council let you speak when the public time had already passed. Now, will you show us the same courtesy and sit down so that we may continue?"

Stanley shook his head, frustration showing on his face. "I know it sounds crazy. I know I don't have that data anymore. But I *do* have this!" He held up the signed consent form. "This is a letter of consent, signed by Mayor Mass and Jim Hargrove, granting their personal permission to allow ParaWorks to operate in Redmain, while understanding the potential risks."

"Mr. Peck," Councilman Daniels said, "Mayor Mass and Mr. Hargrove are the ones who worked with and bargained with the ParaWorks corporation to bring their business here. Any consent form they may have signed was simply in order to move that process along."

"Yes, yes," Stanley said, "but they did so knowing the data clearly showed a risk, a risk they ignored."

"Again, Mr. Peck," Councilman Farmer said, "the EPA, your former employer, also signed off on the safe nature of the ParaWorks facility." She looked at the various members of the city council, then at the crowd of townspeople, who were whispering to each other. "Your claims seem exaggerated and, frankly, disruptive to the people of Redmain."

Stanley worriedly glanced back at Elizabeth. She gave him a small nod, silently urging him on. Stanley swallowed and turned back.

Before he could continue, however, Councilman Daniels jumped on board. "We're trying to build a future here, Mr. Peck, not generate unfounded fears. This project is bringing jobs, much-needed jobs, and unprecedented growth to Redmain. We're not going to just halt progress on the say-so of one man with wild concerns that have no basis in fact."

Stanley held firm. "These aren't unfounded fears!" He tightened his stance but pressed on. "I'm talking about the potential for real health risks—cancer, respiratory illness, and so much more. I've read every report that was commissioned for this project, and the data gathered *does* suggest a potential risk, but that information is buried—hidden—in bureaucratic language and outright lies." He opened his evidence folder, carefully spreading out the pages with charts and photographs on the podium. "I have the proof. I have the evidence." Stanley's eyes quivered with frustration as he connected with the disbelieving and disapproving eyes of the council, but he took a deep breath and kept his calm.

Murmurs rose in the crowd, along with some doubtful and uneasy expressions. Elizabeth and Louise shifted uncomfortably in their seats as the tension in the room grew thicker.

Councilman Daniels was about to speak, but Mayor Mass cut him off. "I'll take it from here, Mr. Daniels." He turned his piercing eye to Stanley. "Mr. Peck," he said, "the economic impact of stopping this project would be devastating to this town. We have to think about the bigger picture, and that bigger picture includes people's jobs, people's livelihoods, some of the people in this very room, as a matter of fact. Are you even a little concerned about that?"

Stanley took another breath, trying to steady himself against the sting of the growing dismissal. "The bigger picture *is* the people who live here, Mayor Mass. It's about the people who work here. The people who drink the water. This isn't about jobs. It's about our families. It's about our health. And the people of Redmain deserve to know the truth before it's too late. Don't *you* care about *that*?"

Councilwoman Hayes raised a hand, cutting off Stanley again. "Even if your reports were accurate, Mr. Peck, and they're not, by the way, this town can't afford to stop progress because of one man's paranoia. Don't you have any concern for that, Mr. Peck?"

Stanley looked out at the audience and caught a few hesitant looks in his direction. A mother clutching her child shifted uncomfortably in her chair. An older man leaned forward, his eyes narrowing as he focused on Stanley.

Mayor Mass cleared his throat, attempting to regain control of the session. "Mr. Peck, we appreciate your concerns, but the council has already approved this project. We have reviewed all the reports, and everything has met local and federal laws. You're wasting your time here."

Stanley adjusted his posture and straightened his tie. "Ladies and gentlemen, I worked for the Environmental Protection Agency for most of my adult life. I know what I'm talking about. The documents I've brought support my claims. It's not paranoia. It's..."

Mayor Mass let out a cruel, interrupting laugh. "We know who you are, Mr. Peck. We know your history. Your reputation is one of disruption and, quite frankly, failure. You were fired from your job at the EPA, and you're bringing that same problem-starting history into this town meeting. You should be ashamed of yourself for trying to stop this project."

The room fell silent as Stanley lowered his head. The

mayor's words cut deeper than any official rejection, any firing, or loss. His hands gripped the podium in front of him. At that moment, Stanley could feel the eyes of every person in the room. He could see Karl Hensley at his seat, furiously writing, with a sickening grin on his face. He could see Christine from City Hall doing her very best to disappear into her oversized coat. It felt like the weight of a thousand suns bearing down upon him. Stanley wanted to bury himself in his collection of files and folders. He wanted to go back to the day he read that newspaper and just throw it away. He wanted to run and hide.

Stanley's hands gripped the podium harder, his knuckles screaming as Mayor Mass's words, *'You should be ashamed of yourself,'* cut through the chamber like a fine razor blade. The crowd's silence was deafening as each pair of eyes bored into him, amplifying the weight of his past failures. He felt the urge to shrink, to vanish into the folder of documents before him. Then Stanley looked over to Louise and Elizabeth. Louise nodded as if promising her support. Elizabeth smiled and gave him a reassuring gaze. If they weren't there, perhaps it would be different. If he were alone in this, perhaps he would turn and leave. But he wasn't alone. He knew he couldn't flee. He knew he had to fight, as much for Redmain as for himself.

Stanley took a deep breath and steadied himself as he leaned into the microphone, channeling the vigor of his youth. "Mayor Mass, Councilwoman Hayes, Councilman Daniels, and Councilman Farmer," Stanley began, "I understand the importance of jobs in this town. I've lived in Redmain long enough to know just how important that is here, to the people here. But I also know that it *doesn't* need contaminated water, polluted air, and a legacy of health problems for our children." He opened his folder, pulling out a specific report, its edges worn from his obsessive review. He waved it at the council. "Let me be clear about the technical risks here. The ParaWorks facility is going to be built on a site with a water table less than 20 feet below the surface. Their own environmental assessment, buried on page 47 of this very document, admits that their chemical waste disposal plan involves deep-well injection. That's a problem when the aquifer in this area is so shallow. One leak, one miscalculation, and you're looking at benzene and heavy metals in Redmain's drinking water. The EPA's own guidelines state that deep-well injection in such conditions risks contamination within five years. I have the data right here if you'd like to see it." Stanley turned to the crowd. "If *any* of you would like to see it!"

Stanley pointed the report at the audience, its charts and numbers glaring under the fluorescent lights. The crowd stirred, with a few heads leaning forward. The council, however, remained purposefully stone-faced. Councilwoman Hayes adjusted her glasses, her lips pursing. "Mr. Peck, professionals reviewed those reports, not *former* employees with a history of overreach. Mayor Mass and Jim Hargrove signed off on it. The EPA itself cleared this project. Are you suggesting they're incompetent?"

"Incompetent?" Stanley questioned. "Not even a little bit. I've been working with someone who worked at the EPA." He looked down at Louise, silently asking for permission to tell her story. She smiled and gave him the okay with a nod of her head. "I say '*worked*' with the EPA because, you see, my good friend over here got fired from the EPA this morning. No doubt because of pressure put on the EPA by certain people in this very room."

Mayor Mass laughed at Stanley's statement. "So your source

is someone so valuable and trusted by the EPA that they fired her?" He shifted in his seat. "Mr. Peck, do you hear yourself?"

Stanley grimaced at the mayor's comments. "Louise Talbot was willing to put her career on the line because she could see that something was wrong. She was willing to risk everything to show me, to show all of you, the data that supports everything I've said here tonight. That makes her valuable and trusted to me. It should make her valuable and trusted by you, too."

Councilwoman Hayes leaned forward to her microphone. "That's very touching, Mr. Peck. But are you suggesting the EPA knew of this data you're talking about?"

Mayor Mass and Mr. Hargrove shifted slightly in their seats, trying their best to remain detached. Stanley's jaw tightened, but he pressed on. "I'm suggesting, Councilwoman Hayes, that the data was cherry-picked. The reports mention '*acceptable*' emission levels, but they omit the cumulative impact of volatile organic compounds over time. ParaWorks plans to emit over 200 tons of VOCs annually, which is well above the threshold for long-term respiratory risks, according to the 1963 Clean Air Act. I've cross-referenced their projections with independent studies from the University of Nevada. The risk of chronic bronchitis and asthma in children rises by 15% in communities near facilities like this. You're gambling with Redmain's health, and the numbers don't lie."

Councilman Daniels spoke up, expression firm. "Numbers can be twisted, Mr. Peck. You're throwing around statistics, but where's the proof of actual harm? This sounds like fear-mongering from a man who's made a career of it."

The jab stung, but Stanley refused to flinch. "Members of the council, I have the data right here for you to review," he said. "Some of you may be more familiar with it than others, but it's here. I have copies for you." Stanley turned back to the crowd, where more and more people were leaning forward. "I have copies for *all* of you."

Mayor Mass leaned into his microphone, his voice booming through the speakers. "Mr. Peck, you will not threaten or bully this council into believing your ridiculous narrative! You can take every copy of that data and park it right next to your corrupted soul!"

"Corruption!?" Stanley shouted. "Would you like to talk about corruption, Mayor Mass?" He shot a glance at Elizabeth and Louise, who both gave him a reassuring nod to keep going. He reached into his folder again, pulling out a stack of printed emails and financial documents. "This isn't just about the environmental risks. There's so much more. I had hoped not to resort to this sort of thing, but you've left me no choice." Hargrove shot a far less subtle look at Mayor Mass as Stanley continued. "I have evidence of corruption tied directly to this project." He paused, letting the weight of his words settle over the room. The crowd's murmurs grew louder. "I've uncovered correspondence between Alan Hargrove and ParaWorks executives, discussing '*off-the-books incentives*.' I also have evidence of shell companies tied directly to Mayor Mass and city planner Alan Hargrove. Mr. Hargrove, you see, has received money funneled directly through those shell companies as '*payments*' for services rendered." He turned to the crowd. "For what services, exactly? I'd like to know! And our dear Mayor Mass has received campaign contributions from another one of these shell companies. Why would he have done that exactly? Bribe money? Hush money? I'd sure like to know that, too!" Stanley grabbed the podium's microphone handle and pulled it in close. "These aren't rumors or theories. These are emails, bank transfers, meeting minutes, and signed consent forms. And it all points to one thing—Mayor Mass and Alan Hargrove have hidden and lied about their financial stake in this project. They aren't interested in Redmain. They're only interested in themselves!"

Mass's face burned red. "You have some nerve, Mr. Peck, coming in here and throwing around claims like that. I've received campaign contributions from all sorts of sources, including businesses. And Alan Hargrove has been part of our City Hall for decades. His services are called upon by other outside companies because he's good at his job. His ex-wife even worked for Redmain. We're a family here. Can't you see that?"

Stanley held his gaze on Mayor Mass. "If you claim these things are innocent, where are your records? Where's the transparency?"

A few feet away, Elizabeth sat up at the mention of Hargrove's ex-wife. She reached for her pocket, instinctively going for her phone to access her emails. Her hand found no prize as she remembered their ineffective kidnapper had taken all of their phones. She looked around the crowd, seeing about half of the people either on their phones or recording with them. She continued to scan the room until she came upon a familiar face—Christine from City Hall. Elizabeth smiled and turned to Louise. "I'll be right back." She got up and started making her way toward the back.

The chamber erupted in gasps and whispers. Hargrove's face paled at the sound of Stanley's claims. His fingers froze mid-tap on the table. Mayor Mass's calm facade cracked as his eyes narrowed and he leaned into his microphone. "Those are incredibly serious accusations, Mr. Peck. Slanderous, I'd say! No matter what happens here tonight, you'll be hearing from our lawyers!" He turned his attention to the audience, whose whispers and gasps weren't so quiet anymore. "But let me assure the people of Redmain that these accusations are without merit. The '*evidence*' Mr. Peck refers to is public information, and it is *not* proof of any wrongdoing. Mr. Hargrove and I have private holdings and investments. There is nothing illegal about that!"

As the back-and-forth at the front of the hall continued, Elizabeth had made her way to the back of the audience and crouched down next to Christine from City Hall. "Hi, Christine," Elizabeth whispered. "Remember me?"

Christine nodded. "Of course I do. You're working with Stanley Peck."

Elizabeth smiled. "That's right. I'm hoping you can do me a small favor. I don't have my phone with me, and I need to check some really important information. Do you think I could borrow your phone for a few minutes?"

Christine pulled back, unsure. Elizabeth quickly followed with, "It's so very important. I promise I'll bring it right back."

After a moment of contemplation, Christine said, "Okay," as she pulled her phone out of her purse. She entered her password and opened it for Elizabeth to use. "Here you go. I hope it helps."

Elizabeth took the phone and touched Christine on the leg. "I hope so, too," she said before slinking her way back to her seat.

Back at the public podium, Stanley held up a stack of financial reports, his voice rising with conviction. "These documents show rental payments from ParaWorks to a shell company called Redstone Holdings, which in turn has been making *'payments'* to Alan Hargrove in almost the same amount. That's over $300,000 in *'consulting fees'* going to Redmain's own city planner. Tell me that doesn't sound dirty." In his seat on the dais, Hargrove shifted uncomfortably as Stanley pressed on. "And there's more. Redstone Holdings is just one of two shell companies tied to this project. Redstone is owned by another company—another mysterious company called Parkview Enterprises. And wouldn't you know that very same Parkview Enterprises made campaign contributions to a certain Redmain political candidate? And who would that politician be?" Water pointed his finger straight at the dais. "That's right. Mayor Jim Mass himself!"

Hargrove shot to his feet, his voice cutting through the gathering storm of chatter in the crowd. "This is absurd! You're peddling conspiracy theories, Peck! Those are privately owned companies with every right to pay for services or to support a local candidate. You're desperate! And you're grasping at straws to make all of your so-called *'evidence'* connect. The people of Redmain deserve better than your delusions!"

A few feet away, Louise watched, literally on the edge of her seat, as Stanley battled the council at the dais. Next to her, Elizabeth entered her email and password information into the divorce records database in the browser of Christine's borrowed phone. After a few seconds of connecting and loading, Elizabeth's email screen refreshed and populated.

At the podium, Stanley continued to defend his claims. "These are no delusions, Mr. Hargrove!"

"Really?" Mayor Mass continued. "Would you like to tell us the connection between those companies you're throwing in the mud? You can't, can you? Because they aren't owned by me, and they aren't owned by Alan Hargrove. They are legitimately owned companies that are doing business with the city of Redmain. You've got nothing here, nothing of any value. Everything you've presented tonight is slanderous lies. It makes me sick to listen to it!"

The crowd's whispers grew into a low roar, some nodding in agreement with Hargrove, others casting doubtful glances at Stanley as the mayor and Alan Hargrove poked holes in his documents and evidence. Stanley felt the room tilting against him, the weight of his past threatening to drown his credibility.

Amidst the crowd, Karl Hensley was writing away, no doubt burying Stanley in *'evidence'* of his own. Stanley opened his mouth to respond, but before he could, Elizabeth stood up from her seat, her eyes wide. She stepped forward, Christine's borrowed phone in her hand and a report glowing on the screen.

"Wait!!!" Elizabeth called out, her voice cutting through the chaos.

The room quieted in half a heartbeat. All eyes turned to Elizabeth as she stepped up to the podium and touched Stanley on the shoulder. Stanley took the cue and stepped to the side. Elizabeth moved in front of the podium and leaned into the microphone to address the crowd. "Please forgive my interruption," Elizabeth started, "but there is more to all of this that everyone here deserves to hear." She turned her attention away from the dais and to the crowd. "My name is Elizabeth Peck. Stanley Peck is my father. I also happen to be an attorney. So I can tell you, from a legal perspective, that everything Mayor Mass and Mr. Hargrove have been saying is true. Much of this is either legal or can be explained away." She turned back to face the council. "Mr. Mayor, you brought up the question of the connection between the two companies, Redstone Holdings and Parkview Enterprises. You're quite right in pointing out that privately owned companies can employ or make campaign donations to whomever they want. But..." She held her phone up to Stanley, who read the contents of the screen as Elizabeth finished. "I'll let my father explain to you a little piece of information that just came my way."

Elizabeth stepped back and took her seat next to Louise, who sat slack-jawed at the unfolding events. Stanley finished reading the information on Christine's borrowed phone and cocked his head, almost in disbelief. "People of Redmain," Stanley said, moving back to the front of the podium. "If you've been keeping up with this *admittedly* twisted tale of corruption and greed, you might be asking yourselves, just as Mayor Mass just inferred, '*What's the connection between those shell companies?*' If they're owned by *some* people, *somewhere*, then maybe we *do* have a case of one old man's delusions. But..." He paused, his gaze locking onto Hargrove, whose breathing froze, his face draining of color. "What if I told you the owner of Redstone Holdings is listed as one Lillian Gaines? And what if I told you that Parkview Enterprises's listed owner is one Mark Marietti?" Stanley raised his hands in resignation to the audience. "Sounds perfectly legitimate to me," Stanley continued. "But what if I told you that these two people, Lillian Gaines and Mark Marietti, two seemingly unconnected people, *do* in fact have something in common?" The crowd fell all but silent and leaned in as Stanley held a pause before continuing. "Lillian Gaines and Mark Marietti, you see, had a daughter out of wedlock many years ago. And that daughter, Lorraine, grew up and married someone, someone in this *very* room." The crowd looked about, as if that person could be sitting right next to them. "Have you guessed it?" Stanley asked the audience. "That's right. Lorraine, the daughter of Lillian Gaines and Mark Marietti, two seemingly unconnected people, married and eventually divorced none other than our very own Redmain city planner—Alan Hargrove!" The crowd erupted into chatter and finger-pointing as Stanley finished things off. "And to add insult to injury, Lillian Gaines and Mark Marietti tragically died in a car accident twenty years ago." Stanley paused, as if waiting for the crowd to catch up with him. "You might be wondering, what does all of that mean? It means Alan Hargrove used his ex-wife's deceased parents' names to act as owners of two fake companies, companies that are directly connected to the ParaWorks project, and are companies that have directly paid out embezzled money to Mr. Hargrove himself and financially contributed to our own city mayor, Mr. Jim Mass."

The chamber exploded in chatter, the crowd's skepticism and eyes shifting from Stanley and instead toward Alan Hargrove and Mayor Jim Mass.

A woman in the front row gasped, clutching her purse.

A man in a work jacket whispered to his neighbor, "Dead parents?" he said. "That's shady as hell."

"This is unbelievable!" a husband said to his wife.

Stanley's heart pounded, a surge of hope breaking through the fog. Mayor Mass looked to the side of the dais and gestured for the technician, who quickly shuffled over. He whispered something into the technician's ear, who then hurried over to the side wall, which hosted all the electronic connections for the night's event. The technician ripped a cord from one of the circuit boards.

Mid-word, Stanley could hear his voice drop away from the amplified loudspeakers as his microphone was unplugged. His eyes lit up as he stepped away from the microphone and addressed the council and the crowd with his own booming voice. "You can silence my microphone, Mr. Mayor, but you can't silence me!" He raised his voice high, challenging anyone in the room not to hear him. "The people deserve to know! The people deserve to know!"

Mayor Mass slammed his gavel. "Order! Order!" his voice strained. "I tell you all, these are baseless allegations from a known trouble-maker, and I won't have this meeting turned into a circus!"

But the crowd was no longer his. A man from the back stood, his voice loud and clear. "Why'd you cut him off, Mr. Mayor? If it's not true, then why shut him down?!"

A man near the front called out, "Yeah! What are you guys hiding!?"

A ripple of agreement from the audience followed. Some nodded while others whispered questions to neighbors. But everyone was talking.

Mayor Mass slammed his hand on the table. "Enough!" he yelled, settling the crowd's voices back down to a whisper. "This council will not be questioned by the lies and rumors of the town nut-job! This council's decisions have been made in the best interest of this town."

Stanley fired back quickly. "Mr. Mayor, are you *sure* the council is doing what's best for us?"

"We are!" Mayor Mass exclaimed.

Stanley continued. "Then we deserve to know the truth, no

matter the cost. What's the point of this project if it destroys our town and hurts its people?!"

The mayor's face tightened, no longer able to hold back his personal hatred of Stanley. "Listen…Pecker!" he yelled. "We've heard enough of your fantasies!"

The crowd of onlookers fell instantly silent at the mayor's accidental slip of Stanley's unofficial and disrespectful name. Stanley swallowed a sudden and giant lump in his throat as he lowered his head in shame at what one word had reduced him to.

Then, a voice from the audience pierced the painful silence as a woman in the back of the audience, Christine from City Hall, stood and pointed her finger at the dais, directly at Mayor Jim Mass.

"Hey!" she yelled. "His name…is **PECK**!"

Heads whipped around toward Christine as another voice joined hers. "That's right! Stanley Peck! We've known him forever. He's one of us!"

One by one, more townspeople rose, their voices swelling to nearly a chant.

"Stanley Peck!"

"Stanley Peck!"

"Stanley Peck!"

"That's right!"

"Listen to him!"

The mayor's angry posture faded as he looked to council members Daniels, Hayes, and Farmer, who regarded him with looks of unquestionable disappointment. He looked nervously at the growing chorus in the crowd, then at his conspirator, Alan Hargrove. Hargrove simply closed his eyes and lowered his head, silently giving in to the rising tide of persecution.

Stanley's shoulders lifted, his breath steadying as he felt the weight of years peel away. His voice softened as he turned to face the people in the crowd. "Together, we can make sure this town stays safe. This town matters. You all matter. I might not have said it the right way forty years ago, but I've spent my life trying to protect people, even when they didn't want me to. And I won't let these men endanger the people of Redmain, because this is *my* town. This is *our* town!"

Mayor Mass, sweating down his neck, cleared his throat and leaned into his microphone. "Alright. Alright. Let's take a short recess to discuss this *new* evidence."

"No!" a man near the front yelled. "Vote now! You've heard the evidence. We want a public vote! And we want it now!"

A chant started from the back rows, low and steady at first, then overtook the crowd all the way to the front.

"Vote!"

"Vote!"

"Vote!"

The pressure was mounting, and the council knew it. Amidst the clamor of the crowd, Councilwoman Hayes turned and leaned close to Councilman Daniels and Councilman Farmer. "If we don't handle this now, it's going to explode."

Daniels agreed. "You're right, and I sure as hell don't want to be associated with any part of *this* mess."

"Agreed," Farmer said.

Hayes nodded, then took her microphone and stood up, assuming control over Mayor Mass. "Ladies and gentlemen," she said to the crowd. "I call for a motion to pause construction of the ParaWorks project pending further environmental review and to respond to allegations of corruption by Mayor Jim Mass and city planner Alan Hargrove." She looked over to her fellow councilmen. "Councilman Daniels, Councilman Farmer, your votes are officially required to pass this motion. Do you agree?"

Daniels stood and raised his hand. "I agree."

Farmer stood next, raising his hand as well. "I also agree."

With that, the crowd erupted in cheers. The people's energy washed over Mayor Mass and Alan Hargrove like an executioner swinging his ax. Hargrove stood and quietly stepped down from the table, heading for the exit behind the dais. Mayor Mass stood immediately after, straightened his tie, stepped off the dais, and walked directly toward the center aisle of onlookers. He passed by them without offering so much as a glance in anyone's direction—until he came upon Stanley at the podium and stopped.

Stanley Peck stood frozen in place, holding his position firm. He looked Mayor Mass up and down. The mayor returned Stanley's gaze, as if taunting him to say or do something, anything.

Stanley deliberated for a few long seconds, then squared his attention on the mayor. Stanley leaned forward, raised the corner of his upper lip—and snarled. "Grrrrrr," was all he cared to say.

Mayor Mass scoffed at Stanley's choice of comebacks. And with that, the mayor proceeded down the aisle, past the attendees, and out the doors.

Elizabeth and Louise, who had been watching quietly, dropped their things on their chairs and rushed over to Stanley.

Elizabeth wrapped her arms around Stanley and yelled, "You did it, Dad!"

Louise followed with a hug of her own. "You really did it!"

Stanley smiled, the first genuine smile he'd had in years. "No, *we* did it."

The trio stood, hand in hand, as the crowd of townspeople filed by, patting Stanley on the back, thanking him, thanking all three of them for standing up for the town. Never in a million years did Stanley, Elizabeth, or Louise dare think that it could have turned out this way. It was done. They won.

Stanley nodded, shook his head, and even smiled at the people as they passed by and showered him with adoration. He knew many of their faces, but this was the first time he felt he was truly seeing any of them.

Then another familiar face approached. Christine. She walked up to Stanley, Elizabeth, and Louise. "Thank you," she said. "Thank you for standing up to them."

Stanley smiled. "It's what I do."

Elizabeth handed Christine's phone back and said, "Thank you for this. You saved us."

Christine took back her phone, smiled, and quietly walked on. Her exit left room for yet another familiar face, who was approaching from the crowd. Karl Hensley. The reporter put up his fists, half-heartedly joking with Stanley to '*put up his dukes*.' Stanley did nothing of the kind.

"That was one hell of a show, Peck!" Hensley said. "They had you on the ropes for a minute there, but then you came back swinging! You blew the doors off this racket and showed those two guys exactly who they messed with." He slapped Stanley on the arm. "Stanley Peck, that's who!"

Elizabeth took a step towards the reporter. "You've got some nerve, Hensley," she said angrily. "After what you did to my father, you have the stones to act like nothing happened?"

Hensley waved away Elizabeth's comments and continued

to look at Stanley. "All water under the bridge, Peck. Like I told you, *you* are the story. And what a comeback story it'll be. Disgraced Stanley Peck turns Redmain's savior!" He leaned in closer to Stanley. Too close. "Sit down with me. Talk to me. Let me tell Redmain who you *really* are."

Stanley regarded Hensley for a moment. "Gee, Hensley. I don't know.." he said, rubbing his chin with his fingers.

"Oh, come on, Peck," Hensley pushed. "Why not?"

Stanley leaned in close. "Well, you didn't use the magic word."

Hensley harrumphed, smiling insincerely as he said with as much sincerity as he could fake, "May I *please* write your story, Mr. Peck?"

Stanley locked eyes with the portly reporter, then pulled away, taking Elizabeth and Louise under each of his arms. "No, I don't think so, Hensley," he said. "You go ahead and write your story. But you'll be writing it without me." Stanley looked at Elizabeth and Louise. "You see, I don't need my story told. The people that matter most to me—know all about it already."

The trio walked past Karl Hensley, past the townspeople, who were still talking and singing Stanley's praises, and quietly walked out of the town hall and into the night.

Chapter Twenty

The day after the town hall meeting, the morning sun started its hours-long rise into the sky as Stanley stepped onto the familiar pavement in front of his apartment. This was the same Stanley Peck who had walked this sidewalk hundreds of times. He wore his usual loose-fitting clothes, consisting of khakis and a faded button-up top. But something was different. Something in his posture had shifted. He looked like the same Stanley Peck, but he also looked like someone new all at the same time. His shoulders were straighter, and his steps were lighter. It was as if the weight of years had lifted from his thin frame.

The town of Redmain moved around Stanley as it always did. The morning air carried the scent of fresh bread from the bakery, and lawnmower engines were spinning in the distance. Even the laughter of children playing down the street at the park was in the wind, if you listened closely enough. It was the same town Stanley had seen and walked by a thousand times before. But today, it too felt different. Today, it made him smile.

As Stanley passed the local bakery, Mrs. Callahan, the owner, who always avoided eye contact with him, popped out from behind her business door. "Good morning, Mr. Peck!" she called, her voice filled with a warmth Stanley wasn't at all used to. "Your coffee's on the house today! And I threw in a blueberry muffin too, fresh from the oven!"

Stanley blinked rapidly, caught off guard by the gesture. He steered himself in her direction, thinking this had to be a joke or the first step in an alien invasion. "Thank you, Mrs. Callahan," Stanley said. "That's really kind of you." He accepted the coffee and the paper bag with the warm muffin inside. Stanley also managed a small, involuntary smile as Mrs. Callahan waved him off with an ear-to-ear grin. Why is my face doing that? Stanley wondered. I don't do that. I don't smile.

Further down the sidewalk, a teenager on a skateboard zipped past Stanley, seemingly oblivious as he knocked over a trash can. The teenager quickly spun around towards Stanley. "Yo! That was awesome last night, Pe… uh," the teenager said as he caught himself almost using Stanley's famous slur. "I mean, Mr. Peck!" The teen flashed Stanley a thumbs-up before he leaned down and picked up the trash can, setting it back where it had been standing. He jumped back on his board as his friends down the way hollered after him with laughter.

Stanley shook his head, thoroughly confused and amused, and continued on his way. As he rounded the corner, Stanley passed the local hardware store. A group of workers in dusty jeans and safety vests were loading supplies onto a work truck. One of them, a big man with a graying beard named Tom, spotted Stanley and stepped into his path. He wiped his dirty hands on a rag and extended his hand. "Peck, you old dog," the man said. "You were right about that ParaWorks site. To tell you the truth, we were all too scared to say anything about it."

Tom leaned in closer. "You know, with the bosses breathing down our necks and all. But thanks for standing up for us."

Stanley shook Tom's outstretched hand. "Takes all of us, friend," he said. "You'd have done the same if you were in my shoes."

Tom snorted. "Yeah, maybe, but I wouldn't have done it half as loud. Ha!"

The other workers laughed. One of them slapped Stanley on the shoulder as he passed. "Keep 'em honest, Peck!"

As Stanley walked further down the street, he noticed an old man sitting on a bench just outside the post office. His newspaper was unfolded and opened wide. He peered over it slightly as Stanley approached, his eyes just making it over his glasses. "Never thought I'd see the day Stanley Peck was the hero," he muttered, a grudging respect in his tone. "Guess you're not as crazy as they said."

Stanley paused and smiled. "Guess not," he said, tipping his head before continuing on. For the first time in years, the town wasn't looking through him. They were looking *at* him.

Stanley stopped by the diner, where Jenny, a waitress who'd served him countless cups of coffee with little more than a side-eye, leaned out the door with a grin. "Look who it is! Come on in, Stanley," she called. "We all heard about the other night. Whole town's talking about you. Pie's on us today."

Stanley raised an eyebrow, accepting the slice of apple pie she slid across the counter.

"Didn't realize I was so famous," he said.

"You're Redmain's own vigilante now," she teased, winking as she poured Stanley a fresh cup of coffee.

Stanley chuckled softly, the sound of niceness and courtesy so foreign to his ears. Some time later, after enjoying his coffee and pie, Stanley made his way out, the bell above the door jingling behind him. The town truly felt different today, Stanley thought. Not just the people, but the air itself. Lighter. Kinder. He wasn't being followed by his past anymore. He was home.

* * *

That evening, the busyness of his recent evenings had faded, replaced by the steady chirp of crickets outside Stanley's small apartment. A stack of papers lay forgotten on the coffee table, their urgency gone with the victory at the town hall. The quiet was strange now, Stanley thought. In such a short time, Stanley's existence had gone from a quiet hermit's life to that of a busy EPA investigator again, and now that it was all over, the quiet seemed strangely out of place.

Stanley sat on his couch, quietly observing the calm of his apartment. He noticed a tear on the side of his recliner, the one the thief and kidnapper had toppled when escaping Stanley's attack with a fake potted plant. Better get that repaired, Stanley thought. He looked at the walls, fixating on the various fingerprint tape and dust marks left by the police when they came by that same night. Going to have to clean that, Stanley thought.

Stanley was about to move on to another element to be added to his to-do list when Elizabeth stepped over from the kitchen and handed him a steaming cup of chamomile tea—her choice, not his—and sat beside him, curling her legs up under her body in her usual way. Elizabeth's suitcase sat by the door, a sad reminder that she'd be leaving for home soon to resume her life. The sight of the suitcase sent a dagger through Stanley's chest, but he pushed the pain of it aside, focusing instead on the time he had with her before she left.

He took a sip of the tea, its mild flavor a far cry from the whiskey he might've reached for in years past. "I still can't believe it," Stanley said, watching the steam curling up from the cup. "I didn't think anyone would listen."

Elizabeth leaned her head on his shoulder. "They didn't at first," she said. "But you didn't back down, Dad. You were honest. You were brave."

He let out a quiet laugh. "Brave's not the word most people have used for me."

"Well," she said, lifting her head to meet his eyes, "they're using it now. And that's what matters."

Stanley looked at Elizabeth, a small lump forming in his throat. Her eyes, so much like her mother's, held a fierce pride that made his chest ache. "Lizzy, I..." He paused, searching for words that felt too small for the moment. "I spent a lot of time being angry. At people, at myself. I thought if I just followed the rules hard enough, maybe I'd matter. But it never seemed to work that way."

Elizabeth reached over, taking Stanley's hand. Her grip was steady, grounding him. "You've always mattered, Dad. I just didn't realize how much until last night." Her voice softened. "You know, growing up, I watched you fight for what you thought was right, even when it cost you everything. I was so young. I didn't really understand it then. But I do now. You taught me to stand up, to keep going, no matter what. That's why I'm here."

Stanley squeezed her hand, his eyes glistening. "I'm so proud of you, Lizzy. Prouder than I've got words for. But…" He hesitated for a moment. "I'm sorry you got dragged into this mess. You've got your big job, your new life. You didn't have to come back here for me, but I'm really so glad you did. I couldn't have done this without you."

Elizabeth shook her head. "Dad, I didn't come back for you. I came back for *us*." She leaned closer. "Besides, my '*big job*' could wait a few days. You think I'd miss seeing my dad take down a corrupt mayor and his shady sidekick? Not a chance!"

Stanley chuckled, the sound easing the knot in his throat. "I'll tell you this much, you're tougher than I ever was. You know that, right?"

"Maybe," Elizabeth teased, nudging his shoulder. "But I learned from the best."

They sat in silence for a moment, the crickets outside filling the quiet. Stanley's gaze drifted to the suitcase by the door, and his heart sank like a rock in a pond. "You're leaving soon," he said, not quite a question.

Elizabeth nodded. "Yeah. Got a big case waiting for me."

"I'm going to miss having you here, kiddo," Stanley said. "Louise will miss you, too. The two of you made fast friends."

Elizabeth smiled. "We sure did. I had lunch with her earlier today and said our goodbyes. We talked about planning a visit where she'll come up and see a bit of what I do."

Stanley's face flushed with warmth. "That's good. I like that."

"But I'll be back, Dad," Elizabeth said, nudging Stanley's arm. "Holidays, weekends, whenever you need me. And you got a new job today. You're gonna be busy keeping everyone honest."

Stanley snorted, a small smile breaking through. "Yeah, laminated badge and all. Can't say I ever saw that coming."

Elizabeth laughed. "You deserve it, Dad. The town's lucky to have you." She paused, her eyes searching his face. "You know, when I was a kid, I used to think you were larger than life. Even after… everything, I never stopped believing in you. And the other night, I saw that larger-than-life person come back. It was awesome."

Stanley looked away, blinking fast in an effort to stop those pesky tears. "I almost quit, Lizzy. More times than I can count. Back in Chicago, after your mom left, I thought I'd lost everything, even you. You were the only thing that kept me going."

Elizabeth's eyes started tearing up. She squeezed his hand tighter. "You didn't lose me, Dad. You never will. And you didn't lose yourself either. You just… took the long way home."

Stanley let out a shaky breath, a single tear slipping down his cheek. "Thank you for believing in me, Lizzy."

"Always, Dad," Elizabeth said. She leaned in, wrapping her arms around him in a tight hug. Stanley held her close and held on to her for a long while.

As they pulled apart, Elizabeth wiped her eyes, a smile returning to her face. "You sure you're gonna be okay here without me?"

Stanley chuckled, brushing a hand through his gray hair. "I think I'll manage," he said. "Got a whole town to keep me on my toes now."

Elizabeth grinned, then stood up and stretched. "Good. Because I'm expecting regular updates. And don't you dare let that badge go to your head."

He raised his teacup in a salute. "Yes, ma'am."

Elizabeth reached over and grabbed her jacket from the couch, slinging it over her shoulder. "Well, I've got to be hitting the road now," she said, "so I can time my stops right." Elizabeth walked across the room to her suitcase. "Get some rest, Dad. You've earned it."

As Elizabeth headed for the door, suitcase in tow, Stanley called after her. "Lizzy?"

Elizabeth turned around, her hand on the doorknob. "Yeah?"

"You're the best," Stanley said.

Elizabeth's smile widened, her eyes bright. "Right back at you, Dad."

Elizabeth stepped out, and the door closed gently behind her. Stanley sat back, the tea cooling in his hands. The crickets chirped on, and for the first time in decades, Stanley felt at peace. For the first time in a long time, he was home.

Chapter Twenty-One

A few weeks later, the town of Redmain had officially halted construction on the ParaWorks site. A full investigation, spurred by Stanley's relentless push, uncovered a web of shady deals and overlooked safety reports. Mayor Mass resigned under pressure, with a new election set to replace him. Alan Hargrove quietly left town, his reputation in tatters. The area where ParaWorks had started construction was now a vacant lot again. Once a symbol of promised progress, it now stood as a testament to the town's resilience and to Stanley Peck's stubborn determination.

Although people asked him to in the wake of the town hall incident, Stanley didn't run for office. He had no interest in the spotlight or in politics. The town council, however, recognizing his expertise, had requested that Stanley serve on the newly formed environmental advisory board, a position Stanley *did* accept. They even gave him a laminated badge, which he wore when called upon. It wasn't a grand redemption arc, but rather a quiet victory.

That afternoon, Stanley stood by the now-empty lot where the ParaWorks construction had stopped, in front of a single bench where the ParaWorks "*coming soon*" sign used to be. The empty desert landscape stretched out before him, untouched for now. Its simplicity was a fitting contrast to the chaos that had unfolded in Stanley's life over the past weeks. Stanley adjusted his jacket, the sun warm on his shoulders, and took a deep breath of the clean air.

Louise Talbot approached Stanley from behind. She carried a paper bag with two sandwiches from the diner, compliments of Mrs. Callahan. Her formal work blazer was gone, replaced by a casual sweater. Louise reached into the bag and handed Stanley one of the sandwiches—a turkey club—and kept a veggie wrap for herself.

"It's a big lot," Louise said, "but they've decided to turn it into a park."

Stanley smiled. "A park?" He nodded his head. "I kinda like that."

"You know, they offered to name the park after you," Louise said.

Stanley snorted, unwrapping his sandwich. "Please tell me you said no."

"I told them to name *this* bench after you instead," she replied, gesturing to the bench they were standing next to. "And to put it where it would always get lots of sun." Louise smiled playfully at Stanley. "So it's always uncomfortable, and no one will want to sit on it."

Stanley chuckled, shaking his head. "That sounds about right."

The two of them sat on the bench anyway, sun be damned, eating in silence for a moment as the desert breeze rustled around them. A pickup truck rumbled by. The driver, a grizzled man in a tight shirt, honked and waved. "Good to see you, Peck!" he called out before disappearing down the road.

Stanley raised a hand in return. "I'm actually getting used to that," he admitted.

Louise smirked, taking a bite of her wrap. "You're practically a celebrity now. Famous, not infamous." She laughed. "You know, I saw Mrs. Callahan from the bakery telling everyone in the shop the other day that you always come by, but that she never lets you pay."

Stanley rolled his eyes, but a smile lingered. "I don't know about '*always*,' but she did give me a free muffin yesterday. At least she doesn't look at me like I'm about to rob the place—like she used to."

A young couple pushing a stroller passed by. The mother offered a shy smile. "Thank you, Mr. Peck," she said. "We can't wait to play here when the park is built."

Stanley nodded, awkward with the praise. "Looking forward to it," he said.

Louise leaned back as they watched the couple walk by. "I'm so glad I got to be a part of this with you, Stanley." She trailed off, her attention dropping to the sandwich in her hands.

Stanley turned to his friend. "How you holding up, Louise?"

She sighed, setting her wrap down on the paper bag. "It's been rough. Twenty years at the EPA, gone like that." She snapped her fingers. "They blacklisted me. No government job will touch me now. Elizabeth made good and offered to represent me, to make a case of it, but I said no. She might have been able to win it for me, but the truth is that I did what they accused me of, and I'm willing to pay the price. But..." Her lips twitched into a determined smile. "I'm not done yet. I've been talking to some folks at City Hall, and I'm throwing my hat in the ring for mayor. Mass's old job!"

Stanley raised an eyebrow, obviously impressed. "The mayor

of Redmain, huh? You'd be damn good at it. Redmain could use someone like you."

She laughed. "That's what Elizabeth said when I called her last night. She's already offering to help with my campaign. Strategy and legal advice, all pro bono. Said she learned from the best." Louise shot Stanley a pointed look.

Stanley's chest tightened at the mention of his daughter, now back at her new job, diving into her next big case. "Lizzy's something else," he said. "She didn't have to get mixed up in all of this, but she did. Neither did you, for that matter, but you did."

Louise nodded, her eyes softening. "She's proud of you, you know. Told me you're the reason she's a lawyer. Said you taught her to fight for what matters, even when it's messy."

Stanley looked out at the lot, his throat tight. "I wasn't always sure I was teaching her anything good. After Chicago, I thought I'd lost my way."

"Maybe you did for a while," Louise said. "But you stepped up when it mattered. You rallied your troops, and you fought the good fight. That's what's important." She paused, her eyes becoming absorbed in thought. "I was ready to walk away after they fired me. I felt like I'd lost everything I'd worked for. But then I think about what you did at that town hall meeting. The way you stood up to Mass and Hargrove, knowing what it cost you before. It reminds me of why I got into this in the first place. To protect people. To do what's right."

Stanley met her gaze, his expression serious. "You're the one who put it all on the line, Louise. I had nothing to lose. You risked your career to get us the ammo we needed. This town owes you as much as it owes me. And if I were a betting man, I'd bet you'll win that election next month."

Louise waved a hand, brushing off the compliment, but her eyes began to tear up. "We were a good team, Stanley. All three of us."

They ate in silence for a while as the sun dipped lower, casting long shadows across the lot. A kid on a bike rode by. "Hey, Mr. Peck! You're the man!" he said before pedaling off.

Stanley shook his head as he smiled. "Kids like him have no idea I used to be the town nutcase."

Louise chuckled. "Oh, they know, Stanley. They know. They just don't care anymore. You're *their* nutcase now."

Stanley laughed, full and unguarded. "Guess I can live with that."

Louise finished her wrap, wiping her hands on a napkin. "You know, running for city mayor's gonna be a fight. Mass and Hargrove still have friends in town, and they're not happy about what we did."

Stanley shook his head. "I wouldn't worry about them. Any friends Mass and Hargrove may have had will be busy helping them fight the kidnapping and harassment charges we filed against them. And the ones that don't help them will want as much distance from them as they can get."

"Then I guess I have no excuses," Louise said, smiling.

"You've got my vote, Louise," Stanley said. "Always will. And I'll be right there with you, flashing my new fancy badge." He patted his pocket where the laminated badge sat, a playful glint in his eye.

Louise grinned, standing and brushing crumbs from her sweater. "It's a deal then, but you're buying the sandwiches."

"I get them at a discount these days," Stanley said with a smile.

Louise chuckled and started to walk away. Stanley called after her. "Louise!"

She turned, raising an eyebrow. "Yeah?"

"You're gonna make one hell of a mayor," he said. "And if anyone gives you trouble, you know where to find me."

Louise's smile widened, her confidence returning. She made a heart gesture with her two pointer fingers, then waved goodbye as she headed off, her steps purposeful, already looking like someone ready to take on the town. Stanley watched her go, then turned back to the empty lot. The desert stretched out before him, quiet and unassuming, much like Redmain itself.

Stanley glanced down at the bench that was to be his namesake. He squinted his eyes and cocked his head as he questioned out loud, "The Peck Park Bench?" He shook his head. "I don't like that. The Stanley Peck Park—now that I like." Stanley chuckled amusingly to himself.

"I'll have to talk to someone about that."

Epilogue

The bell above the door gave its usual half-hearted jingle as Stanley Peck stepped into *Beans & Brew*, the only decent coffee shop in Redmain and Stanley's favorite place to sit and sip and contemplate his day. The barista, a young girl probably still in high school, watched him come in and flashed him a smile.

"Good morning, Mr. Peck. The usual?"

Stanley gave a stiff nod. "Black. No syrup. No froth. Just coffee."

She scribbled on the cup with deliberate strokes. Stanley watched her like a hawk.

A few minutes later, he received his order. He turned the cup in his hand. Written on the side—*PECK.* No joke. No insult. No 'Pecker' written in Sharpie and in all caps like in years past. And no matter how many times he performed this little ritual, it always made Stanley smile, and today was no exception.

Sometimes he would just take his coffee and go, but that morning Stanley found a spot along the long counter in front of the window, sat down, and let the heat of the cup settle into his palms. He stared out across the street and watched a dog tug its owner along the sidewalk, and watched the trees sway in the breeze. He watched the town. Familiar and comfortable.

Eventually, Stanley let his eyes drift back into the coffee shop. And when he did, his heart all but stopped.

There, sitting at the far end of the counter he himself was sitting at, sipping something undoubtedly too sweet and too expensive, was none other than **Leonardo Vincent**. The same smug disposition. The same perfectly refined suit and hair. And the same arrogant aura. He was older. Grey now, just like Stanley, but it was him. It was definitely him.

Stanley blinked furiously and rubbed his eyes.

He looked again.

He was still there. It really was him.

From across the counter, Leo Vincent caught Stanley's eye and returned a half-hearted smile, the kind a famous person gives to a fan who noticed them on the subway. Vincent started to look away, but then performed something of a slow double-take as he looked Stanley up and down.

"Do I… know you?" Vincent asked inquisitively.

Stanley's throat went dry as he choked on his own version of stage fright. Every speech, every scathing comeback he'd ever rehearsed in the mirror or muttered under his breath was suddenly gone. Gone! Gone right along with the years and the pain he had held on to for so long. Stanley sat in silent amusement at the fact that this man, this man who had humiliated him in front of a city, this man who had been the bane of his existence—had no idea who he was.

Stanley took a breath and steadied himself. Then he smiled.

"No," Stanley said. "You don't know me."

And with that, Stanley stood, taking his coffee with him. As he reached the door, Stanley paused and looked back at his lifelong foe. Vincent, unaware, had already gone back to eating his jelly-filled donut.

Stanley turned to address the dozen or so patrons of the coffee shop. Loud enough for all to hear, he announced:

"Ladies and gentlemen. *This* man is a human ball sack!"

Gasps!

Confusion!

The barista even dropped her spoon.

Then, Stanley snapped out of his little daydream fantasy.

He was still in his seat at the end of the counter in front of the window. He was still clutching his coffee, the warm steam still wafting into his nose. Leo Vincent, however, wasn't there. He was never there, nor would he ever be.

Stanley smiled and allowed himself to laugh at the daydream joke, the true zinger that he had been waiting so many years to deliver at Leo Vincent's expense.

But, Stanley mused, he didn't need to say it anymore, didn't need to prove anything anymore. Not to Leo Vincent. Not to anyone. He had what he needed—his daughter, his friends, his dignity, and the respect of a town that once laughed at him.

However, Stanley thought, somewhere in a bustling city on the other side of the country, a man without a clue would never know just how close he came to getting roasted in the middle of a little coffee shop by one Stanley Peck.

Stanley lifted his cup and took another sip.

Content.

About the Author

Justin Bradley lives in Southern California, where he works as an elementary school teacher. He enjoys writing in many different genres, including drama, science fiction, and children's stories. Writing has been a lifelong hobby for Justin, and this book represents his second novel in that journey.

Also by Dry Ink Publications

Also available from Dry Ink Publications

A Journey Through the Looking Glass by Justin Bradley